A LESSON IN MANNERS

The three men were dressed like what they were—ranch hands. They wore flannel shirts, neckerchiefs, heavy denim pants, worn boots and chaps. Stained work-worn hats rested on their heads. Gunbelts were buckled at their hips.

"You boys appear to be lookin' for trouble," Wolfe said.

"Me, Curly and Aud came to teach you somethin' about respecting your betters," Ike said.

"We're tired of your smart-mouthin'," Curly snapped.

"Enough talk," Aud said suddenly, his left hand moving toward his pistol.

Wolfe jumped sideways, his right hand pulling his Peacemaker. Aud's shot screamed wide, and Wolfe fired, hitting the man squarely in the chest.

As a slug from Curly's pistol burrowed into the dirt, Wolfe swung and fired, winging Curly in his shooting arm. Then he wheeled, fired again, and Ike smashed against a boulder behind him, his shirt soaked with blood.

Wolfe turned back to Curly, pulling back the hammer.

"I still got a shot left, Curly. I'd be happy to oblige you with it if you insist."

HIGH COUNTRY SHOWDOWN

JOHN LEGG

ZEBRA BOOKS
KENSINGTON PUBLISHING CORP.

For my agent,
Scott Siegel,
without whom
I wouldn't be riding
this trail.
Thanks, Scott.

ZEBRA BOOKS

are published by

Kensington Publishing Corp.
475 Park Avenue South
New York, NY 10016

First printing: April, 1991

Printed in the United States of America

Prologue

"Come on, dig faster, you old coot," Jeb snapped to the tall, reedy, formerly red-headed man next to him. Sweat poured down his face and dripped into the dust.

"I cain't dig no faster'n this, damn your eyes," Russ Scarborough said back in the same tone. He threw dirt as fast as he could. "Damn, I'm too old fer sich doin's."

"You ain't gonna git no older, them Mojaves catch us out here like this."

"This here's foolishness, Jeb," Scarborough complained. "Pure, plumb foolishness."

"You're the one wanted this stuff so bad. Dig!"

"I'm diggin', damnit."

Two hours later, Wolfe and Scarborough were hard on their way again, rushing as fast as they could, knowing the Mojaves were not far behind.

The next day, they were hunkered down amid the crumbling stone and adobe of a centuries-abandoned pueblo in the shadow of three hulking mountains. They took turns firing as about two dozen angry, half-naked Mojave warriors swarmed around on horses or on foot, firing arrows and guns at the two white men.

But the Indians didn't dare get too close to these two, not out in the open, and not with the way the two men handled their Hawken rifles. It seemed to the Mojaves that every time one of the two white men fired, one of the Indians went down.

"This the same bunch killed most of Jed Smith's boys down on the Colorado so long back?" Wolfe asked during one of the lulls in the fighting. It had to be close to twenty years now, he thought. He wiped sweat off his face and neck with a bandanna. He bit off a chaw and gnawed it down some.

" 'Twas Mojaves put all them boys under that time, and these here niggurs is Mojaves. Cain't say if'n these's the same band, though. Goddamn red devils."

As usual, Wolfe marveled at Scarborough's speech. The old mountain man was nearly unintelligible half the time.

"Wish we hadn't of let all them horse beasts go," Scarborough griped.

"They ain't worth all that much to you, are they?" Wolfe said with a growl. The two had been up for two days, constantly harassed by the Mojaves, and he was edgy.

"We went through some hard times to get 'em. Seems a pity to let these fractious, goddamn savages have 'em just for the askin'. Not even with a fight for 'em."

The two old mountain men had made a trip to California, leading a wagon train of gold seekers. It was a shining time at first. But they quickly ran out of money, and so they had taken to stealing horses to make a livelihood.

Soon they had a heap of stolen horses, and nowhere to get rid of them—in California. But Wolfe, who owned a store back in St. Charles, Missouri, knew that the folks back East, especially the hordes of gold-hungry immigrants, would be wanting—and needing—horses. Wolfe and Scarborough could make themselves a small fortune with the horses there, and maybe make up for some of the hardships they had suffered in the past year.

So they started driving the herd of stolen horses eastward, making their way across the vast wasteland of sear-

6

ing, hellacious desert. It was only with some luck—and some fine shooting—that they made the Colorado River. It was not hard to get across the wide, heavy flowing river. They were not bothered, and soon they were on the east bank—with all the horses.

But soon after they began pushing on, a small band of Mojaves attacked.

Wolfe took charge of the herd. He got the horses running, leaving Scarborough to fend off the Indians by himself.

An hour later, while Wolfe waited nervously with the horses in the meager shade of some scrub pines, Scarborough showed up. He was covered with sweat and bleeding lightly from a shallow bullet wound in the arm.

"We best not set here on our rumps," Scarborough said, looking back over his shoulder. "Them niggurs'll be on our tail feathers soon enough."

They moved on, and began an on-again, off-again running battle with the Mojaves, who added men as they went. Wolfe and Scarborough kept just ahead of the Mojaves. When they found the Indians closing in, they always managed to get to some sort of protection, drive the Mojaves off, and then race ahead again.

On and on it went, mile after mile. They finally hit some pine forests and followed a clear, cold stream. Not seeing much sign of pursuit, they thought they had lost the Mojaves, and so they slowed, letting their own mounts as well as all the stolen horses recover from their exertions.

"How'n hell'd I ever let you talk me into such foolishment as racin' a bunch of savages across the desert, goddamnit?" Wolfe grumbled as they made their camp that night.

"Your stick don't float here, goddamnit, take it somewhar else," Scarborough said only somewhat cryptically.

"Bah."

They followed the creek as it wound northeast, and two days later came out on rolling brush and piñon-covered high plains, having come out of the thick pines and around a small knob of mountain. To the east, and a little north, three jagged peaks thrust up almost arrogantly. And in those directions were more pines, heavy, thick stands of them.

It was then that Wolfe said, "We best cache what plunder we got, Russ."

Scarborough argued over it for a while, but he finally agreed, though he was still not happy with it. "But how we gonna git some breathin' room so's we got us some time to do it?" he asked, his voice on the edge of whining.

Wolfe shrugged. "We'll let all these animals go," he said simply, figuring they had no choice.

"You're goddamn *loco*," Scarborough exploded.

"You got a better idea?" Wolfe asked. He was not in the best of humors either. "Them shriekin' red niggurs are gonna be breathin' down our necks any minute. We don't do somethin' to throw 'em off, they'll be down on us before sundown. We can't keep runnin' from 'em forever."

"Like hell we can't."

"Booshwa. Like as not, our hair's gonna be hangin' from a Mojave lance, and they'll have the goddamn horses anyway."

"Hell," Scarborough growled. But he knew Wolfe was right. Unhappily, he nodded.

They turned out all the stolen horses, and Scarborough watched glumly as the animals raced off. "Come on," Wolfe snapped. He was none too happy about all this either.

Wolfe led the way to a spot he thought would be likely, and the two men began digging a cache. They finished and moved on eastward, the Mojaves almost in sight.

Wolfe and Scarborough made a cold camp that night, and kept a close watch, but they were not molested. They pushed on at first light, but by midmorning they became aware of a cloud of dust following them.

They passed the three mountains that were still slightly north of them now, and made their way into a land of glazed, black rock, spit out millennia ago by the volcanic cones of the San Francisco Peaks. The jagged rocks cut the horses' hooves, and, swearing, Scarborough turned them north, out into the high, flat country again.

The Mojaves, worried now that they were in Navajo country, hurried to catch up. Scarborough and Wolfe just managed to make the crumbled remains of an old pueblo, where they were protected by crumbling adobe and stone walls, before the Mojaves attacked again.

It was an odd place, but strong defensively. All around was flat land reaching off miles to the horizon. But right where they were was a small canyon, perhaps twenty feet deep. The old pueblo, not used for several centuries, had been built from the canyon bottom, up the wall and beyond.

The two men defended themselves easily from their vantage point in one of the "apartments" of the old Indian dwelling. They brought their saddle horses and pack mules into the "house," leaving them in the lower level.

"Goddamn, fractious, horse-stealin' savages," Scarborough roared, and shot another Mojave when the Indian, slinking along the ground, poked his head up a few inches.

But after losing two more warriors, the Mojaves had had enough. Besides, they had the horse herd and were happy enough about their hollow victory. They grabbed their dead and wounded and rode off, whooping.

"Such arrogant doin's don't shine with this niggur no how," Scarborough said. He raised his Hawken rifle and tried to shoot another Mojave. He missed, but the shot made the Indians ride off at a faster pace.

The two white men stayed that night in the old pueblo, after first making sure it was as clear of rattlesnakes and scorpions as they could make it—something they had not had a chance to do earlier. But the next morning, Scarborough said, "This old niggur's got to thinkin' that his

9

medicine's gone plumb bad." He looked even more sorrowful than usual.

"Hell, it's just some bad Injins, Russ. This ain't the first time a couple old mountaineers like us been took after by a pack of vexatious Injins."

"Well, that's true enough. But it don't shine with this ol' niggur to be sharin' my travels with no other coon no more. No, sir. Goddamnit, I need me some solitude to set my stick a-floatin' whar thar ain't no others about."

Wolfe wasn't all that put out. He had had more than enough adventure for a spell, and he was more than a little tired of Scarborough's quarrelsome nature and long bursts of unintelligible jabbering. Plus, he had wasted several months and had nothing to show for it. He missed his Rachel more than he was willing to admit to anyone but himself, and he wanted to get back to her something awful. He just nodded.

"Damnit, though, I hate to've lost them horses," Scarborough grumbled for perhaps the thousandth time.

"Hell, they were all stole anyway, damnit. We didn't lose nothin' by it."

"That's a fact, I reckon," Scarborough said dryly, trying to grin but failing miserably. "But we best leave them possibles cached a spell."

"How long?" Wolfe asked. He had been figuring on using that plunder to more than compensate him for the loss of two trapping seasons.

Scarborough shrugged. "We'll meet up one day and jaw it over."

"But . . ."

"That's what my stick floats, damnit," Scarborough said harshly, climbing onto his Indian pony. "Take it or leave it," he shouted as he rode off.

Wolfe stepped into his stirrup and pulled himself into his saddle. He slowly rode up the incline of the small canyon wall. At the top, he saw a speck riding away to the east across the flatness of the high country. He thought for a moment of heading back to the cache and digging up the plunder. He would only take his half, leaving the rest for Scarborough.

But he decided against it. The Mojaves were out that way; and if there were any Navajos in this vicinity, they most likely would be coming to see what all the ruckus had been about. Wolfe figured he had better get moving.

He touched his heels to the horse's sides, and rode off at a trot, heading north.

Chapter One

Though he was still in his early twenties, Lucas Wolfe knew from long experience that the best place to get information in a new town was at a saloon. So when he rode into Kaibab, Arizona Territory, he found the first likely looking saloon and stopped.

He dismounted and tied his horse to the hitching post out front of the High Country Saloon and took a quick glance around town.

Kaibab was a small place—he had heard it had just been settled, if that's the word one could use, in the past three years or so. It was typical of the area, with buildings made of adobe, brick, stone or pine wood. Some were stone with wooden false fronts on them. From inside the saloon, Wolfe could hear the tinkling of a cheap, out-of-tune piano.

He pushed into the saloon, making sure the two doors were shut behind him. Several men, townsmen from the look and dress of them, sat at tables. Three lean, hard cowboys, wearing work-soiled, frayed clothing and plain Colts riding high on their hips, stood drinking at the bar.

The bar itself was the most—well, it was really the only, Wolfe decided—impressive thing about the saloon. It was of heavy, dark, rich wood. It took up the left side of the short, narrow saloon. A brass foot rail ran the length of the bar, curving around the corner at each end.

Wolfe stepped up to the bar and ordered a bourbon. The bartender, a tall, heavyset, powerful-looking man with thick, greasy black hair and a graying black mustache, pulled the cork from a bottle and poured some liquor into a small glass.

"Leave the bottle," Wolfe said quietly.

The bartender hesitated until Wolfe dropped some coins on the bar. They landed with a dull ringing sound that got faster and faster, until it stopped when the coins were flat. Then the bartender nodded and set the bottle back down.

"Anything else?" the barman asked.

"Information," Wolfe said flatly.

The bartender looked at Wolfe with brown eyes that were sharper than they appeared to be. What they saw was a slim, hard-muscled man about five-foot-ten, perhaps one hundred seventy-five pounds. He was twenty-six years old, and his light brown eyes were clear. He had dusty brown hair, and his cheeks, chin and upper lip were stubbled. A blue, light-wool shirt was tucked into worn, blue denim pants. A dirty, white-patterned red bandanna encircled his neck, hanging in a triangle on his upper chest. He carried a Colt Peacemaker on his right hip. There was nothing fancy about the pistol, but the bartender—a shrewd judge of men—figured the young man knew how to use it.

"Information don't come easy," the barkeep growled quietly. "Or cheap."

"I ain't lookin' for clues to the lost gold of the Conquistadors, pard," Wolfe said softly. He chugged down the shot and silently refilled the glass.

The bartender looked a little disappointed. Then he shrugged and said, "Ask."

"There a place owned by the Corvallis family around here?" Wolfe asked.

"Yep. Owen Corvallis owns the Lazy O Ranch."

"Can you tell me where it is?"

"Yep."

Wolfe was aware that the three cowboys down the bar had gotten a little more alert and were staring at him. Wolfe downed his shot and pulled out another coin. "Such information can't be worth more'n this," he said quietly.

The bartender knew better than to mess with this man. "Reckon that'll do," he said, taking the coin and slipping it into a pocket. He poured another shot for Wolfe. He pointed and said, "Ride west maybe five miles. A small road forks off to the northwest. Take that. It'll bring you right to the ranch house."

The bartender looked at Wolfe with a question in his eyes. It was common enough for drifting cowpunchers to seek work at ranches in the area. And the Lazy O was the largest ranch between the Colorado River and the Hashknife Outfit far to the east. But this hard young man did not look much like a cowboy, the bartender thought. There was a quiet deadliness in the cool brown eyes and in the way the man carried himself.

But Wolfe gave the bartender no satisfaction. He simply nodded curtly and said, "Thanks, mister."

"Call me Orville," the bartender said. His tone indicated he expected a name in return. He did not get one.

Wolfe snapped the shot down his throat in one fluid move. He set the glass down, corked the bottle and grabbed it by the long, thin neck. Without another word, he walked out.

A little more than an hour later, he topped a juniper- and piñon-covered hump of land and looked down at the wide, softly undulating valley tucked between pine-forested hills. Cattle grazed off to the west, the tiny brown dots widely spaced as the animals searched for enough graze in the short, brown grass and amid sagebrush.

The house, a long, low, lonely looking place of blue-painted clapboard, was straight ahead.

Wolfe lightly touched his bootheels to the palomino's sides, nudging the horse forward. As he neared the sprawling house, Wolfe saw two men come out onto the long porch and stand in the shade, waiting for him. One had his thumbs hooked into his gunbelt. The other looked to be holding a riding quirt. Wolfe stopped the horse a few feet from the porch steps. "Howdy," he said politely.

"How do," the younger of the two men said. There was a distinct lack of friendliness in the voice. The man was about Wolfe's age, and a bit shorter, but bulkier. He wore good wool pants and a well-made cotton shirt. The Stetson he wore cost as much as four of Wolfe's would have, Wolfe guessed. And he wore two ivory-handled Colts. Wolfe figured him to be the ranch owner's son. "I'm Aaron Corvallis. This is my spread."

"Your old man's, you mean," Wolfe said quietly.

Anger flickered across Aaron's face and disappeared. He pointed to the man next to him. "This here's Ev Eyman, our foreman. You're looking for a job, you'll have to go through him."

Eyman was tall and thin, with a great hooked nose that dominated his face. He had thin lips and a bony chest covered by a threadbare, gray cotton shirt. Large, leather batwing chaps covered worn Levi's pants. His eyes were shaded by the porch roof and the weather-beaten felt hat.

"You ever run cattle before?" Eyman asked, his voice sounding like an ungreased windmill screeching in a gale.

"Your old man home, boy?" Wolfe asked Corvallis, paying Eyman no heed.

"I told you," Corvallis said angrily, "that Mr. Eyman here does the hiring."

"What makes you think I'd want to hire on with this outfit?" Wolfe asked nonchalantly. He wrapped his reins around the wide knob of the saddlehorn. He stretched up and back, working the kinks out of his muscles.

"Why else would a broken-down saddle tramp like you show up here?" Eyman asked quietly. There was no anger in his voice. Nor any real worry. Still, he was wary. He had run into enough hardcases in his lifetime to know that this young man was no run-of-the-mill cowpuncher.

"I'll discuss that with his old man," Wolfe said, pointing to Corvallis.

Corvallis had the loop of the short, hard-leather quirt wrapped around his wrist, and he held the whip in his hand. Now he snapped it against his thigh. "I got a good mind to horsewhip you, punk, and then run your butt off."

Wolfe calmly took out his fixings and started rolling a cigarette. "Do I make water in my pants now?" he asked sarcastically as he put away the fixings and licked the cigarette paper. "Or should I wait a spell?" He scraped a match across the rough seam of his pants and fired up the cigarette. He flicked the still-burning match at Corvallis.

Corvallis was hard-pressed not to leap out of the way, but he managed to stand his ground. The match hit his chest and bounced off. His eyes blazed hotter than Wolfe's cigarette. His right hand glided toward one of the ivory-handled Colts.

Suddenly Eyman's hand snaked out and grabbed him. "Don't, Aaron," he said.

Corvallis stared at Wolfe, hate smoldering in his eyes. But his hand dropped.

Wolfe and Eyman stared flatly at each other for a few moments. Each knew that Eyman had just saved Corvallis's life. What they didn't know was whether they had also saved Eyman's life—or possibly Wolfe's.

"Now, I asked you once, boy, and I'll even ask this one more time. But you best be warned, I'll not ask a third time. Is your old man around?"

"Who should we say is callin'?" Eyman said, cutting off a retort from Corvallis.

"Tell him Lucas Wolfe is here to see him."

"He ain't here," Corvallis said sharply.

Before either of the other men could say anything, a man in his fifties stepped out of the house onto the

17

porch. "Who ain't here?" he asked in a pleasant baritone.

"You Mr. Corvallis?" Wolfe asked, stubbing out his cigarette on his saddle.

"Yes, sir," the man answered. "And you are?"

Corvallis was, Wolfe thought, a dignified man. Still tall and strong looking, his face was creased with years of riding open ranges in all kinds of weather. His hair was graying, but was still thick and full, as were his muttonchops and mustache. His clothes were expensive and tailored, an interesting counterpoint to the hard life reflected on his wide face.

"Name's Lucas Wolfe."

"Any relation to Bill Wolfe?"

"He was my father, sir."

"Well, a pleasure to make your acquaintance, Mr. Wolfe. I knew your father some back in the old days. How is he?"

"Been dead several years now," Wolfe said offhandedly. He and his father had not gotten along all that well, though Luke had cared for his father. Still, Bill Wolfe had not been a big part of Luke Wolfe's life, for many reasons. "Him and all the rest of the family were killed by Apaches down in the Seven Springs area of this territory."

"I'm sorry to hear that, Mr. Wolfe. You have my condolences. Bill Wolfe was a fine man."

Wolfe shrugged. "Life's like that, Mr. Corvallis, as I'm sure you know."

Corvallis nodded. This young man was wise beyond his years. "Well, what can I do for you, Mr. Wolfe?"

"I'd be obliged for some of your time, Mr. Corvallis. I'd like to bend your ear a bit."

"Oh? And about what?"

"This land," Wolfe said quietly.

"Want me to run him off, Pa?" Aaron asked, almost eagerly, Wolfe thought. He stared at Wolfe, though he was addressing his father. "Me and Ev were about to do

so when you come out. But if he's being a pest or something . . ."

This boy's in a real hurry to die, Wolfe thought. He
was .of half a mind to oblige. But he thought it best to
wait.

"No, son," Corvallis said. "We don't turn people away
here. He looks like he's had a long ride. Hospitality says
we offer him a meal, something to drink. And maybe
even a little time for talk." He smiled up at Wolfe.

"But . . ."

"I said that's the way it's going to be, boy," Corvallis
said sharply. "And I'll hear no argument of it."

Wolfe wondered at the exchange. To him it seemed
that Corvallis was very disappointed in his son. At the
same time the elder Corvallis was trying to be civil to his
son. Perhaps he was the only heir, and while Owen Corvallis might not like his son much, he had to be at least
somewhat considerate of his only heir.

"Light and tie, Mr. Wolfe," Corvallis said. "Ev will see
that your horse is well taken care of."

Wolfe glanced at Eyman, who nodded once, curtly,
but with no disrespect, in his direction. It told Wolfe that
Eyman did not think it an onerous task.

Wolfe dismounted and stepped up onto the porch. He
shook Corvallis's outstretched hand. The two Corvallises
and Wolfe entered the house and sat in a well-appointed
living room. The room reeked of Western maleness, with
guns and animal heads and skins hanging on the walls;
other skins were spread on the floor. Several chairs were
made of elk antlers.

A young woman entered the room, and Wolfe's breath
caught in his throat. She was perhaps five-foot-two, and
quite curvaceous, even accounting for the petticoats
under her neck-to-ankle wool dress. Reddish-gold hair
hung, long and straight, onto her back, and framed a
delicate, sun-tanned face of elegant cheekbones, shimmering blue eyes, finely crafted eyebrows and perfect
lips.

19

Wolfe scrambled to stand as Corvallis said, "Mr. Wolfe, my daughter, Sally."

Wolfe, uncomfortable in the presence of such radiance, mumbled something and was rewarded by a soft, pleasant giggle. He was a little more prepared a few minutes later when she came and handed him a tumbler full of bourbon.

"To your health, sir," Corvallis said, raising his glass.

Wolfe nodded, and raised his, noting the sour expression and lack of effort on Aaron's part.

"Now, Mr. Wolfe," Corvallis said with a smile, "what do you want to know about this land?"

"I don't want to know anything about this land, Mr. Corvallis," Wolfe said, also smiling. He liked Owen Corvallis, he found. "I just want to say something about it."

"And that is?" Corvallis asked, still jovial, despite knowing what was coming.

"This land is mine, sir," Wolfe said quietly.

Aaron Corvallis almost choked on his whiskey. But Owen just grinned.

Sally Corvallis appeared in the doorway to the room. "Dinner is served, gentlemen," she said.

Chapter Two

Dinner was a rather strained affair. Owen Corvallis was wary, his son angry, his daughter interested, and Lucas Wolfe almost smug. But they all retained a semblance of civility as they passed along baked chicken, chickpeas, boiled potatoes, fresh baked bread and rolls, and coffee.

After the meal, the three men retired to the den once more. Aaron, surly, grabbed a tumbler full of bourbon and sat heavily in an antler chair. His father threw him an angry look, but he composed himself before turning to Wolfe. He handed Wolfe a glass of bourbon.

Sally Corvallis entered the room, not at all uncomfortable in a world of such blatant and uncompromising maleness. She picked up a box of cigars from the large, solid wood desk in one corner. Coming over to Wolfe, she held out the box, opened. With a charming smile, she asked, "A cigar, Mr. Wolfe?"

"Thank you, ma'am," Wolfe said politely, pulling a cigar from the hard-cardboard box. He sniffed it a moment, appreciating its rich aroma. He bit off an end and spit the piece into the fireplace to his right. He scraped a match on the arm of the chair and lit the cigar. He sat back, enjoying the thick, blue smoke.

The elder Corvallis also lit a cigar. He slumped into a chair across from Wolfe and said, "Now, sir, let's talk about my land."

"Like I said, Mr. Corvallis, it's my land."

"And where'd you ever get such a notion, boy?" Corvallis asked, a slight smile curling his lips. He liked this brash young man, and was not at all shamed by wishing that Wolfe, not Aaron, was his son.

"My Grandpa Jeb laid claim to this land years ago. I reckon it's mine, and I come to take it back."

"This here's my land, Mr. Wolfe," Corvallis said, not angry. He was almost bemused. "I won it fair and square. I even got the papers – signed by your father – to prove it."

"You mind tellin' me just how you come to have possession of those papers – and the land?"

"He already told you, you stupid clod," Aaron snapped. He had finished the brimming tumbler of whiskey and was halfway through another already. His face was a bit flushed.

Sally, standing behind her father, rubbing on his shoulders, cast a disapproving glance toward her brother. But when she looked back at Wolfe, her face was serene and she was smiling. Everyone ignored Aaron.

"Well, sir," Corvallis said, staring through a swirling cloud of cigar smoke. "It was almost ten years ago now I got the land. Me and your father had met down in Prescott, where we were working the mines, each trying to get a grubstake up."

Though it was less than twenty years ago, they seemed a lot younger then, full of energy and ambition. Owen Corvallis, tall, broad-shouldered, imbued with some book learning and a little culture. Bill Wolfe was shorter and slighter, a whipcord strong, generally peaceful man. But he was one who could not be pushed too far. If he was, he would explode, and become like another man.

The two men had met in Prescott, Arizona Territory, three years after the end of the Civil War. They worked in the mines together. Each had a family, and the two men would talk together nights in the saloon, sharing their thoughts. Sometimes, when times got hard, they would split a loaf of days-old bread and some jerky or beans, trying to stretch out what little they had.

But their friendship fell apart just about ten years ago. They were still living in Prescott, working in the mines. Corvallis, though, had moved ahead, which put heavy strains on his friendship with Wolfe.

Corvallis was the son of a fairly well-off merchant in Pittsburgh, and so had some education. He was good with money and figuring and such. Because of that, he had several years earlier moved up the ranks from miner to shift foreman, and recently to a job in the office working with the company's books.

Wolfe, the son of a former mountain man and a dirt-poor farm girl he had met in St. Charles, had taken on many of his father's ways. Not the least of those ways was his penchant for blowing money on foofaraw. His wife did not like such a thing, and it was a constant source of friction between them.

It wasn't so much that Wolfe was a bad man. He was not. But he did have a mighty free hand when it came to money. It was common for him to buy the house a round or two on the day the boys at the mines got their pay. It bothered him that Corvallis kept getting ahead while he never went anywhere. But he would never tell his old friend so. Still, a simmering resentment lingered, and he was not introspective enough to see that he was angry at himself for his foolish, free-spending ways.

Still, they often were seen together, drinking in the Prescott Palace Saloon, and playing cards. It was a card game that finally ended their friendship.

Six men were playing, and no one was winning or losing much, though Corvallis's luck seemed a little better than that of the other men. Wolfe had been drinking freely, and was getting both boisterous and obstreperous. Finally the deal came around to him again, and he chose to deal seven-card stud.

"I think you're luck's runnin' a little too good, Owen," Wolfe said, words slurred a bit. "I reckon it's time for that to change."

Corvallis ignored the insult, and its implications, saying only, "Deal 'em, Bill."

Wolfe did. The man to his left, Corter, had a nine and a queen showing; the next, Hotchkin, a two and a seven; then Corvallis, a nine and an eight; Pohlski, with a three and a ace; McSwerley, a six and a jack; and finally Wolfe, who had an ace and a seven up.

Pohlski tossed a dollar into the pot, and was called by all. Wolfe passed out another up card, in order, an ace; four; another nine, giving Corvallis a pair of nines; ten; five; and another ace for himself, giving him a pair.

Wolfe carefully lifted up the corner of his hole cards and checked them. Keeping a straight face, he threw a five-dollar gold piece into the pot. Corter dropped out, but Hotchkin, Corvallis, Pohlski and McSwerley called.

Another face-up card was dealt, bringing Hotchkin a six; Corvallis another eight, giving him two pair showing; a five for Pohlski; and queen for McSwerley; and a deuce for Wolfe, who scowled before composing himself.

"Two pair's got the bet," Wolfe said.

"I know," Corvallis said with a confident grin. "I'm just trying to decide how much to charge you boys to stick around a bit."

"Whatever it is, it's too damn much for me," Pohlski said, tossing his cards in.

"Same here," Hotchkin said, following suit.

Corvallis threw two five-dollar gold pieces into the growing pot and sat back.

Wolfe grinned. He saw the bet and added two five-dollar bills to the pile. He turned to face McSwerley.

The miner was dirty of face and clothes, like all his compatriots except for Corvallis. He shoved back his stained cloth hat, contemplating. Finally he shrugged and tossed in twenty dollars.

Corvallis nodded. He saw the ten-dollar raise and then put in another twenty-five dollars.

McSwerley sucked breath in past his teeth, and Wolfe's eyes grew wide. Wolfe checked his hole cards again, and smiled inwardly. He nodded and added thirty-five dollars in various bills to the pot. As Corvallis looked at McSwerley, Wolfe glanced down at his stash. What had started out as a decent pile of money was down to thirteen dollars and seventy cents. Betsy was going to kill him if he didn't win this pot.

McSwerley shook his head. "This 'un's too rich for my blood," he muttered, scraping up his cards and tossing them toward the center of the table.

Wolfe, suddenly dry of mouth, flicked a down card toward Corvallis, and then slapped another onto his hole cards. He set the remainder of the deck down and carefully lifted up the corner of the last card.

Corvallis looked at his last card, too, though he did not seem all that interested. "Let's cut the crap," he said pleasantly. It was another thing that annoyed Wolfe. Owen Corvallis was always pleasant. Corvallis picked up a pile of bills and set them atop the pot. "Fifty dollars," he said quietly.

Wolfe managed to stifle the sinking feeling of fear that gripped his belly and to keep a straight face. But there were several gasps, and a number of miners began gathering around to watch.

"I ain't got that much," Wolfe croaked, embarrassed.

Corvallis shrugged and reached for the money in the center of the table.

"You can't do this to me, Owen," Wolfe said, trying hard to keep the pleading out of his voice. "We been friends too long."

Corvallis stopped and leaned back. "What do you propose?"

"I'll use what I got," Wolfe said with some relief, "and pledge the rest out of my next wages."

"Not good enough, Bill. You owe too much money

25

around town as it is."

Wolfe sat thinking for some moments. Then, with a sense of dread, but his usual feeling of bravado, he pulled a piece of paper from a shirt pocket. With a careless flip of the wrist, he tossed it onto the pot. "It's the title for some land I own north of here," he said casually.

"The land you've always talked about? Up near that mountain named for some old mountain man?"

"Yep. My pa named me for the same old mountain man—Bill Williams."

"How much land?"

"Fifty thousand acres."

Corvallis kept his face composed. "I reckon that'll cover my bet."

"Plus some," Wolfe countered.

Corvallis acknowledged it with a nod. "Then I'm called," he said quietly. Never taking his eyes off Wolfe's, he turned over two of the three face-down cards, revealing two eights. "Four of a kind," he said, still in a soft voice.

"Damn," Wolfe breathed as he turned over two cards, showing three aces and two sevens. He watched in disgust as Corvallis spread his hands around the pot and pulled it toward him. Corvallis did not gloat, which Wolfe would have done. Wolfe fought back the tears of frustration as he gathered up his thirteen dollars and seventy cents. Sticking the money in his pocket, he downed the last of his whiskey and stumbled out of the saloon and into the night.

"So you see, Mr. Wolfe," Corvallis said to Lucas Wolfe, "it was all on the up and up." He shrugged and threw the cigar butt into the fire. "I left Prescott a couple years later and came up here. I had been working all that time for a stake to buy land, as well as cattle. I had some money saved up, but it wasn't enough. Without having to buy the land, though, I didn't need too

26

much more to buy cattle and other stock."

"And we've all lived happily ever after," Aaron Corvallis said drunkenly. " 'Till you come along causin' trouble."

Wolfe glanced at the younger Corvallis briefly, and with irritation. He looked back at Owen. "You seem a nice man, Mr. Corvallis. And your daughter's certainly a fine woman." He coughed a moment in embarrassment. "But your boy here could use a few lessons in manners."

"You gonna give 'em to me?" Aaron Corvallis asked, his voice slurred.

"Wouldn't put me out none," Wolfe said easily.

Aaron Corvallis stood, weaving a little. His handsome, though cruel, face was flushed from the alcohol. His right hand twitched near the butt of his Colt pistol. "Come on, then," he said, trying to sound tough.

"Aaron!" his father said sharply. "That's enough! Either take yourself up to bed, or go on out to the bunkhouse till you sober up." There was no equivocation in his voice. He did not even look at his son.

Aaron Corvallis stood, sneering at Wolfe, who was mildly amused at the petty arrogance—and attendant stupidity—of the younger Corvallis. Aaron knew better than to argue with his father. He lurched off after a few moments.

When Aaron was gone, Owen said, "My apologies, Mr. Wolfe. Since Aaron is my first born—and my only son—I'm afraid he has been indulged more than a little. My wife . . ."

Sally Corvallis playfully swatted her father. "Don't you go blaming Mama now, Pa. You're just as bad when it comes to that boy."

Corvallis grinned and rolled his eyes up, trying to see his daughter. "And I suppose me and your ma've been so cruel to you, eh, girl?"

Sally giggled, and the sound sent a thrill racing up Wolfe's spine. "I didn't say that, Pa."

"That's true, you didn't," Corvallis said, patting one of

Sally's hands on his shoulder. He looked at Wolfe. "Just the same, Mr. Wolfe, I apologize."

Wolfe shrugged it off.

"Another drink, Mr. Wolfe?" Corvallis asked.

"Reckon so. But only one." He grinned. "And I'd be obliged for another of those cigars."

"Daughter, please," Corvallis said.

Sally refilled Wolfe's glass and then Owen's. She handed the young visitor a cigar, smiling warmly at him.

Chapter Three

Lucas Wolfe sipped his drink for some minutes, thinking. He did not know his father all that well, and perhaps Corvallis was telling the truth. Corvallis seemed a nice enough man, and Wolfe had warmed up to him quite rapidly.

"That ain't the way I heard it," he finally said in tones calculated not to raise ire.

"Oh?" Corvallis questioned. "How'd you hear it?"

"Well, sir, I remember Pa tellin' Gramps about it. If old Grandpa Jeb wasn't ailin' at the time, I do believe he would've come down here and took his land back."

Corvallis raised his eyebrows at Wolfe but said nothing.

"Pa told Gramps that he lost the title to the land in a card game. That much is true enough. But . . ."

Much of what Corvallis had said was similar to what Bill Wolfe had told Jeb. Still, there were discrepancies.

"Well," Wolfe continued, becoming embarrassed by what he had to say, "my father intimated that you cheated in that game."

"I'd expect a man who had lost title to fifty thousand acres in a card game to say he'd been cheated," Corvallis said with a sympathetic chuckle. "Hell, I'd do the same."

"He seemed quite sure of it," Wolfe insisted, growing

29

more discomfited. "And my father wasn't much takin' with lyin', at least as far as I knew him."

"I wasn't callin' Bill a liar, son," Corvallis said quietly. He smiled. "But just how was I supposed to have pulled off this wondrous sleight of hand?" Corvallis asked. He was rather amused, though still understanding.

Wolfe shrugged. All he knew was what he had heard his father tell his grandfather.

Bill Wolfe was excited as he looked at his two hole cards, but he kept his face bland. He had a pair of aces showing on the table. And in the hole, he had another ace and another seven, giving him a full house, aces over seven.

Across from him, Owen Corvallis had two pair showing, nines and eights. Even if he had a third of either in the hole, his full house could not match Wolfe's. Wolfe figured that finally he would be able to get his old friend.

Old friend! he thought then. Not with the way Corvallis had been treating him—and the other dirt-poor, hump-breaking miners who toiled away for the Prescott Gold Extraction Company. Ever since Corvallis had gotten his promotion into the office, he had been treating the others rather poorly, and Wolfe did not like it. He and Corvallis had gone through too much together in the eight years since they had met.

It wasn't so much what Corvallis did, Wolfe thought, as it was the way he acted. All of a sudden he thought he was better than the other miners. He was arrogant and condescending when talking to the miners he had once worked shoulder to shoulder with. And he wore better clothes now—suits made of wool, and white shirts and polished boots. That, to Wolfe, seemed to rub the miners' noses in the fact that they could afford only work clothes, and those quickly became permanently soiled.

Wolfe wanted to gloat over his good fortune now. With the hand he had, he figured he could not lose. Still, he looked down at the small pile of bills and coins at his side—thirteen dollars and seventy cents. Not enough to counter whatever Corvallis was going to bet, he knew.

Sure enough, Corvallis bet fifty dollars. Wolfe's heart sank and he had a sick feeling in his stomach, especially looking at the self-satisfied smile on Corvallis's face. Damn, it made him mad to have Corvallis buy a pot like this. Wolfe figured Corvallis knew damn well he couldn't win and so was trying to drive Wolfe out with such a large bet.

He was also angry at himself. He was one of the guys, and enjoyed that feeling. He was not above buying a round or two now and again for the others. Most of the other men would reciprocate, and though maybe he was a little more open-handed than most of the boys, at least he wasn't as tight-fisted as Corvallis. Still, he knew that if he had been a little more circumspect with his money, he would have been able to cover the bet.

"I can't cover that, Owen," he said quietly, sadly. "You know that."

"Reckon I won, then." Corvallis began reaching out to rake in his pot.

"Wait!" Wolfe said urgently. He could not let this pot get away from him. There had to be something he could do.

Corvalis stopped and then sat back, waiting expectantly.

"I'll use what I got," Wolfe said with some relief, "and pledge the rest out of my next wages."

"Not good enough, Bill. You owe too much money around town as it is." It wasn't said nastily as much as it was said condescendingly, irritating Wolfe all the more.

"It's the best I can do, Owen."

"Then you've lost, Bill."

"You can't do this to me, Owen," Wolfe said, trying to keep the pleading out of his voice. "We been friends too long."

"Friendship ain't got no place in a card game, Bill. You know that. You ain't got the cash to pony up . . ." He shrugged. There was nothing he could do; Bill Wolfe knew the rules of the game as well as anyone. "Unless," Corvallis said with false benignity, "you got something else of value you'd care to put up." He looked at his friend questioningly.

Wolfe thought, but he owned little of value. He sat, staring straight ahead, the sick feeling spreading.

"What about that land you told me you have title to?" Corvallis asked slyly.

"No, Owen," Wolfe said with a slight note of desperation. "I couldn't do that."

"It'll cover the bet."

"More'n that, I'd say."

"I reckon you got yourself a good hand there, Bill," Corvallis said soothingly. "Or else you wouldn't be so pushy on all this. I reckon if you think it's that good, you'll put up your land. You ain't got much to worry about, I imagine."

Wolfe had told Corvallis about the land—fifty thousand acres! Corvallis remembered—several years back. Wolfe had told Corvallis that he was trying to raise enough of a stake to go to the land and start a ranch. That had been enough to get Corvallis to thinking. And for the past several years, he had been wondering how he could get that and. He, too, was working to get a stake—but he would have to buy a hunk of land before investing in cattle and what else he would need. But if he could get title to fifty thousand acres, he figured he would be set.

He had been too honest to steal it, but he wanted to be able to take advantage of any opportunity that came along. Finally one had presented itself. He knew, though, that he could not push Wolfe too far, or Wolfe would simply drop out, leaving him only the pot. Not that the cash in the pot was anything to sneeze at, but it wasn't fifty thousand acres, either.

And Corvallis had no doubt he would win the hand. He was certain Wolfe could not best him, even if he did have a full house, as Corvallis suspected he did.

He started to reach for the pot in the center of the table again. "Well, Bill, if you ain't gonna put that title up to cover what I've wagered, I reckon this's all mine."

"Wait," Wolfe said again, but this time it came out as a croak. He took a slim leather wallet from a breast pocket. From that he extracted a folded piece of paper. With a trembling hand he reached over and set it carefully on the top of the money. "I call," he whispered, fear clogging his throat.

If it wasn't for the crashing thump of his heart, Wolfe would have thought he had died and gone straight to hell when Corvallis spread out the four eights on the wood table top. Wolfe found it hard to breathe suddenly, and his eyesight blurred as he watched the slip of paper that had been his future being dragged away by the greedy arms of Owen Corvallis. And he was barely conscious of what he was doing when he scooped up the few meager dollars he had left and stumbled out the door.

"You still haven't said how I could've cheated, Mr. Wolfe," Corvallis said.

"Double-dealin'," Lucas Wolfe said unconvincingly.

"Your father dealt that hand, Mr. Wolfe," Corvallis said softly.

"Hidin' cards maybe," Wolfe said without much hope.

Corvallis hesitated, then said, still quietly, "I didn't cheat, Mr. Wolfe. I won that land fair and square. Your father was so sure of winning that he gave no thought to the consequences of losing when he put that title into the pot."

"Hell, Mr. Corvallis," Wolfe said a little heatedly, "you could've offered to sell the title back to him. Surely you know how much a man values land."

"I do know. I value it as highly as any man. Your father and I are about the same age. When I won that title, I saw my chance. I care for my family as much as any man, Mr. Wolfe. And with that piece of paper in hand, I could see my way clear to taking proper care of my family."

Wolfe nodded sadly.

"Speaking of such things," Corvallis said, "I don't recall you being with your father—your family—down in Prescott. There was a boy in the family. No, two. And a girl. But you don't seem the right age for it."

"I wasn't there. Me and Pa never got on real well." He was not embarrassed by it; it was simply a fact. When he was only three years old, his father had gone off to fight in the Civil War, leaving the young Luke Wolfe with his mother, Betsy, and grandmother and grandfather, Jeb and Rachel, in St. Charles, Missouri.

Bill Wolfe was almost a stranger to his son when he finally mustered out three and a half years later, and the father had more things on his mind than getting reacquainted with his son.

By the time the boy was almost ten, Bill Wolfe was ready to move west, two years after the war. But Lucas was much like his grandfather by then—independent and hard-headed. He refused to go with his father, mother and two young siblings.

So the Bill Wolfe family had headed west to seek their fortune with only seven-year-old Mark and almost two-year-old Betty along with them.

Wolfe broke away from his reverie when Corvallis asked, "Then why are you so concerned about land your father lost?"

"More for my Grandpa Jeb than for my father," Wolfe

said after several moments' hesitation. He had to be sure he didn't say too much. "Grandpa come through here back in the late thirties, forties with Bill Williams . . ."

"The mountain man for whom the mountain and river near here are named?" Corvallis asked, eyes bright with interest.

"The same. Gramps said he fell in love with this land when he come through here. He wasn't able to get back for some years, though, and lay claim to it. He had a store up there in St. Charles that kept him busy. He didn't want to give that up just to come down here and try'n work the land. Or try'n get a town started. Soon after the war, he gave the title to my pa."

"It's good land, that's for sure."

Wolfe nodded. "Gramps passed on late last year, and told me about the land here, and how you 'stole' it from Pa. He asked me to try'n get it back."

"I reckon you've come a long way for nothing, then, Mr. Wolfe," Corvallis said, seemingly apologetic. "I've held title to this land for nearly ten years, and I've been running the Lazy O Ranch almost that long. I've provided well for my family here and have no intention of just giving it up to fulfill some man's dying wish."

There was no rancor in the man's words, just determination.

Wolfe nodded, understanding. He had liked Owen Corvallis right from the start, and he saw no reason to change his opinion now, just because Corvallis was doing what any other man would do under the circumstances. "Well," he said finally, "I hope you don't mind me pokin' around some, maybe droppin' in to try'n talk you into changin' your mind."

"Don't mind a'tall," Corvallis said with an easy smile. He was aware of his daughter's hand still on his shoulder. It had gripped hard when it seemed that this might be the last they saw of Lucas Wolfe and relaxed at her father's last statement.

35

"I'm obliged, sir," Wolfe said, standing. "Well, reckon I'd best be gettin' on back to Kaibab and find a room."

"You're welcome to stay here at the house, Mr. Wolfe," Corvallis said, knowing Sally would be pleased at such a thing. He doted on his daughter, and wanted to indulge her as much as reasonably possible.

"Thanks, Mr. Corvallis. But I reckon it'd be best all around if I was to stay in town and just pay my respects here occasional."

Chapter Four

Kaibab wasn't all that much of a town, though it had grown considerably in the three years since its founding. The main street—Corvallis Road—was a ragged track that meandered roughly east and west between the store fronts. One large street—Williams Street—cut across Corvallis Road about in the center of Kaibab, and several other, smaller streets entered at various points.

On the northwest corner of Corvallis Road and Williams Street was the High Country Saloon; catty-corner from it was Fletcher's Hotel. It was the cleanest looking hotel in Kaibab.

Wolfe stopped in front of the hotel and tied his horse to the hitching post. He realized the hotel and Rice's Mercantile across Williams Street were the only two places in Kaibab that he had seen with sidewalks in front.

It was dusk as he stepped into the hotel. A well-dressed, still-attractive woman of about forty was behind the counter. She smiled sweetly at Wolfe as he entered. Wolfe appraised her as he neared the desk. She was a little on the plump side, but not overly so, and wore too much rouge. Clouds of perfume wafted up off of her. She had dark eyes that sparkled with life and humor. When he stopped at the desk, he noted that the woman was displaying an ample amount of cleavage. He didn't mind.

"Need a room?" she asked in a pleasant voice.

"Yes'm."

"How long?"

"Ain't certain," Wolfe shrugged.

"Room's four bits a day; three dollars if you take a week."

"Let's put me down for a week, then."

Wolfe signed the register in his scratchy handwriting and gave over three dollar bills.

The woman nodded. "I'm Alma Fletcher. I own this place. I also own the restaurant next door. It's closed now, but if you're hungry, I imagine we could rustle you up something."

"I've ate, ma'am. Thank you."

"I'm also part owner of the High Country Saloon across the street. That's still open." She smiled, making her look some years younger.

"I reckon I got me enough of a dry built up that I could go'n cut it some."

Alma smiled again and said boldly, "I also own the place right around the corner here on Williams Street." She chucked a thumb in a southwesterly direction. "In case you got a thirst of a different kind."

Wolfe looked at her blankly a minute, confused. With a huge grin, Alma pulled open the already gaping bodice of her loose, silk dress, baring her breasts. "You do like girls, don't you, mister? she asked sweetly.

Wolfe reddened and stammered, "Yes'm."

"That's good to know," Alma said, grinning as she covered herself up some. She handed him a red poker chip emblazoned with the words "Fletcher's Hotel" in gold letters. "If you're interested, give this to the folks over there. Gets you a discount."

Wolfe was losing his embarrassment fast. "I expect that might not be such an awful thing," he noted. He took his key and headed upstairs to his room, his saddlebags slung over his left shoulder, and his Winchester in his left hand.

The room was typical of such a place, though perhaps a bit bigger than most he had seen. It contained a sagging, quilt-covered bed with four short wood posts; to its right, at the window was a small, round table on which a coal-oil lantern sat; a chair that had once been plushly upholstered was next to the table; on the other side of the room was a very small table with a basin and pitcher, with a face towel folded up next to them; under it was a chamber pot; above it was a small, murky mirror.

He dropped his saddlebags and rifle on the bed. He stretched and went to the smaller table. He was surprised to see that the pitcher was full. He poured some water into the basin and then rinsed off his face and hands. After drying off, he tried to flatten down his hair, grimacing into the mirror.

Giving it up as hopeless, he left. Outside, he turned left and then left again onto Williams Street. The first building he came to was large and more ornate than any other he had seen in Kaibab. It, too, had a sidewalk in front. Without hesitation, he climbed the seven steps to the porch and then entered.

A plump, fairly attractive young half-breed wearing only a thin silk robe over a scanty chemise greeted him. "Welcome, sir," she said, smiling brightly. "Can I help you?"

"I expect," Wolfe said, feeling the heat growing in his groin. "You available?"

"Of course." She smiled while she paused. "But perhaps you'd rather see who else is available?" she questioned.

"Can't be none other as pretty as you are," Wolfe said gallantly, smiling.

"Thank you, sir," the woman said with a smile and a

curtsy. "My name's Esther."

"Pleased to meet you, Esther," Wolfe said, touching the brim of his hat. "I'm Lucas Wolfe."

Esther took his hand and led him toward and then up the stairway. She opened the door to a room and allowed him in first. Inside, she said, "I hate to bring this up, Mr. Wolfe, but I'll need to be paid before we get down to business."

"Don't you trust me, Esther?"

She grinned. "Oh, sure, I trust you, Mr. Wolfe. But I don't expect Miz Alma'll think kindly of me was I to get taken by you, or any other man. Them's the rules."

"Yes'm," Wolfe said with a grin. "And speakin' of Miz Alma . . ." He dug out the poker chip and handed it to Esther. She nodded and took it, then the cash he held out.

An hour later, Wolfe was strolling into the High Country Saloon. The place was about half full. Wolfe went to the bar and ordered a bottle.

"You find the Corvallis place all right?" the bartender asked.

"Yep. Thanks, Orville."

"My pleasure."

Wolfe took the bottle and a shot glass and wandered off to a table, the back of his chair to the northeast wall, where he could watch the door.

Before long, Aaron Corvallis, Ev Eyman and three other men came in. They went to the bar and talked with Orville for a moment. The bartender pointed in Wolfe's direction, and the five men turned and headed that way. Watching them, Wolfe loosened his Colt in the holster, and left his hand resting lightly on the butt. He drank with his left hand.

The five stopped in front of the table, spread out a little, with Corvallis in the center, Eyman to his right.

"Evenin', boys," Wolfe said pleasantly.

"The hell with you, Wolfe," Corvallis snapped. His eyes were bloodshot, and Wolfe figured he must have a fair-sized hangover.

"You must've gone to some big, fancy-pants college back East to be so well-versed with words, Aaron," Wolfe said with a sneering grin.

Eyman fought back a chuckle, though the three other cowboys stayed stony of face.

"I don't need fancy words for what I've got to say to you, Wolfe," Corvallis snapped, his anger bolstered by Wolfe's unconcerned attitude.

"And I don't need to hear anything you got to say, Corvallis, so you can take yourself — and your fellow idiots — and get the hell out of here."

"Don't let me catch you out at the Lazy O Ranch again, Wolfe," Corvallis said, seething. "Or I'll not be responsible for what happens."

Wolfe laughed, then said, "Lordy, someone of you boys best hold me down so I don't fall to pieces. I'm quakin' so hard with the fright."

Eyman stood back, saying nothing, his face bland, but Wolfe had a suspicion that the ranch foreman was rather enjoying seeing Aaron Corvallis taken down some. He could not enjoy taking orders from the arrogant, foolish young man.

Corvallis's chest heaved with the anger that burned inside. "Just heed my warning, Wolfe."

Wolfe set his glass down carefully on the table. Warily watching all five men facing him, he stood slowly, his hand near the butt of his Colt Peacemaker.

"Now listen to me, boy," he said quietly but fiercely. "I'll ride wherever the hell I please, whenever the hell I please. You get in my way, and you'll **not** see the next sunrise."

"You're mighty goddamn cocky for a man outnumbered five to one," Corvallis said, gaining back some of his usual arrogance.

"I've got five rounds in my Colt—that evens the odds, Corvallis."

They faced each other, waiting, the tension rising. It was silent now, except for an occasional cough from one person or other hiding behind an overturned table. Many of the other customers had already fled.

Suddenly Corvallis relaxed. He nodded, trying to grin. "I get it," he said. He reached into a pocket and pulled out a wad of bills. He tossed most of them onto the table. "There," he said. "That ought to compensate you for your travels and such."

The malevolence on Wolfe's face was weighty, and it was all directed at Corvallis, who was taken somewhat aback. Corvallis licked his lips, thinking perhaps he had underestimated Wolfe. He tossed the rest of the bills on the table with the others. "All right, that's more than fair," he said boldly. "Just take it and ride on out of Kaibab. I don't care where you go, as long as it's nowhere near the Lazy O Ranch."

Wolfe was far more angry than Corvallis realized, but he kept himself in check. He did note, however, that one of the cowboys had shifted his hand so that it almost rested on his pistol.

"Ev," Wolfe said quietly, though he still glared at Corvallis, "you better get this pissant punk away from me—if you value his life at all."

Eyman was about to respond, cutting off Corvallis's smart aleck retort, when the cowboy who was fingering his pistol snatched at the Colt.

Things moved in a blur as Wolfe ripped out his Colt, thumbed back the hammer and fired, all in one oiled move. He could risk only one shot, since there were four other men, and he only had four slugs left. He was fairly certain Eyman would not join in the fracas, but he was not at all sure about the others—particularly Corvallis.

42

But the one shot was all he needed for the moment. The bullet shattered the cowboy's sternum before ripping through his lungs and sending a shower of bone into the heart. He had not even gotten his pistol all the way out when he fell, half-twisted, coughing out blood and his life on the floor of the saloon.

The two other cowboys started to go for their weapons. Corvallis did, too, but Eyman swung in front of him and yanked Corvallis's pistol away from him before spinning back toward Wolfe, the pistol held loosely, non-threatening.

Wolfe had the drop on the other two cowboys, who had let their hands fall and were standing nervously, waiting for Wolfe's next move.

"I expect such stupidity from Aaron here, boys," Wolfe said, directing his words toward the two cowboys. "I got no complaints with you two, unless you insist on comin' against me again. In which case, the undertaker's gonna plant your butts straight off."

"We're just doin' our job, Mr. Wolfe," one said.

"Did Owen Corvallis send you out here for this?" Wolfe queried.

"No, sir. Aaron asked us to come along."

"Then you ain't doin' your jobs. Your job—both of you—is punchin' cows, ridin' fences and other such things. It ain't gunnin' for folks on the say-so of some goddamn idiot." He paused for a breath. "Now take your friend and get the hell out of here. You can wait outside for the other two."

The cowpokes needed no further prodding. They grabbed up the dead man and hurried out. Wolfe turned to face Eyman and Corvallis. He nodded barely perceptibly at Eyman. "You're a lucky bastard, Corvallis," he said.

Corvallis was enraged but said nothing. His hands itched, though, as if he wished he had a gun in them.

"It wasn't for Ev here, they'd be haulin' you out along

with that cowpoke."

"Crap," Corvallis muttered.

"He would've killed all of us, Aaron," Eyman said softly.

"I would've killed him," Corvallis hissed.

"One of us might've got lucky enough to put him down, but not a one of us would still be alive to brag on it."

"Crap."

"Hell, you ought to be a schoolmarm, Aaron," Wolfe said with a sneer. "You're so good with words and speechifyin' and such." His face hardened. "Now, you listen to me this time, boy. I don't look kindly on folks tryin' to gun me down. And killin' folks don't set well with my digestion. You come at me again, and I'll plant your butt in the boneyard so fast you'll not know what hit you."

"I'll kill you, you son of a bitch," Corvallis screamed. His face was livid, and his eyes crazy. "I'll kill you!"

"Come on, Aaron," Eyman said softly, tugging on Corvallis. "Time to get you home." He looked back at Wolfe, almost as if apologizing. Then he hauled Corvallis out of the saloon.

With a weary sigh, Wolfe sat and poured himself another drink.

Chapter Five

Marshal Sam Trumble wasn't much of a marshal. He was past fifty, medium height, softly plump. His clothes were old and worn, from the threadbare short-brimmed Stetson to the worn cotton shirt, faded to a dull pink from the crisp magenta it had once been; from the dreary wool pants to the boots with the holes in the bottom. He wore his old Colt pistol hanging almost directly in front, where it flapped against his crotch.

Trumble had been "elected" marshal because he was nearly useless and would get in no one's way. Any heavy duty marshaling would be done by Owen Corvallis—or men he would designate. It had worked well so far.

Marshal Sam Trumble strutted into the High Country Saloon shortly after Wolfe had gunned down the cowboy. He stopped just inside the doors and hiked up his belt, eliciting a few low chuckles. Most of the men no longer laughed at Trumble, since this pathetic excuse for a lawman had long ago passed the stage of being funny to the people of Kaibab.

Then the marshal thumped over to Wolfe's table, not knowing the disrespect with which he was followed by bored eyes. He pulled out a chair, swung it around and sat down, with his arms resting on the chair back.

Wolfe gazed at him a moment, impressed by the man's foul odor. He must not have had a bath in months, maybe years, Wolfe thought. The marshal smelled of tobacco, wood smoke, spiced food, sweat and things Wolfe did not want to contemplate.

"You're new in town, ain't you, mister?" Trumble asked.

"Yep."

"Plan on stayin' long?" Trumble grabbed the bottle from the middle of the table and tilted it up to his mouth, downing a fair amount. He set it down, and glared at Wolfe. "Well?"

"That depends."

"On what?"

"Orville," Wolfe called, facing the bar. "Bring another bottle over here. And a glass."

"You didn't answer me, son."

"That's 'cause it's none of your business."

Trumble was taken aback, and he tilted the bottle up again. "It is," he gasped, still not recovered from his latest dose of redeye, "when you go around shootin' people."

"He drew first, Marshal," Wolfe said diffidently. "Or tried to." He nodded his thanks as Orville set a new bottle in front of Wolfe and the glass in front of Trumble. Wolfe poured himself a drink and downed it. He poured another and sat back.

Trumble took another big drink. Setting the bottle down, he said, "Let me tell you some facts about the town of Kaibab, Mr. . . . Mr. what?"

"Lucas Wolfe." He paused, then said, "Tell me these facts, Marshal." Wolfe pulled out his fixings, rolled a cigarette and fired it up.

"First off, Kaibab's a peaceable town. I want to keep

46

it that way. Folks hereabouts don't take kindly to shootin's and such in public. It's especially problemsome when the shootin' involves the Corvallis family."

"That cowpuncher was no member of the Corvallis family," Wolfe said in irritation.

"No, but he's one of the Lazy O boys. And that means damn near the same thing."

"You tellin' me Owen Corvallis owns you?"

Trumble bristled. "Nobody owns me, Mr. Wolfe," he snapped before downing another healthy slug of whiskey.

"But he runs things around here, if you catch my meanin'," Trumble said a little contritely. He knew he was not fooling Wolfe. "I got me a cushy job, pays well. If some real bad trouble kicks up its heels here, Mr. Corvallis'll supply enough manpower — and firepower — to see that it's all set to rights soon enough. I cross him, and I'll lose this job. I'm too old for ridin' drag somewhere and punchin' cows."

He paused to belt down some more liquor. He slapped the empty bottle down on the table and stood shakily. "I'd be obliged, Mr. Wolfe," he said with voice thickened by whiskey, "if you was to cause me no more trouble like tonight's excitement."

"Or?" Wolfe asked. He was tired of threats. There had been too many of them for one day. He would prefer to spend more time with Esther over at Alma Fletcher's bordello.

"Or you'll find yourself feelin' the wrath of Owen Corvallis. I'd think considerably on that before you start somethin' else in this town."

"Let me tell you something, Marshal," Wolfe said unpleasantly. "If you'd gotten off your lazy butt and did your job, that cowpoke'd still be alive, and I wouldn't be sittin' here listenin' to you flap your gums at me

47

while I got to sit here and smell you."

He paused for a breath, then said, "But since you think your goddamn job is to set on your butt in your office, boozin' till you can't stand, you ought to just keep on doin' so. Just stay out of my way. And if you know what's good for you, you'll tell Aaron Corvallis to keep his distance, too. Unless you want to plant him and then be the one to go explain it to old man Corvallis."

Wolfe sneered at the marshal and flicked the remains of his cigarette butt at the disreputable lawman. The flaring butt bounced off Trumble's arm and fell onto the table, since the marshal was too drunk to be able to move. "Now go on back to your office, Marshal." The last word was thick with derision.

Trumble staggered out amidst the laughter from the other patrons. This, the customers thought, was a bit out of the usual, and worthy of laughter.

Wolfe had another shot of bourbon, but he was starting to feel the liquor a little bit now. He stood and corked the bottle. Lifting it in a salute to Orville, he headed slowly toward his room at Fletcher's Hotel.

Alma Fletcher was still at the counter. "Don't you ever sleep, ma'am?" Wolfe asked politely.

"On occasion." She smiled. "Hear you had a little excitement tonight."

"Sure did," Wolfe said with a satisfied grin. "That Esther was really something. Hoo-ee."

Alma laughed, a deep, raspy laugh that created visions of lust in most men. It did in Wolfe. "Glad you enjoyed it. But that ain't what I meant."

"I know."

"You'd better watch your step around the Corvallises, Luke, if you know what's good for you."

"I'll try, ma'am." He did not sound at all convincing

48

either to himself or to Alma.

She stared at him a minute, knowing he did not mean it, and knowing there would be more trouble in town. Alma Fletcher had nothing against Owen Corvallis, nor was she under his power. Still, she had felt his grip over the town, as well as over her own saloon, and did not appreciate it. She liked Lucas Wolfe. He was young, handsome and full of vigor. And, more, he seemed willing to stand up to Owen Corvallis. That made her like him.

"Look, I don't usually do such things," Alma said with a soft, pleasant smile. "But I can arrange to have Esther come pay you a visit tonight."

Wolfe grinned. "I'd like that," he said. "But there's another I'd rather have," he added on a whim.

"Oh?" Alma asked, surprised. Esther, with her dusky, creamy skin, and plush figure, was one of the favorites over at the brothel. Men were attracted to the dark, well-proportioned half-breed, and frequently asked for her, sometimes to the annoyance of the other girls. "And who would that be?"

"You, ma'am," Wolfe said with a straight face. Esther was twenty years younger, and far more beautiful that Alma Fletcher. But Wolfe, despite his young years, felt a sense of loneliness within Alma Fletcher. She was a woman who had been stunningly beautiful in her youth, and was still far more beautiful than most women. But because she was no longer a fresh-faced, bright young girl, many men would prefer another to her.

Wolfe thought of Esther, and knew from experience that she could be mighty pleasureable. But he knew Alma would be so, too. In fact, despite his youth, he had enough experience to suspect that what Alma Fletcher lacked in youthful exuberance and vitality she

49

would make up in expertise and caring.

"It's nice of you to pity an old woman, Mr. Wolfe," Alma said, not certain whether to be flattered or insulted.

"You ain't old, and I've never been accused of havin' much pity, ma'am," Wolfe said simply.

Alma stared at the hard young man, and she was sure he was telling the truth. Perhaps, she wondered, she just wanted to believe he was telling the truth. But if he was lying, he was a mighty convincing liar. It would probably make him a convincing lover, too. Suddenly she smiled brightly, and released another of her throaty, somewhat naughty laughs.

"I ain't done such a thing in a coon's age, you understand," she said huskily. "But I reckon a girl can always use herself a last fling."

"Who's to say it'll be your last, Miz Alma," Wolfe said as he held out his arm for her to take.

Alma hurried out from behind the counter and flew to the front door. She turned over the sign so it would read "Closed" from outside. She clicked the lock and pulled the curtains over the front-door windows. Then she took Wolfe's arm. As they walked up the stairs, she felt her face flush with the heat of desire.

Wolfe was gone by the time Alma Fletcher awoke. She stretched lazily, luxuriating in the feel of her nude flesh against the sheets, and luxuriating in the feelings Lucas Wolfe had left inside her. He was a skilled, thoughtful lover, though he was still young. Alma knew Wolfe did not love her; nor would she want his love. Still, the night had been mighty pleasurable. It had been years since she had abandoned herself to a man in such a way. She had worried some at first that he would think poorly of her for it. But that had not been the case.

Wolfe thought well of the night, too. He had been right in his assessment that Alma Fletcher would be more of a woman, if that's how one could phrase it, than the delightful half-breed Esther. And the night left him with a heaping helping of pleasantly lustful thoughts as he rode northwest toward the Lazy O Ranch.

He veered off the road long before he got to the Corvallis ranch house, and made his way through the stunted junipers and piñons, up a ridge and then down. He stopped atop another sage-covered ridge and dismounted. He loosened the horse's saddle and let the animal crop grass. He took his canteen and drank mightily. He wiped sweat off his brow. This might be the high country, he thought, but it was still hotter than blazes in the daytime, even if it cooled considerably at night.

Wolfe hung the canteen back around the saddlehorn. From his shirt pocket, he pulled out a piece of paper and unfolded it. He studied it a bit, then began searching the landscape with his eyes, turning slowly. He checked the map, looked at the land, turned a little, and repeated the process.

He spent most of the day doing the same thing. Riding from ridge to ridge, and then stopping to check the landscape against his map. At one point, he saw into a valley, where scores of beef cattle were grazing. He thought he saw Ev Eyman, but at this distance it was too hard to tell. He was sure he did not see Aaron Corvallis, since the ranch owner's son would be carrying the ever present quirt.

Wolfe ate cold biscuits and jerky for lunch, and washed them down with water from his canteen.

Shortly after noon, he had the sense that he was being followed. He dipped into another small valley between two humps of ridges, and then cut around, weaving into a pine forest. He stopped, dismounted and waited.

But an hour later, he still had not seen anyone. "Damn fool," he muttered to himself as he remounted the horse and rode on.

Wolfe spent the next several days doing the same thing. He would ride about the ranch, always keeping out of sight of the cowpunchers. He never disturbed anything, but he was certain that Owen Corvallis was getting reports of his presence every day.

He did not find what he was looking for, but he was not about to give up. He would search most of the day, then ride back to Kaibab. There he would wash up and then eat well at Alma Fletcher's restaurant. Afterward he would spend an hour or two in the High Country Saloon, playing cards, swapping yarns with Orville or some of the regulars, or just drinking. Neither Aaron Corvallis nor Eyman showed up there, for which Wolfe was thankful. He was not here for killing people, only to get "his" land back.

After that, he would go back to his room. Alma Fletcher had taken a liking to him, and appointed herself his temporary mate. Wolfe did not mind, though he occasionally thought that a turn with Esther might be a fun interlude. But he liked Alma and enjoyed her company.

On more than one of his trips to the Lazy O Ranch, he again had the feeling that someone was following him—or at least watching him. But though he stopped and waited a while, he saw no one trailing him. It had bothered him at first, since he was not the sort to live easy with the thought that someone might be on his trail. But after a few days, he figured that if someone really was following him, and he wasn't just jumpy, the person probably meant him no harm.

He even got to thinking that it might be Owen Corvallis himself following him, just to keep an eye on him and try to figure out what he was doing. It didn't seem likely, but he could think of no other explanation.

Wolfe paid another three dollars for a week's room rent — ov Alma's protestations — and prepared himself mentally for spending a long time at his task.

Chapter Six

Luke Wolfe sensed someone following him again. For some reason it was more irritating this day than it had been before. With a growing sense of determination to put an end to this, he pulled behind some boulders that had skidded down off a slope. He left his horse, and scrambled up the slope, down the other side and then around the base of the hump. He waited behind a towering pine, shielded by thick brush.

Less than a quarter of an hour later, Wolfe heard a horse clopping unhurriedly in his direction. He wiped sweat from his forehead, settled his hat on more firmly, and hefted his Winchester.

A horse hove into view, but Wolfe could not see the rider because of the heavy bushes in front of him. He waited until the brown patch of horse moved past the brush, then shoved his way through and into the clear, bringing the Winchester up. "Whoa, there, pard," he roared.

He felt like an idiot, as Sally Corvallis stopped, gasping in fright, and turned her horse to face him. "Mr. Wolfe!" she breathed, her face ashen under the bright red calico bonnet.

"Damn," Wolfe muttered as he lowered the rifle. "My apologies, Miss Sally," he said in embarrassment. "I . . . I . . ." He didn't know what to say. He could not tell her how foolish he felt, or even explain to her why he had done this. Such explanations never came out right anyway. Better just to stand and face her wrath or anger than her laughter, he figured.

"I understand, Mr. Wolfe," she said softly. Her voice was melodious and exciting to Wolfe. "You sensed someone was following you and waited, is that it?"

"Yes'm," he mumbled, his face growing red.

Sally smiled at Wolfe. "I'm sorry that I brought such a thing on," she said. "And I must confess, this is not the first time I've followed along your trail, Mr. Wolfe." She looked a little embarrassed, but not too much. She was a strong-willed young woman, and not given to worrying overly much about things. When she wanted something, or when she thought something was right, she went along and did it, and to hell with the consequences. It might get her in trouble of a time, but, generally, such an attitude had served her well so far.

Wolfe nodded. So that was it! he thought. It had been her all along. That was a relief to him to know, but he would not let her know that. "And why've you been doin' that, ma'am?" he asked politely, but with a hard edge that made it obvious that such things were not pleasing to him.

He watched her as he waited for her answer. She wore a dress of material that matched her bonnet. It covered her fully from throat to ankle. High-top boots peeked out from under her dress, since she had one leg curled around the odd horn of the sidesaddle. She looked uncomfortable sitting on it, and Wolfe wondered why she even used such a contraption. Sally

55

Corvallis did not look like the type of woman to stick too hard to convention. Besides, in this day and age, out here, most women would ride astraddle, if they rode a horse.

"I . . . well, I . . ." She flushed and could not finish.

"Could it be," Wolfe asked sharply, "that you're spyin' on me for your pa?"

She flushed again, but this time with anger. "I should say not," she snapped.

"Then why?" Wolfe persisted.

"I . . ." Sally stopped. She took a moment to compose herself. With a discomfited smile, she said firmly, "I took something of a liking to you when you visited our home, Mr. Wolfe. I thought perhaps I would try to see you—to speak with you a little. But the couple of times I saw that you were on the Lazy O and followed, you always disappeared, and I turned back."

Wolfe was rather dumbfounded. Such a thing seemed so unlikely that he suspected it was true. Women didn't just do such things—taking a liking to someone at first glance. Or if they did, they certainly didn't talk about it or act on it. Her saying such a thing made it all the more believable. Besides, he acknowledged that he did not want to believe she was a liar. Like any other man, he took vast pride in the thought that such a beautiful woman would take a liking to him, even though he knew that such an idea was foolish.

"I don't know as I believe such an outlandish tale, ma'am," he said blandly.

Sally took no offense. "And why is that, Mr. Wolfe?"

He gulped and said, "Well, ma'am, it ain't likely a woman of your beauty and nature to take a shine to a

56

saddle tramp like me."

"I would expect a gentleman to say such a thing, sir," she said with a small smile.

"I've never been so insulted, ma'am," Wolfe said with a laugh, unable to bristle at her.

"I think it's you who are telling tales, Mr. Wolfe," Sally commented in amusement.

Wolfe knew he could either believe her—or at least seem to—or call her a liar here and now. He much preferred the former to the latter. At least until he learned otherwise. "Perhaps," he said with a grin. "Well, ma'am, I've got to get my horse. I'll be back directly."

"Where is it?"

"Yonder around this hill."

"May I join you?"

"Don't see why not," Wolfe said with a shrug.

"Help me down, please." She didn't really need any help, despite the uncomfortable saddle. But she wanted to make him feel needed and thought this a good way to do that. She was used to riding astraddle, but she was afraid that if she caught up to Lucas Wolfe, he might think her a wanton woman if she was riding that way. Hence the sidesaddle.

Wolfe nodded. He set the Winchester down against a bush and stepped up to the horse. He reached up and grabbed Sally under the arms. He jerked his arms up, lifting her easily. She swung her leg free of the horn and straightened both legs as Wolfe set her down. Wolfe was rather amazed at how light she was. And then, when she was standing, he was surprised at how small she was. At a distance, even the small distance of across the room, she had seemed bigger, somehow more substantial. Still, she was solid under his hands, and her hands resting on his biceps felt

57

quite nice.

"Thank you," she whispered, looking up into his eyes. She took her hands away after letting them linger a few moments longer than was strictly necessary.

"My pleasure, ma'am," Wolfe said, stepping back. Her touch had excited him in a way he had never felt before. He stared at her, gazing deep into her shimmering blue eyes framed by long, thick lashes. There seemed to be an invitation in those eyes.

He broke his gaze away, thinking himself foolish once again. There was no invitation in her eyes, he decided; only in his imagination. Almost angry at himself, he grabbed his Winchester. Taking the reins of Sally's horse in his other hand, he strode off. Sally walked at his side, her hands clasped behind her back as she walked.

Wolfe tied Sally's horse to a bush while he brought his own mount out from behind the boulders. He was confused, not sure what he should say to Sally Corvallis, if anything at all. Finally he managed, "Would you still like to talk, Miss Sally?"

"I would, Mr. Wolfe." She hesitated, then said, "I've brought some lunch. We could have a picnic." She looked eager.

"That'd be real nice," he said, speaking truthfully. "Where should we go?"

"There's a place along Havasu Creek, that way," she pointed, "that's real nice."

"How far?"

"Four miles, maybe."

"Let's go."

They rode through the heat of the day, along a thready ribbon of dirt trail between sage, prickly pear and juniper. Eventually they started winding up a grassy hill. They topped it and let the horses move stiff-legged down the slope at their own pace. Soon they had entered a pine forest, with thick stands of trees, a soft carpet of dead needles, and cool, quiet shade.

Sally finally stopped her horse. Wolfe, following her, stopped too. He dismounted and helped Sally down from her horse once again. Sally took a blanket that was tied behind the saddle, while Wolfe took the basket that dangled from her saddle on the far side, and carried it as he walked behind Sally.

"This looks like a good spot," Sally said, stopping in a small circular clearing covered with needles, a few yards from the creek. She spread the blanket out, and Wolfe set the basket on one corner of it. "Sit," Sally said. Wolfe did, as Sally began pulling food from the basket.

But Wolfe could only sit so long. After a few minutes, he built a fire a few feet from the blanket, between it and the creek. He put on a pot of coffee.

Finally they both sat, and Sally served her and Wolfe cold baked chicken and biscuits. They ate in silence, Wolfe content to just cast surreptitious glances at Sally; she happy just to be with a man who did not work for her father, a man she had a considerable interest in, she realized.

After their meal, complete with thickly sugared coffee, Sally pulled out two tins of peaches. Wolfe opened them, and they spooned out the syrupy fruit. When they'd finished eating, Wolfe got them each another cup of coffee. Then he sat, rolled a cigarette and lighted it.

"You're an uncommon man, Mr. Wolfe," Sally said, her smile bright, her eyes sparkling with joy.

"Why is that, Miss Sally?" he asked, surprised, but covering it well.

"Well, for one thing, you don't wear any spurs. I think you're the first man I've met who didn't."

Wolfe shrugged, but he was secretly pleased. "Somethin' I picked up from Gramps," he said.

"Gramps?"

"My Grandpa Jeb. He was an old mountain man, back in the days of Jim Bridger and Bill Williams and all."

"And he taught you not to wear spurs?" Sally asked, interested.

"Well, I reckon he did. He never wore 'em either. Always wore moccasins, even after he was years away from the mountains. I once asked him why. He told me, 'Luke, Crows is the best horsemen this ol' coon's over seen. And ye ain't ever seen one of them niggurs wearin' spurs, have ye?' "

Sally giggled. "He sounds like an uncommon man, too, Mr. Wolfe."

"He was that for sure," Wolfe said with a grin.

"You liked him a lot, didn't you?" Sally asked, smiling softly to take the edge off any pain he might feel.

And he did feel some. Despite having grown into a tall, strong, independent man, Luke still felt hurt at the loss of his grandfather. "I still like him a heap, Miss Sally. Just 'cause he's gone now don't mean . . ."

"I'm sorry, Mr. Wolfe." Sally looked horrified at having caused his pain. "I didn't mean to say that . . ."

"I know," Wolfe said, smiling. "I know you only meant well. It's just that sometimes I really feel it that he's gone."

Wolfe seemed to grow distant. "Even after I grew, I could always talk to him, tell him what I was feelin' and such. I never did much, since I was off on my own most times. Still, it just don't seem right that he's gone. Damn!" He realized again where he was. "Sorry, ma'am," he muttered, embarrassed.

"It's all right," Sally said. She smiled brightly, trying to ease his discomfiture. "Tell me more about your grandfather."

Wolfe shrugged and smashed out the cigarette in the dirt next to the blanket. "He was a wild ol' coon," Wolfe said, smiling at the remembrance. "At least, that's what I hear. He was settled and runnin' a store long before I come along. But ever once in a while some of the old boys who were in the mountains come by for a visit. I'd sit and listen to 'em for hours on end."

"What'd they talk about?"

"The old days mostly. And told yarns."

"What kind of yarns?"

"All kinds," Wolfe said with a hearty laugh.

"You remember any of them?"

"Sure," Wolfe said, laughing again. He was comfortable here with Sally Corvallis. More comfortable than he had been with a woman in as long as he could remember.

"Tell me some."

"I can't remember a one that could be told in front of a lady, Miss Sally," he said, his voice reflecting the mixture of humor and embarrassment inside him.

"Are you callin' me a lady?" Sally asked, looking askance at him in mock anger.

"Yes, ma'am." He was beginning to like Sally more and more. She had a refreshingly open attitude about life and such. It was not common among women.

"Now it's my turn to be insulted, Mr. Wolfe," she noted feigning distaste.

"Oh?" he asked, surprised and a little confused.

"I seem to recall your reaction not long ago when I

61

called you a gentleman . . ." She giggled, and Wolfe laughed, their sounds intertwining to drift up into the warm, blue, high-country sky.

Chapter Seven

It was as splendid a picnic as Wolfe had ever had. He found himself drawn more and more to Sally Corvallis, and not only because of her beauty. She was an interesting young woman, full of life, knowledge and chatter.

But she was reluctant to talk about herself much. "Ain't got much to tell," she told him. "I've lived a sheltered life here," she shrugged. She did not look particularly sad about it, just stating the facts. She smiled. "But how about you?" she asked.

"What about me?"

"Tell me about yourself." She seemed interested enough.

"Well," he said slowly, "I take after my father a little. And he took after Gramps a little, too. All of us are independent cusses. But I reckon I take after Gramps the most."

Even as a boy, Lucas Wolfe had been independent, never fond of taking orders. His father went off to the Civil War when Luke was barely three years old, leaving the boy and his mother with Jeb and Rachel. When Bill returned, it seemed Luke was no longer his son. The boy was wild, though not in a bad way; mostly just filled with exuberance, and spoiled by his grandparents.

He had the run of his grandparents' store, and he had the run of their house. He missed Jeb when the grandfather went off for several months, taking "Uncle" Casey with him, near the end of the war. It bothered the six-year-old Luke that Jeb would take Casey and not him. But then Jeb was back and life returned to normal.

"Uncle" Casey was actually the son of an old friend of Jeb's — Russ Scarborough. The young man had come to the Wolfe place several years before Luke was born, telling of how his father and mother had died. Jeb and Rachel took him in. Luke got along mostly with his uncle, who seemed to take a shine to the baby. But Bill Wolfe, who was only three years older than Casey, did not. Tension built after Bill had come home from the war, until finally Bill decided to try his fortunes in the great, opening West.

Preparations were made, but when the time for leaving drew near, nine-year-old Luke boldly told his father, "I ain't goin', Pa."

"Don't talk that way to me, boy," Bill warned.

"What's the problem?" Jeb asked, walking up.

"I told Pa I ain't goin' with him and Ma."

"Oh?" Jeb asked, somewhat amused at this cocky little man. "What're you plannin' to do?"

"Stay here with you and Grammer." The boy had no doubts in his mind.

"We'd expect you to earn your keep, boy," Jeb said, annoying his son, who felt that Jeb was usurping his parental powers.

"I can help at the store."

"Doin' what?" Jeb asked, chuckling.

"Anything. I can do whatever you want."

Jeb believed him.

"You're going with us, and that's all there is to it," Bill ordered.

"No I ain't."

Bill raised his hand to strike the boy. "Then you'll be whupped," Bill snapped. He took up a length of knotted rope, and came for the boy. Until his own father stepped between them.

"You can whup me all you want, Pa," Luke said defiantly. "But I ain't goin'. If you force me to go, I'll just run away first chance I get."

Bill stood with arm raised. He could not condone such defiance. But he knew his son was speaking truthfully. They were too much alike, this father and son, fiercely independent, quietly confident in themselves.

"He can stay here, son," Jeb said quietly. "If you give us your say-so. That fair to you, Luke?"

"Yep, Gramps."

Bill shrugged. "Don't come lookin' to me or your ma for sympathy when you get to be missin' us."

"I won't."

"Bah," Bill growled. "Git out of here now."

As the boy ran off, Jeb said, "Hell, son, don't be so hard on the boy."

"Don't tell me how to raise my family, Pa."

"I ain't tellin' you how to raise your family, son. But you got to see somethin' from the boy's part. You ain't been a big part of his life. You went off to war when Luke was only a babe. By the time you come back, four years'd gone by. He's used to me and your ma, mostly. He spent more time with Rachel than he did with his own ma. He'll be all right, son."

Bill scowled and stomped off. But he was secretly pleased that his son was showing signs of growing.

A week later, Luke said polite goodbyes to his

mother, seven-year-old brother and year-old sister. He said a very reserved farewell to his father. By the time the large, canvas-topped wagon had pulled out of the yard and onto the wide dirt track that served as a road, Luke was off playing.

Luke grew into a tall, strong boy, and caused more than his share of mischief. Still, he was industrious and hard-working. And, much to Jeb's surprise, the boy was smart enough to know that Uncle Casey would be a bad influence, and the boy kept his distance.

Luke did not miss Casey when Jeb sent him packing. Luke was thirteen at the time, and felt a sense of relief. But he was also becoming a little upset at the confines of working in the store, as well as the confines of St. Charles itself. He would see the old trappers come to visit his grandfather, and he would listen to them talk of the good old days, when they were free to roam the mountains, living by their wits and their guns. And he would see the Indians come to town, far fewer of them now than he remembered as a small boy; and the river-boat men; and the gunmen; pioneers heading west after the war; soldiers, whoring and drinking in town before heading off to the Indian wars; and former soldiers, discontented with the boredom of life without war. Many of the latter would turn to outlawry, others to bounty hunting.

Luke watched them all with interest and a strange yearning. Jeb could sense it, and finally began taking the boy out to the woods and fields around St. Charles, teaching him the proper use of a gun—both rifles and pistols.

Wolfe was no gunslinger, and had gone West when flintlocks were still the height of weaponry. Now there were myriad versions of six-shooters, and repeating rifles and such. But Wolfe knew his guns, and, more importantly, he knew men.

"You might see some of them young punks back from the war," Jeb growled, "guns slung low, lookin' for trouble."

"Like Uncle Casey?" Luke asked.

"Yep," Wolfe said, still angry at his old friend's son. "But that fast-draw crap ain't gonna save your hide. You ever have to use your gun close up, boy, best learn to take your time aimin'. Best to be a little slow on the draw and be accurate than be faster'n greased lightnin' and a piss-poor shot. More folks get killed firin' all their shots at once to no effect, and then got to stand there while some angry son of a bitch just plants a couple slugs in 'em."

Luke learned well. Plus he was, like his grandfather, a natural-born shot. Within six months, he was roaming the countryside around St. Charles, hunting on his own. And, unbeknownst to Grandpa Wolfe, he practiced his quick draw — as well as firing accurately from the draw.

Three years later, Luke was a strapping young man of almost seventeen, and feeling the confines of St. Charles. He wanted to leave, but he was unsure of himself.

But two wild-looking, down-on-their-luck men made up his mind for him. The two wandered into the store one day while Luke and his grandfather were working. Jeb was busy helping someone, while Luke was just checking stock. He turned when he heard the jingle of the bell suspended over the door. He was ready to offer his service, but the look of the two men stopped him. He kept quiet, almost hidden behind bales and boxes and piles of goods. And he watched, mouth dry with fright.

The men looked around a little, trying to seem inconspicuous. Jeb ignored them, his attention focused on Mrs. Labrea, who was being her usual troublesome self.

Suddenly the two men had their pistols out, aimed at Jeb and Mrs. Labrea. "We want all the money you got in the till," one said. He was big and stupid-looking; filthy of appearance and clothing. "And all the paper cartridges you got for a forty-four."

"Anything else?" Jeb asked dryly, coolly.

"Food. Jerky, salted beef, hardtack. Some coffee, flour, sugar, canned peaches."

"You got a wagon?" Wolfe asked, edging away from Mrs. Labrea.

"We don't need no goddamn wagon," the other outlaw said. He was a depraved-looking soul, broad of shoulder and low of brow. "Now just do what I told you."

As Wolfe went to do what he was told, the two outlaws followed him with their eyes and their guns. Mrs. Labrea, who had spent the best portion of her fifty-seven years on various frontiers, moved slowly away from the two men. She didn't figure she could escape, but she wanted to get to the best possible point out of any line of fire, should someone come along to help.

Luke watched her move, and he drew his pistol. He was scared spitless, but steady of hand, as he poked the revolver up over a pile of goods. As soon as Mrs. Labrea was out of the way, Luke shouted, "You two best drop your pistols."

"Who's that?" the bigger one asked, looking around while his partner stood dimwitted.

"The man's gonna send you to meet your Maker you don't drop that piece right now!" Luke was sweating and fearful. This was an entirely different story than hunting deer or elk.

The big one spotted Luke and started to swing his

pistol in the youth's direction.

Jeb stood frozen, wanting to grab the double-barreled shotgun under the counter, but unwilling to do so when the second outlaw had him in his sights.

Luke had never been so frightened in his young life. But he had never been as sure of what had to be done, either. He did not hesitate; he just fired. The ball from the .44-caliber Colt Dragoon his grandfather had given him slammed into the side of the outlaw's head, just above the temple. The man went down as if poleaxed.

"You, drop your weapon," Luke shouted to the other.

But the man was already moving. He had crouched and was swinging toward Luke.

Once again the youth did not hesitate. He fired twice, wanting to make certain he hit his moving target. Both bullets found a home, one breaking the man's upper arm bone, the other hitting the heart. The man went down, not dead, but close to it.

Luke cautiously came out from his haven, while Jeb grabbed his shotgun and moved around the counter. But the man would do them no harm. "You shined here, boy, you sure did," Wolfe said, throwing an arm around his grandson's shoulders. He whooped and hollered.

Luke grinned wanly. He looked down at the gore he had wrought. Then he spun and ran out, getting sick against the back wall of the store outside. He was embarrassed about that, but that wore off soon, and the episode convinced him that it was time to move off on his own.

"What're you gonna do, boy?" Wolfe asked gruffly when his grandson told him of his decision. He would never admit it to anyone, but he would miss the boy terribly. Rachel, though, knew how he was feeling, and she came to rest a hand on her husband's shoulder.

"I thought I'd take to huntin' buffalo." There had been plenty of hide hunters leaving from St. Charles in the past few years. Luke was an excellent shot, and figured he could handle the work.

"You'll do well, son," Wolfe said sadly. He could not bear to stop his grandson from leaving, no matter how much it might hurt.

Luke left soon after, outfitted well from his grandfather's store. He spent four years doing that work, but by then the buffalo was no more. Once, when visiting St. Charles, Luke felt his grandfather's pain at the rapid depletion of the noble, shaggy animal. And for the first time he realized just how much the buffalo had meant to men like Jeb Wolfe — and to the Indians, with whom Luke had only limited contact. He was saddened that he had added to the problem, but there was nothing he could do about it now.

Luke Wolfe spent the next several years living by the gun. Sometimes he hunted men down for the bounty. He felt less concerned about that than he had about hunting down the buffalo. But most often he worked as a lawman, a marshal for one town or another, drifting on as the demands of the cow towns and railroad towns and such changed.

Then, one day, he got a wire from Grandma Rachel telling him that Grandpa Jeb was dying and wanted to see him. With as little hesitation as he had shown in that first shooting back in Jeb's store, Luke headed fast for St. Charles.

"You've led a rather colorful life, haven't you?" Sally said. She was confused. She liked Wolfe considerably, but such a past was a little much to take all at once.

"Reckon I have," Wolfe said with a grin. He grew

70

serious. "But if it bothers you, I'll not come around any more."

"Oh, no," she said. "I wouldn't want that." She smiled.

He nodded. But the time came for them to part. Wolfe was sad when Sally left, but they made plans to meet the next day.

Wolfe's evening was much the same as the others since he arrived in Kaibab, but this time his mind was on Miss Sally Corvallis.

Lying next to him that night, Alma Fletcher sensed something was wrong with Wolfe. She knew, because of her experience, that another woman was concerned. With a sad smile, Alma left him in the morning. She did not offer to join him the next night, or any after that.

Wolfe and Sally met each day and picnicked, enjoying each other's company. But five days after their first picnic, as they were eating their lunch and talking, Aaron Corvallis and Ev Eyman rode up. Wolfe, sitting on a small log, shifted so his gun was clear, alert.

Chapter Eight

Eyman remained on his horse, but Corvallis dismounted. Snapping the ever-present quirt against his leg as he walked, he came to the small fire Wolfe had made for his picnic with Sally. Smoke from it wafted into the air, carrying with it the scent of cedar. Corvallis squatted and reached for the cup Sally had been using. "You don't mind, do you, Sis?" he asked, not caring what the answer was.

"I do mind," Sally said, growing angry.

Corvallis paid her no heed; he lifted the cup and filled it with fresh coffee.

"That's mighty nice of you to freshen your sister's cup, Aaron," Wolfe said calmly. He was sitting on a small log, and he shifted to make sure his gun was clear.

"Huh?" Corvallis asked, startled, stopping with the cup halfway to his lips.

"I said . . ."

"I heard what you said, Wolfe," Corvallis snarled. "I just ain't payin' it no heed." He laughed.

He stopped abruptly when a bullet punched a hole through the cup, and hot coffee poured onto one knee. He howled at the pain, dropped the cup and jerked upright. Eyes ablaze, he reached for his pistol.

"You ain't that damn stupid, are you?" Wolfe asked

calmly. His cocked Colt was aimed at Corvallis's chest. Eyman sat on his horse, wrists crossed on the saddlehorn as he rested on it. He knew better than to try anything at the moment.

Corvallis dropped his hand, and stood fuming. It took several moments for him to regain enough calmness to be able to speak. In the meantime, Wolfe uncocked his pistol and put it away.

"My father might not mind you sashayin' all over the Lazy O, Wolfe," Corvallis snapped, his anger still holding the upper hand over him. "But I sure as hell do."

Wolfe shrugged and grinned ingratiatingly, making Corvallis all the more furious.

"And I don't want you comin' out here no more, you hear?"

"I hear you, but I ain't payin' it no heed," Wolfe said with another smirking grin.

"You best get on home now, Sis. Pa'd be mighty angry if he knew you was sneakin' off to spend time with this punk."

"He already knows," Sally said icily. "And even if he didn't, I ain't taking orders from you. Not till you grow up and start acting like a man."

"I said you're to go home," Corvallis hissed. "I got business to discuss with Wolfe here."

"Any business you got with Mr. Wolfe can be discussed in front of me, dear brother." There was no love lost between the two.

"You want me to throw you across your horse and drag you home?"

"That wouldn't be advisable," Wolfe snapped before Sally could say anything. His pistol was out again, though uncocked.

Corvallis stood, chest heaving with rage. Finally he spun and stomped off, the quirt tattooing his thigh. He leaped into his saddle. With a vicious yank, he tugged the horse around. He jabbed his spurs into the animal and galloped off. Eyman shook his head. He touched the brim of his hat at Wolfe and Sally and loped after Corvallis.

"You'll be all right when you get home, Miss Sally?" Wolfe asked after Corvallis and Eyman had left.

"Sure." She sighed. "My brother's a fool, Mr. Wolfe. My father isn't."

"Aaron won't do nothin' to you?"

She chuckled. "What's he going to do to me?"

"I don't know," Wolfe said with a shrug. "But someone as wild as him's likely to try anything."

"Don't worry about me."

He nodded. They cleaned up and Wolfe escorted Sally part of the way back to the ranch house before he turned his palomino toward Kaibab. He washed up, ate his supper at Fletcher's restaurant, and then wandered over to the High Country Saloon. He was feeling good when he left. Not drunk or anything, but pleased with the possibilities Sally offered. She was a fine woman, finer than any he had hoped to find.

He just started up the stairs of Fletcher's Hotel when he heard a noise. He started to turn, hand going for his Colt.

An ax handle smacked Wolfe half across the side of the face and half in the front, cracking on his cheekbone and eye socket. He went down, stunned but conscious. As he got the Colt out, someone kicked him in the ribs. Fire exploded there.

Wolfe fired three times before someone kicked the gun out of his hand. He knew he hit at least two men, but how seriously, he did not know. He just heard their grunts or howls of pain.

Then the men—and he never knew just how many there were—started pounding on him in earnest. A fist exploded against his ear, and a boot smashed into his

74

groin, crushing his genitals. Lights burst in a pattern before his eyes, and he had trouble breathing.

Despite the searing pain that blazed out from his crotch, and the agony brought forth by each fist or boot that connected with bone, he refused to give up. He fought — not only his attackers, but the waves of nausea that swept over him from the pain. He felt a momentary flaring of satisfaction when his knuckles broke a nose, and then a rib, and his boot cracked someone's kneecap.

He heard gunshots, as if far off, and then the attackers were gone, and he was lying in the street, just off the wood sidewalk, pain coursing through his body with every heartbeat.

Marshal Trumble bent over him. "You all right, Mr. Wolfe?"

Even with all his pain, Wolfe flinched from the man's fetid breath and foul body odor. "Hell, no, I ain't all right," he croaked.

"Let me help you."

"Get the hell away from me," Wolfe snapped, shoving the lawman away. "I don't want no help from the likes of you."

Grumbling, Trumble stood. Alma Fletcher knelt at Wolfe's side. "You'll take my help?" she asked, smiling, trying to ease his pain with soothing words and kindness.

"Yes'm."

It took a considerable effort on his part, but Wolfe finally managed to stand, leaning far more weight on Alma than he had planned. But he could not help it. Once he was standing, on his feet but bent, Alma asked, "Can you walk?" She was worried and lost her light-heartedness.

"In a minute," he gasped.

She nodded, bearing up as best she could under his weight.

Trumble, who had drifted off a bit, shuffled up.

"There's two dead here, Mr. Wolfe," he said.

"Too goddamn bad."

"I reckon I'll have to take you in."

"Take a hike, Sam, and leave folks to go about their business."

"But, Alma . . ." Trumble whined in protest.

"But, hell, Sam. If you was any kind of lawman, you'd set about findin' out who did this and bring them to justice, 'stead of botherin' folks that've been set upon by animals."

"But . . ."

"Shush now, goddammit, before I get real mad. Go fetch Mr. Wolfe's gun and then get Doc Windsor. Bring 'em both to Luke's room."

Trumble knew better than to argue when Alma Fletcher got like this. As much fear as he had of the Corvallises, he had almost as much for Alma Fletcher, though for far different reasons. Was Alma Fletcher to get real mad, she might put a stop to his free visits over to her bordello. And, though she allowed him a very limited choice of the girls there—usually only those real new to the place or those who had put their better years far behind them—it was still more than he would be able to do without Alma's beneficence. He hurried off, scooping up Wolfe's Colt as he headed for Doc Windsor's.

"Think you can walk now, Luke?"

"Yes'm." Wolfe was still in agony, his groin the worst, but he began to think he would live. He ignored the small crowd that had gathered and watched silently as he allowed Alma to steer and help him turn. Getting up the stairs was the worst. He felt like his genitals were swollen up to the size of pumpkins, making each step seem like one of the Rocky Mountains to be conquered.

But he made it. The shuffle across the lobby was far easier, but then he faced the stairs to the second floor. Suddenly, Charlie Free was there. "I'll take him, ma'am,"

76

Free growled.

Alma nodded, and let the huge, lumbering black man take Wolfe and lift him. Free carried Wolfe up the stairs without strain and set him gently on the bed.

"Thank you, Charlie," Alma said.

The man nodded. He had been working for Alma Fletcher in various places for nearly fifteen years. He was a fine handyman, and his size and strength made him an excellent protector for the girls she hired. There rarely was trouble in any of Alma Fletcher's bordellos when Charlie Free was around. He left, heading back to the bordello.

Alma was working Wolfe's shirt off when Trumble and Doc Windsor arrived. She stepped aside and took Wolfe's gun from Trumble as Windsor bent to look Wolfe over. "You can leave now, Sam," Alma said with some derision.

"Can I stop by the 'house,' Alma?" he asked, voice pleading.

"I reckon," Alma said in disgust. "Tell Charlie you get Velma."

Trumble winced. Velma was only thirty-three, but she had lost the bloom of youth years ago, and had never been blessed with the gift of any sort of beauty. Plus she weighed in at better than two twenty-five. Still, she was about the only one at the cathouse who would accept him stoically. He nodded and hurried out.

Windsor hummed and ahemed and clicked his tongue as he peeled Wolfe's clothes gently off and then checked him. He put disinfectant on the bleeding wounds, and stitched up a cut—caused by the ax handle—on his cheek. Alma stood to the side, fidgeting, but knowing enough to stay out of the doctor's way.

Windsor stood, and Alma asked anxiously, "How is he, Doctor?"

"He'll be in some pain for a while, that's for sure.

And," he added, winking at Alma as he snapped his bag closed, "he ain't going to do no pokin' for a spell. But he'll be fine."

Alma's stomach twisted at the doctor's humor. But she was relieved. She had worried that he would never be able to do anything with a woman again, and she still had hopes of a rematch with Wolfe one day. "Thanks, Doctor," she said. "How much do I owe you?"

"I'll think on it." Alma had been more than fair to Doctor Abel Windsor since he had pulled into Kaibab two years ago. He felt odd about taking money from her for such a thing.

"Thanks." Alma saw Windsor out. She had stayed out of the way while Windsor worked. Now she went to Wolfe. She felt like a criminal with what she was about to do, but she could not help herself. She had to look. She pulled back the sheet covering Wolfe. And she gasped.

Wolfe was in too much pain to be embarrassed as he lay there naked under Alma's gaze. The woman checked him over carefully in the light of the lantern. His face was coloring, and his chest, sides, stomach and thighs were bruised. She looked between his legs and gasped at the amount of swelling. She wished there was something she could do for him, but knew there was not.

As gently as she could, she lifted the sheet over him. He smiled wanly up at her. She lightly kissed his forehead. "I'll be here all the night, in case you need me, Luke," she whispered. She turned down the lantern and then took the quilt from the bed. She sat in the threadbare chair and pulled the quilt around her.

Wolfe awoke numerous times during the early stages of the night as the pain racked him. Every move he made sent a stabbing spear of agony lancing through him. And each time Wolfe groaned, Alma would awake and sit there, heart pounding, worrying about him.

78

Along about midnight, after Wolfe had come awake again, Alma got up. In bare feet she padded to her room and got a bottle of bourbon.

"Drink," she ordered, holding his head up and putting the mouth of the bottle to Wolfe's lips.

He did so, almost eagerly, as a baby reaching for mother's milk. He got half the bottle down, before his eyes rolled up drunkenly and he fell asleep, snoring loudly and irregularly.

Alma went back to sleep in the chair, and was not disturbed the rest of the night. Daylight coming through the window woke her, and she left quietly. She went about her business, checking on Wolfe frequently. At last he awoke. "How're you feeling?" Alma asked, knowing it was a foolish question under the circumstances.

"Ready to dance," Wolfe tried to joke. Then he groaned. "Tell you the truth, I feel like I been run over by the entire herd from the Lazy O," he moaned. With a supreme effort he shoved himself up and back, sliding his buttocks across the bed until his back was against the head of the bed. His body throbbed with pain, and his head pounded from the hangover. But he was alive and was sure he would survive.

He spent all that day in bed, and all the next day. But by the time he awoke the next morning, he decided he had better get up. The swelling in his groin was almost gone, and the pain, while still there, was not really all that debilitating.

"You sure you want to do this?" Alma asked, worried.

"Yes'm." He wasn't really sure, and doubt grew when he sat on the side of the bed. Waves of nausea competed with a flickering blackness threatening to flatten him again. He sat, eyes closed, breathing deeply, hoping to calm himself.

Gathering his strength—and determination—he shoved himself up. And vomited as he could no longer control

79

the nausea. He sank back onto the bed, sitting, sucking in air through his vomit-fouled mouth.

"I told you you wasn't ready for this," Alma scolded.

"Bull," Wolfe croaked. He steeled himself and tried again. He met with more success this time. "See," he crowed.

"Looks good to me," Alma said with a lecherous grin.

Wolfe realized he was still naked, and he flushed in embarrassment. He looked down at the floor, and saw his vomit, and was more ashamed. "Get me some water and a rag," he said in much less arrogant tones. "I'll get to cleaning the floor."

"I'll have one of the servants do it."

He nodded, still embarrassed. Making him all the more so were the colorful bruises all over his body. They were not pleasant to look at. "My clothes?" he asked.

"You need a bath first. Sit, while I get things set up."

Wolfe lay on the bed, covering himself gratefully with the sheet. Within minutes, a Mexican girl came in and cleaned up the mess Wolfe had made. He stared at the ceiling, unwilling to even look at the girl cleaning up after him, so ashamed was he. As soon as she had left, Charlie Free carried a huge brass tub into the room. He, the Mexican girl and a black girl toted in buckets of water and poured them into the tub.

When they had left, Alma came back in. "All right, into the tub, Luke," she ordered.

He nodded. He was in no position to argue, and he needed a bath. And he figured the hot water would make him feel better. He shuffled over and gingerly entered the water. It was like Nirvana.

Alma had left again, but soon returned with a paper-wrapped package. She tossed it on the bed. "New clothes for you," she said.

Wolfe nodded. "I'm obliged."

"If you need help getting downstairs, give a call."

80

Wolfe nodded again, but he was determined to get about by himself. He got out of the tub, dried himself, and dressed in longhandles, Levi's pants, sky blue wool shirt, clean socks, and his old boots; he put a new bandanna around his neck. He spent some time cleaning his Colt, oiling it, and then reloading it. Last, he buckled on the gunbelt. He plopped his old hat on and headed out the door.

He felt pretty good, except for lingering aches and pains, and he found it still a little difficult to walk. But he made it down the stairs. "I'm headin' next door, Alma," he said.

She grinned at him.

After eating, he went to Doc Windsor's.

"Come back in a couple more days," Windsor said after checking him over. "I'll take those stitches out. Other than that, you're fine. Nothing was broken, surprisingly. You're one tough old boy, ain't you?"

"That's what some have said," Wolfe said modestly.

After a nap and some supper, the world was looking better to Wolfe. He headed for the High Country Saloon.

"You're lookin' good, Luke," Orville said with a chuckle.

Wolfe noted his purple-yellow-blue face in the mirror behind the bar and grinned. "Some guys are just naturally handsome, Orville," he said, chuckling himself.

He took a bottle and glass and headed for a table. He had originally thought of standing at the bar to chat with Orville a while, but he realized he wasn't quite strong enough yet.

Most of the people left him alone, for which he was grateful. About an hour later, though, Aaron Corvallis, Eyman and two cowhands entered the saloon and headed for the bar. Corvallis glared at Wolfe as he leaned back against the bar.

81

Chapter Nine

Wolfe was irritated at Corvallis's glaring, but he did not let it show. However, he was also very angry, since he was certain Aaron Corvallis was responsible for the beating he had taken the other night. And Lucas Wolfe was not the type of man to take such things lightly.

But odds of four to one were not to his liking either, and he decided that waiting for a better opportunity would be the smart thing. Unless he was pushed too far.

So he sat drinking his bourbon slowly, trying not to think of the pain that still pulsed within him. And he tried not to think of the nearness of the man who was responsible for that pain.

Wolfe turned down an invitation to join a stud poker game at a nearby table and rolled a cigarette. He puffed, staring straight ahead, but managing to keep Corvallis and his cronies in range of his peripheral vision.

But he couldn't shut out the comments that began coming from the two cowboys with Corvallis and Eyman. The words started slowly, but picked up in intensity, as well as volume and daring after a few minutes.

"Damn, if he don't look to be a man of color to me, Curly," one said.

"That he does, Ike. I can't figure why Orville'd even let him in the place."

Back and forth it went, on and on, as Wolfe puffed his cigarette. He was outwardly calm, but the anger was building in his chest. It started at a low simmer, an almost soothing, slow burning. It grew slowly into a seething cauldron of rage.

"Maybe he ain't really a colored boy after all, Curly. 'Least not the kind of colored boys we're used to. Look at him. He's a man of all colors. Got him some nigra, some Chinee, even some I ain't even sure of. But he's got a streak of yellow, that's certain. It goes with the rest of the colors."

"You mean he's a yellow-bellied, low-lyin' skunk, Ike?"

"Must be, Curly."

"I don't know. I think I disagree. It takes a real hero to come sit in a good saloon lookin' like that. I mean, if I had gotten the snot whaled outta me so bad as to look like that, I'd not want to show my face anywhere."

"You could be right. I'd not want to do that either. Reckon he is a tough guy." He laughed crudely.

"Nah, he ain't tough," Curly chuckled. "He's brave. Lordy, I'd like to go shake his hand, just to see if some of that bravery'd rub off on me. 'Course," he added reflectively—or as reflectively as he could manage—"some of his foolishness might rub off on me, too. 'Cause he's gotta be one dumb sumbitch to get hisself smacked around like that."

Other men in the saloon were beginning to listen to

the two arrogantly stupid cowpokes, some in sympathy with the sentiments expressed, some with feelings toward Wolfe. But most were interested not only in what Ike and Curly had to say, but also in what Wolfe would do about it. A few were beginning to wonder whether he would do anything at all.

Wolfe's rage was bubbling deep inside, though on the outside he still looked disinterested in it all. Still, the lava of anger was consolidating in his chest, gathering its strength for the eventual eruption.

Wolfe stubbed out a cigarette on the top of the table and slowly poured himself another shot of whiskey. He drank it down, letting its fire join the flames of fury in his midsection.

With slow, deliberate movements, Wolfe rolled another cigarette. He scratched a match across the top of the table and held it to the end of the cigarette. A thin stream of blue smoke curled up from the tip of the cigarette, and got caught in the other swirling eddies of smoke in the close saloon.

"I reckon," Curly said, the volume of his voice growing, "that somebody's gotta beat the snot out of that boy, just to get his attention."

"You think he might be deaf, Curly? Or do you reckon he's just stupid?"

"Hard to tell, Ike. He does look cow-like—you know, with that dumb look cows have. Like his lantern's gone out, ya know." He chuckled, trying to hold back guffaws.

"Maybe it's just that he ain't got no stones, ya know, to make him a man."

"Could be," Curly said with a snort. "I hear," he announced loudly, "that whoever thumped him squarshed his stones, and he can't use 'em no more." He did laugh this time, making a sound similar to a braying ass.

" 'Course," Ike said around his own laughter, "if he had any stones to begin with, he wouldn't have gotten his butt stomped quite so easy."

The eruption of Wolfe's rage came, though it was all internal. Outside, Wolfe's demeanor looked no different. But inside, the fury roiled and rolled, taking on its own life. It drove and pushed Wolfe, until he stood and walked slowly toward the bar.

Ike and Curly saw the blazing rage sparking in Wolfe's eyes, and suddenly they were not so sure of themselves. No, not sure at all. After all, Wolfe had gunned down Barnet before Barnet had even cleared leather. It did not instill bravery in these two men.

"You know," Wolfe said quietly, seeing no need to shout, "if either of you boys had a brain half as big as your mouth, you could rule the world."

"Leave my ranch hands alone, Wolfe," Corvallis warned.

"Keep your fool mouth shut, boy, before I shove that glass down it."

Corvallis blanched, but then his beady eyes narrowed in anger. "I'll . . ."

But Wolfe was not paying any attention to him. He had turned back to face Ike and Curly. "Either of you clods know who it was attacked me?"

"No," Curly said with a smirk. "Didn't you see who it was done it?"

"Can't say as I did," Wolfe said regretfully. "But it's kind of hard to see who comes up against you when they come at you from behind. It's the kind of thing I'd expect from a couple idiots who take their orders from somebody like Aaron Corvallis."

Before anyone could say anything, Wolfe took the stub of his cigarette and dropped it down the front of

85

Ike's shirt. He slammed his palm against Ike's chest over the cigarette.

The cowpoke gasped, and his eyes widened as the ember singed his chest despite the flimsy protection of his long underwear. "You son of a bitch," he hissed.

"Got a problem, Ike?" Wolfe asked, face appearing innocent.

"You thought you got thumped the other night, just wait'll next time," he warned.

"You best bring more boys with you next time, god-damn it," Wolfe snarled, anger rising to the surface.

"We will."

"Shut up, Ike!" Corvallis snapped.

"It's too late, Aaron," Eyman said quietly.

"Like hell it's too late," Corvallis snapped. This had all gotten out of hand. He had come in here to have his boys poke a little fun at Wolfe, maybe make him do something foolish like go for his gun. Then they could've killed him in good conscience, and be rid of him once and for all.

But somehow, quickly, Wolfe had taken the game away from him and his boys, and Corvallis did not like it the least little bit. And damn, he was determined to gain the upper hand once again, no matter what it took.

"You can't be so goddamn stupid as to think I didn't know who arranged that little party for me the other night," Wolfe said sharply, turning cold eyes on Corvallis.

"I don't like the implications you're makin', Wolfe."

"I ain't makin' no implications, Corvallis. You—and your boys here—are chicken-livered little farts that ain't got the stones to come up against me face to face. No, you got to find a bunch of weak-kneed little snots to come at me from behind—in the dark."

"I'm gonna kill you, Wolfe," Corvallis screeched. His hand snaked for his Colt.

Wolfe took several quick steps backward, right hand going for his Colt. His eyes flicked from Corvallis to Ike to Curly. One swift glance had told him that Eyman was no threat.

Instead of going for his gun, Eyman had spun and grabbed Corvallis's gun arm. "No," he said sharply. It was an order.

"Let me go, goddamn it," Corvallis roared.

"No." His hand gripped Corvallis's arm like a vise. Corvallis struggled, trying to pull his arm free and drag his gun out at the same time.

"Calm down, damn it," Eyman said. He was not having much trouble keeping his grip on Corvallis. But, still, the struggle was wearing, and he hoped neither Ike nor Curly would go for their pistols. If they did, there would be lead flying all around the High Country Saloon, and he would, he figured, wind up in the line of fire.

"Get off me, Ev, or I'll have your butt fired soon's we get back to the Lazy O."

Eyman was unfazed about getting fired from the job at the ranch. At least if it meant saving the life of the boss's hot-headed son. "We'll let your pa decide that later. But I'll say this, I'd rather have your old man send me packin'—though I reckon such ain't likely just on your say-so—than have to cart your dead butt back to the Lazy O and tell him you was killed for bein' such a goddamn idiot."

"Goddamnit, get outta my way, Ev," Corvallis shouted, fighting all the more.

"No!" Eyman insisted. "I ain't gonna be responsible for you gettin' yourself killed because you're a fool."

"I'll kill him, Ev," Corvallis said, almost whining.

"Easy."

"You'll never even get your piece out before he fills you full of lead, damnit. Listen to me. This ain't no saddle tramp you're gunnin' for. That sumbitch knows how to use that Colt, and a lot better'n you do."

"Damnit, Ev, get out of my way. I'll take care of that bastard, if you're afraid to. Ike and Curly'll back my play."

Eyman swung himself more fully in front of Corvallis, and used his body to shove Corvallis up against the bar, pinning him. He was sweating from the exertion, and, he admitted to himself, a healthy dose of nervousness at having Wolfe standing behind him. "Ike, Curly," he said sharply. "Get your butts outside and wait there for us. Now! Move it!"

Neither man was foolish enough to argue when the ranch foreman gave an order in that tone. Especially when they were facing an enraged Lucas Wolfe. They might not like it, but they did as they were told, sliding out between Wolfe and Eyman, clanking away and out the door.

"Now," Eyman said in some frustration, "you're gonna follow 'em, Aaron. Nice and easy."

"Like hell I will."

"You'll do like I told ya, or I'll break your arm here and now." The two men were nose to nose.

Corvallis flinched first. Eyman released Corvallis's arm and moved back a step. Then he grabbed Corvallis's shirt front. He pulled, turned, dragging Corvallis with him, and then shoved the ranch owner's son away, in the general direction of the door. "Move your butt," he ordered.

Corvallis swiped a hand across his mouth, and then wiped the hand on a pant leg. Suddenly he reached for his pistol.

"Goddamn fool," Eyman breathed as he stepped forward and punched Corvallis in the jaw. As Corvallis stood there, stunned, trying to shake off the effects of the punch, Eyman grabbed Corvallis's Colt and shoved it into his belt. He grabbed Corvallis by the shoulders, spun him around and propelled him toward the door with a healthy shove on the back.

Corvallis hunched his back with the anger that surged through him as he stumbled toward the door. His ears and face burned red with the laughter that followed him.

With a sigh, Eyman turned part way toward Wolfe. He touched the brim of his hat.

Wolfe wondered at the blatant stupidity of someone like Aaron Corvallis. And he wondered why a capable man like Eyman was forced to baby-sit for Corvallis. Eyman was just doing a job he had been hired to do, and appeared to be a good man. Indeed, Wolfe was even starting to like Eyman. He didn't necessarily trust him, and he knew that Eyman would do what his boss required, but Wolfe liked him nonetheless. Wolfe nodded at Eyman, who spun and walked away, chaps slapping and spurs clanking.

Wolfe went back to his table and sat, grateful. He was still riddled with pain, and so much standing around—as well as the tension—made it no easier. He finished off his shot of bourbon, and had one more before heading back to his hotel.

It was a cool night, though the day had been warm. Wolfe stopped outside the hotel, looking up at the bright blaze of stars. He smiled, realizing he was almost daring someone to attack him again. But the chill sank into him, setting his still-fresh bruises to throbbing a little. With a last look around, he went up to his room. Alma Fletcher was nowhere in sight, and

Wolfe was not sure whether he was sad or grateful.

The next morning, as the sun warmed up the land, he saddled the palomino and rode out of Kaibab, heading for the Lazy O Ranch.

Chapter Ten

Sally Corvallis saw him first. She was saddling her chestnut mare in front of the barn off to the side of the house. When Wolfe rode up, she glanced at him, anger burning on her pretty face. He stopped near her and dismounted, tying the palomino to a railing of the corral.

Sally steadfastly ignored him, concentrating much more than she really had to on tightening her saddle.

"Ain't you going to say hello?" he asked cheerfully.

"Humph."

"I'm sorry I couldn't meet you the other day, Sally," he said apologetically. "Somethin' came up."

"Oh, really?" she said sarcastically. "I suppose some saloon girl," she added, blushing, "batted her eyes at you and . . ." she turned to look at him, and then gasped when she saw his face. "My God, Luke, what happened to you?"

"I had a little accident."

"I hear he fell off his horse," Aaron said, walking up, an arrogant smile on his face.

"You don't get marks like that from falling off a horse," Sally said firmly. "Were you in a saloon brawl, Luke?"

"Not exactly," Wolfe said dryly, casting a sidelong

glance at Corvallis.

"Oh?" Sally said, looking from Wolfe to her brother. Neither said anything. "I've seen the marks of fighting before," Sally said sharply, not pleased at either man at the moment. "Now just what happened, Mr. Wolfe?"

"You might want to ask your brother," Wolfe said quietly, watching Corvallis. Wolfe leaned his back up against the rails of the corral.

"Aaron?" Sally said, turning toward her brother, her face lingering on Wolfe for a few extra moments.

"How the hell should I know what happened to the fool?" Corvallis said with a shrug. "I heard down in the saloon that he fell off his horse."

"Mr. Wolfe?"

Wolfe shrugged.

Sally's face was a study in barely contained anger. Her cheeks colored red with it, and her eyes snapped fire. "Mr. Wolfe, you had best tell me what happened," she said in a low voice full of warning.

He grinned a little. Then his face grew hard. "Your brother here sent a few of the ranch hands down to Kaibab to whale the livin' tar out of me," he said simply.

"Why?" she asked, not surprised.

"You'd have to ask him that."

"Aaron?" she asked, once again turning.

"He's a goddamn liar."

"Watch your language."

"Bah. He's still a liar, no matter how I say it."

"For some reason, Aaron, I believe him more than I do you. Now why's that, do you suppose?"

" 'Cause you're a damn fool, too," Corvallis snapped before spinning and stomping away.

"That what really happened, Mr. Wolfe?" Sally asked. "Or'd you just say that to get Aaron angry?"

92

"Oh, it's true, Miss Sally." Quickly Wolfe explained what had happened. "So that's why I didn't come to see you the past couple days."

Sally stepped up and touched the three stitches on Wolfe's cheek softly. "You still hurt bad?"

"Not much."

"I'm glad you came to see me today," Sally said brightly. She was, too. She had been heartbroken when Wolfe had not shown up three days ago. She thought he had ridden off and left her. Or maybe had gotten killed in a gunfight somewhere, though she knew in her head—if not in her heart—that she would have heard if such a thing had happened.

"I come to see your father, too," he said, smiling.

Sally looked hurt—and worried.

"You might want to listen in when I talk to him."

Hope burst anew in her heart. "All right."

Together they strolled to the house. Sally went in first, calling for her father. They entered the study— Owen Corvallis's domain. Corvallis and Wolfe shook hands. Wolfe sat in a heavy chair, while Corvallis stayed behind his desk. Sally served them each a glass of whiskey, despite the early hour, and cigars, before she sat in another chair near Wolfe. Aaron Corvallis entered. He grabbed a drink and sat, scowling.

"Well, what can I do for you, Mr. Wolfe?" the elder Corvallis asked pleasantly. He leaned back in his chair, the cigar clenched between his teeth.

"You could give me my land back," Wolfe said with an ingratiating grin.

"Goddamn," Aaron muttered, barely audibly.

"Ain't likely," Corvallis said with a laugh. "Other'n that, what can I do for you?"

Wolfe took a deep breath. This was a new experience for him, and he was nervous about it. "You could let

93

me come courtin' your daughter," he managed to say in clear, firm tones.

Corvallis had suspected it was coming, but the reality still gave him pause. He thought for a bit. There was really no reason to deny the request. He realized that Wolfe might be trying to get the Lazy O through Sally. But if that was so, what better way to keep an eye on what the young man was doing that to have him nearby and under watch all the time? And, if Wolfe was true in his attentions, well, what the harm?

Aaron was Owen's only son, and thereby his rightful heir. But Corvallis had little liking for his son, and would not be all that adverse to having a son-in-law he liked. There was no certainty, of course, that the courting would end in a marriage, but it did not seem out of the question.

Besides, he thought, glancing at his daughter, Sally certainly seemed to have taken a liking to Wolfe. She had seemed quite radiant of late, and Corvallis finally put it down to her growing attraction to Wolfe.

"I reckon that wouldn't be such a bad thing," Corvallis allowed gruffly. "If my daughter wants your attentions?" He turned his face, eyebrows raised in question, toward Sally.

Her eyes sparkled with eagerness, and her face was bright. But when she spoke, her voice was even. "I'd not mind if Mr. Wolfe was to come around now and again."

"Hey, what about me?" Aaron snapped. "Don't I get no say in all this?" He might act foolish sometimes, but he was shrewd enough to know that if the relationship between Wolfe and Sally turned serious, his own claim on the Lazy O might become a lot more tenuous. He had no trouble seeing Wolfe as a threat to his eventual—and, he thought, rightful—inheritance of the ranch.

"I don't expect Mr. Wolfe wants to come courtin' you, Aaron," Corvallis said dryly.

Sally giggled, and Wolfe chuckled.

"That ain't what I mean," Aaron snapped angrily. "I mean . . ." He stopped. He suddenly felt like a fool. He wanted Wolfe away from here forever, so that his own inheritance was not jeopardized. But he could not just come out and say that to his father. He couldn't, he knew, so he shut up quickly. He stood, face flushed with rage, and headed for the door.

"You might want to stick around a spell," Wolfe drawled. "I got one more bit of business with your father, and I expect you'll be interested in what I got to say."

Aaron looked malevolently over his shoulder at Wolfe. But he returned to his seat, looking pained.

Wolfe pulled off his hat and hung it off the end of one chair arm. "As you can see, Mr. Corvallis, I've had me a spot of trouble of late."

Corvallis did not think he was going to like where this was heading, but he said nothing.

"I don't reckon you know anything about this, Mr. Corvallis, but Aaron here sent some of your hands out to bushwhack me the other night."

"He's a liar!" Aaron shouted.

Corvallis ignored his son. "How can you be sure it was Aaron?"

"You missing any of your hands of late?"

"Simms and Walcott left a couple days ago," Corvallis said thoughtfully. "Rode off, Ev told me. Said they got tired of range work." It was a common enough problem, and no reason for him to have gotten alarmed.

"Maybe you ought to check with Klockschmidt down

95

at his funeral parlor."

Corvallis glowered. "What're you sayin' Mr. Wolfe?"

"I'm sayin' that you'll most likely find them two boys either in Klockschmidt's — or in the boneyard already, if Klockschmidt ain't dawdled in plantin' 'em."

"That true, son?" Corvallis asked, facing Aaron. He knew in his heart it was, but he could not bring himself to admit it.

"No, sir," Aaron said adamantly. "I got no idea what he's talkin' about."

"These are serious accusations, Mr. Wolfe," Owen said thoughtfully.

"I didn't mention it to make accusations, Mr. Corvallis. I mentioned them as a way to save a life."

"Oh?" Corvallis said, surprised.

"Yessir." Wolfe tossed his cigar butt in the fireplace, where it lay smoldering. Wolfe took a deep breath. "I'm an easygoin' sort of man most times, Mr. Corvallis. I don't bother folks who don't bother me. Sometimes, though, folks take that as a flaw, and try to have their way with me. Such a thing don't set well with me." He paused to hold his glass out, indicating to Sally that he wanted a refill.

"Get on with it," Corvallis said tightly, as Sally got the decanter of whiskey.

"Well, sir," Wolfe said, as Sally poured bourbon into his glass, "I've had three run-ins with Aaron and some of his boys now, and I do believe I've about come to the end of my rope as far as turnin' the other cheek. I . . ."

"Turnin' the other cheek?" Aaron blurted out. "You killed three of the ranch hands." He realized he had said something he shouldn't have, and clamped his lips shut. He glared at Wolfe. His father stared at him, and Aaron was not sure whether it was with hate, anger, or pity.

"As I said," Wolfe went on blandly, as Owen Corvallis slowly craned his head back around to stare balefully at him, "I'm some tired of turnin' the other cheek. And if you value your son's life, Mr. Corvallis, you'll keep him away from me."

Corvallis sat with his elbows on his desk. His fingers were steepled before his face, and he suddenly felt old. He knew Aaron was a troublemaker, and a poor excuse for a son—and as a man. Still, Owen harbored a hope—and would not yet admit that hope was forlorn—that Aaron would amount to something.

He glanced at his son out of the corner of his eye, and was not pleased with what he saw. Aaron was a handsome man, but despite his relative youth he had an almost burned-out look about him, the result of too much whiskey, too soft a life, and too much of getting his own way. And too much of his mother's softening influence. Owen thought he still loved Aggie Corvallis, but he thought she held too much civilizing sway over her son.

Owen remembered back over the years to when he was Aaron's age. He was slogging through wheat fields and marshes and woods and streams in places like Antietam and Chickamauga and Spottsylvania. There was death and pain and horror all around. Yet he had survived and grown, becoming a strong, hard man, but one still with compassion. He had learned that from one of the Yankees he had fought. A man who had helped a wounded Rebel rather than killing him.

That had affected Owen Corvallis—who had been the wounded Rebel helped by a kind-hearted enemy—immensely, and through the rest of his life he had tried to live by decent principles, while still remaining hard enough to help his family and friends get through life.

97

But Aaron apparently had picked up none of those traits and none of Owen's hard-earned wisdom.

Owen knew that realistically Aaron was hopeless, that his son would never do anything well — or right. But, as a father, he continued to hold out that hope. Still, there were times when reality reared its head enough that one could not avoid it. Now, he was afraid, was one of those times.

"I appreciate your concern, Mr. Wolfe," Corvallis said softly. "And I will do what I can to keep Aaron away from you. I cannot guarantee anything, though, no matter how much I would wish it so."

"I understand," Wolfe said, also softly.

"I don't, goddamnit," Aaron shouted, shoving up out of his chair. "I don't need your protection, Pa." He turned rage-blazed eyes on Wolfe. "And as for you, goddamnit, you'd best stay out of my way. Or you'll end up dead!" He stomped out of the room, leaving behind a wake of awkward silence.

Chapter Eleven

Wolfe did not think his words—or Owen Corvallis's promises—would have much impact on Aaron Corvallis, and so he was rather surprised when he saw neither hide nor hair of the younger Corvallis for several days. Except in passing, of course, when he rode out to the Lazy O Ranch to court Sally, which he did every day.

He and Sally picnicked daily, and he still spent considerable time checking out the ranch. At fifty thousand acres, give or take several thousand, it might take a while to find the spot he was looking for. And he had several suppers at the Corvallis home, chatting with Owen and Sally, while Aaron generally made himself scarce. The last pleased Wolfe. He was not, by any means, afraid of Aaron Corvallis, but, still, that constant tension of waiting for Corvallis to make some move was wearing. And it did not go well with trying to court Sally.

Wolfe didn't see much of Eyman, either. When they did come in contact, both men were polite, if a little standoffish. Wolfe came to realize that he wasn't sure he actually liked Eyman. But he did respect the wiry ranch foreman, and in his world, that was enough.

A week later, his bruises were mostly faded, and he felt no ill effects of the beating. He would never admit it to anyone, but he was scared to death that his genitals would never work properly again after the smashing they had undergone. He could not expect Sally to prove to him that he was a whole man again; no good woman would be so inclined, he figured. So one evening he steeled himself, fighting down the worry that nipped at his stomach, and strolled over to Alma Fletcher's bordello.

He knew that Alma would be put out at him for not having come straight to her. But he knew that if things did not work, he would not be able to face her. So he went to the bordello and asked for Esther.

Lovemaking had rarely been as good for him as it was that night. Esther knew what had happened to him, and she instinctively understood his fears. So she was cautious and comforting at first, using her soft hands and softer mouth on him. It soon became evident that he needed no babying, and they both abandoned themselves to their passions.

Alma was stony-faced when he staggered past her on his way back to his room that night. And her voice was cold as ice, stopping him, "You'll have to vacate your room come morning, Mr. Wolfe," she said.

"Why?" he asked, turning. Since the reason was obvious to him, he was not surprised.

"I need the space for other customers." Not an iota of warmth touched her voice.

"Like hell," he muttered.

Alma was about to say something else when Esther entered from the hallway that led to the door at the back. The door was only a few feet from the back door of the brothel. "You wanted to see me, ma'am?"

100

Esther asked politely. But it was obvious she was nervous.

"Yes, Esther." She stopped, staring at Wolfe, waiting.

He grinned maliciously at her. "I reckon I'll just wait around to hear what you got to say to Esther," he said harshly.

"As you wish," Alma said icily. She turned her attentions to Esther and said, minus any sympathy, "I'll not need your services any longer, Esther. I expect you to have your room at the house cleaned out and be gone by daybreak."

"What . . ?" Esther said in shock. Tears brimmed in her wide green eyes and overflowed, coursing down her plump, dusky cheeks.

"You heard me, young lady. Are you deaf?"

"I . . . But I . . ."

"If you was a man, you'd be dead now," Wolfe hissed at Alma.

She ignored him.

"You selfish, heartless bitch," he continued. "You just can't stand that I went to . . ."

"You may go now, Esther," Alma said coldly and loudly enough to override Wolfe.

"Yes, ma'am," Esther whispered. She rushed down the hallway to the back, tears flowing, sobs lingering in the air after she had gone.

"Good night, Mr. Wolfe," Alma said. Her face still seemed to be carved of granite.

Wolfe did not move. "As I was sayin' before you rudely opened your big mouth, you just can't stand it that I went to Esther tonight, and that's why you're actin' like such a goddamn fool."

Alma continued her impersonation of a statue.

"You think throwin' me and Esther out is gonna

101

make you feel better?" he asked derisively. "Shoot," he commented, drawing the word out. "All you're gonna do is become a dried up old woman without friends or sympathy."

"Is that right?" Alma asked, face and rigid body unchanged.

"Yes, it is. And worse, it's like you're cuttin' off your nose just 'cause it's runnin' from a cold. Esther's your best girl over at the house. You fire her, and you'll be hurtin' yourself."

"I've been hurt before."

"Reckon you have. But you ain't the only one's ever been hurt by somebody else." He paused. "Now, I can understand you being mighty put out with me. But Esther was only doin' her job—and damn well at that," he added with a jab.

Alma's stony facade began to crack as her lower lip quivered. Now Wolfe was surprised. He really had thought she was heartless. But he was not about to ease up on her just yet. "If you want me out of here come mornin', I'll be gone, but I'll be damned and blasted before I let you take out your nastiness on Esther."

Alma was trying to regain her hardness, but was not having much luck with it.

"Now, what you should've done is come to me and told me you was out of sorts with what I'd done. You ever think there might've been reason I done what I did?" She shook her head and he said, "Naw, I didn't think you did. Damn fool. All you do is go flyin' off the handle."

"Tell me now," Alma whispered.

"Hell, it's too late now." He paused a moment, chewing on his lip. "Unless it'll save Esther."

"It might."

102

"You lie to me, woman, and you'll live just long enough to regret it," Wolfe warned. He thought a minute, wondering whether he should say anything. He decided he should, since he could not be responsible for Esther's firing. He told her quickly, and without embellishment, of his fears of what would happen.

Alma's toughness crumbled completely, as she began to cry. "Damnit, Luke," she said. "You should've come to me. I care about you. I would've taken good care of you. I've got a lot more experience — and feelings — than that young trollop, damn you. Damn you."

"It's *because* you care that I couldn't face you if I wasn't a man," he said, embarrassed.

The two stood, awkward, not sure what to do — or say. Minutes dragged by, before Wolfe finally asked softly, "What about Esther?"

Alma searched his face, and smiled wryly. "She can stay."

Wolfe was relieved. He started up the stairs, but turned when Alma called, "Luke." When he looked at her, she said, "You know, I don't mind losin' you to that fancy-pants girl from out of town, but I couldn't face it to lose you to one of the girls in my own place."

"I'd never do such a thing to you," he said earnestly, with a reassuring smile. "Well, time I was asleep. You'll tell Esther right off?"

Alma nodded, and Wolfe headed up the stairs.

Some time later, something awoke him from a deep, pleasurable sleep. He was reaching for the Colt hanging from the bedpost near his head before he was fully conscious. The giggle stopped him when he had the Colt half out of the holster.

"You don't need *that* gun," Alma said with another soft giggle.

He rolled over, facing her. She was in his bed, under the covers, waiting.

"You know we can't do this no more," he said in the morning after they had done so again.

"I know," Alma said dreamily. "But I had to make sure you were all right. And I wanted to say goodbye to you in my own way."

He nodded and got up. Warm sunlight streamed through the partially opened curtains. He padded, naked, to the basin and filled it with water. He washed up and started getting dressed. "Damn, I'm hungry," he muttered. He was pulling on his boots when Alma rose and walked over to him. She was nude, and enticing as she bent to kiss him. Then she wrapped a sheet around her and headed out of the room. Wolfe, watching her, smiled. Alma was her old cocky self, with head held high and back proudly straight.

After a huge breakfast at the restaurant next door, Wolfe got his horse and rode toward the Lazy O Ranch. The sun beat down, bringing out the sweat on Wolfe's back and head. He thought ruefully after a bit that perhaps not all the sweat was from the heat of the day. He had to admit he was feeling more than a little guilt at having spent the past evening and night in amorous pursuits with two prostitutes, while now he was riding out to meet his sweetheart.

He managed to calm his guilt a little by telling himself repeatedly that Sally was a good girl, and good girls would not even think of such things, let alone do them. Besides, he did have to find out if he was still all right in that way. Sally most likely would expect to have children if his courting of her proved successful and they married someday.

If Wolfe showed any of the guilt outwardly, Sally seemed not to notice it, for which Wolfe was grateful. She was, as usual, bubbly, excited, full of life. They ate lunch in the shade of some tall, spindly aspens near a small spring.

Aaron Corvallis and Ev Eyman rode up and stopped for a few minutes. Both men were friendly enough so that Wolfe was suspicious. It was not like Corvallis to be so outgoing toward him. Worse, Corvallis sat there with a knowing smile—damn near a gloat, Wolfe figured—plastered on his face.

The two men did not stay long. They soon bid farewell to Wolfe and Sally and rode off, leaving Wolfe wondering.

"Something don't seem right with those two," Sally said after her brother and Eyman had left.

"You sensed that, too, eh?"

"Yeah. But I can't figure out what's wrong."

"Those two are plottin' something. I wish to hell I could figure out what it is, though."

"Why?" Sally asked, stroking Wolfe's arm lightly.

" 'Cause whatever it is, I know damn well it don't bode well for me." He shrugged. "Reckon I'll find out soon enough."

"You just be careful the next few days, Luke," Sally said, concern in her voice. She looked longingly at him. He smiled and bent a little to plant a kiss on her.

Sally accepted it; indeed, she joined in with fervor. Suddenly, though, she pulled back, face flushed. "We shouldn't . . . I . . ." She was too flustered to continue.

"Nothin' wrong with two folks in love kissin', you know," he said with a disarming grin.

"But it might . . . it could . . . maybe it'd lead to

. . . Well . . . it might . . ."

"You worry too much sometimes," Wolfe said with a small laugh. Sally stared at him, embarrassed. He leaned over and kissed her again. She responded hungrily, and did not pull away in fright.

"Well?" Wolfe said as he pulled his lips away. "Have you been ravished yet?"

"No," Sally admitted, managing a grin.

"You'll not go to hell for it either, I'd wager."

Sally's face flushed pinkly again. "Come on," she said gruffly to cover her discomfit, "it's time I got back. Help me clean things up."

While Sally began packing away the remnants of their picnic, Wolfe saddled her chestnut and his palomino. Then he loaded the picnic basket onto her horse. Together they rode off, toward the ranch house. Wolfe stayed there only long enough to say a stilted goodbye to Sally, and exchange a few words with Owen Corvallis, who was standing there. Then he headed back down the road toward town. He veered off, however, after a mile, and worked up a piñon-covered ridge. Since he didn't know what Aaron Corvallis and Eyman were planning—and he was certain they were—he figured to be extra wary.

Alma was a lot more friendly when he arrived back at the hotel after putting the palomino in the stable. She smiled warmly. He went upstairs, washed off and then went to supper.

Afterward, he headed for the High Country Saloon. There were several other saloons in town, but all looked like dark, evil places compared with the High Country. He found he enjoyed many of the regulars, and he liked Orville, the bartender.

He ordered a bottle of whiskey. Taking it, he headed for a table. But soon he was bored, and he decided to join in a card game for a while. He played without much interest — or luck.

But Wolfe had had enough excitement and such for a while, and he called it a night early. He was rather glad that Alma was away from the hotel desk when he went in. He did not feel like dealing with her tonight.

He turned in, welcoming the comfortable crispness of the sheets. There were some advantages to having gotten in good with the owner of the hotel — things like clean, fresh sheets every other day; and enough water in the pitcher; and the extra servings and larger portions he got in the restaurant these days. He decided he could get used to such things very easily, but he better not.

He rode out to the ranch the next day late in the morning. Sally was pacing out in front of the house, watching the road anxiously. "Where've you been?" she asked.

"Slept late," Wolfe said with a disarming grin. "Had new shoes put on the palomino. You didn't miss me, did you?"

It was obvious to anyone how much she had missed him, but she grinned and said, "Not a bit."

"Now you've gone and hurt my feelings," he said, feigning anger.

"Oh, pooh," Sally said, then giggled.

They rode out and had their picnic. Afterward, Wolfe brought Sally back to the ranch house before riding to an area he wanted to explore. Once again he had the irritating feeling that someone was following him.

He stopped. Rolling a cigarette, Wolfe knelt, pretending to look at his map. But he was concentrating. He knew when the others had moved up behind him. He stood, turned and faced Ike, Curly and another ranch hand Wolfe did not know. Their hands rested uncomfortably close to pistols. Wolfe did not like the look of this, but he remained outwardly calm as he lit his cigarette.

Chapter Twelve

"You boys appear to be lookin' for trouble," Wolfe said. "If you are, I'd suggest you turn yourselves around and take your trouble somewhere else."

"We don't take kindly to the treatment you gave us — and Mr. Corvallis — that night a week or so ago," Curly huffed. He was chunky, with a fat man's florid and puffy face. A nasal condition made him breathe like a broken bellows most times, and his eyes squinted. His teeth were yellow.

"Don't mean a damn thing to me what you like or don't like, Curly," Wolfe said off-handedly.

"Well, me, Curly, and Aud here have come to teach you something about respectin' other folks — especially your betters," Ike tossed in, trying to look mean — and not succeeding.

Ike was as tall as Curly, and as thin as Curly was hefty. He had a tic in one eye that was irritating as all get-out to Wolfe, and one ear was larger than the other. His nose was pushed off to the side, bent at the end.

The third man — the one Ike had called Aud — was a quiet, arrogant-looking man of more than medium height. He had a full chest, flat stomach and seemingly no hips. He stood silently by, thumbs hooked into his gunbelt, with the right hand not far from the butt of his converted Colt Dragoon.

All three were dressed like what they were — ranch hands. They wore cotton or flannel shirts, neckerchiefs, heavy denim or twill pants, worn boots, and chaps. Stained, work-worn hats rested on their heads.

"You couldn't teach a dog to piss on a tree, Ike," Wolfe said sarcastically. He was nervous, though he didn't show it. He did not like being caught by three men; particularly men who were angry and could potentially be dangerous. He took a drag on the cigarette and blew out a stream of smoke.

"We've had enough of your goddamn smart-mouthin', Wolfe," Curly snappped.

"So? What you aimin' to do about it?" Wolfe sneered. "You gonna bring around another five or six boys and try'n beat the stuffin' out of me again? Shoo-oot." He tried to unobtrusively unhook the small leather loop over the hammer of his Colt, hoping the movement of the cigarette to his mouth with his other hand would distract the others.

"We're done whuppin' on you, Wolfe," Ike said with a sneer. "I mean, hell, any man stupid enough to come back after such a thumpin' and try'n cause more trouble's for the folks that thumped him has gotta be dumb as a fencepost."

"That's something you ought to know a lot about, Ike," Wolfe said with a malicious grin. "Hell," he added with an irritating chuckle, "bein' dumb's a fencepost is something you could aspire to. Give you some hope for the future, eh?" He laughed, hoping to anger Ike at least, and, hopefully, all three. They were ranch hands, men used to punching cattle for a living. They were not gunfighters, and, while they might possibly be danger-ous, they most likely would not shoot as well if they were angry. And Wolfe was quite certain that a shootout was where this was leading.

110

"Enough talk," Aud suddenly said. His left hand moved quickly from where it had been hooked into his gunbelt toward his pistol. But by the time the Colt was in hand, Wolfe had flicked the cigarette at Ike's face, hoping to slow him if even for a moment, and threw himself sideways.

His right hand went for his Peacemaker, while his left moved out to break his fall and then shove him partway back up. Ike jumped back a step as the cigarette dinked off his cheek. Ike's movement threw Aud's aim off, and his first shot screamed wide, ricocheting with a piercing whine off a rock behind Wolfe.

Wolfe fired twice, hitting Aud in the chest with one shot. The other bullet missed. "Damn," he swore as he scuttled backward, looking for maneuvering room.

A slug from Curly's pistol burrowed into the dirt near Wolfe's left hand, and he jerked the appendage out of the way. Wolfe fired, winging Curly. Wolfe had a momentary flash of fear as he figured his life was about to end. Ike swung toward him, pistol cocked, and Wolfe knew he did not have enough time to either kill Ike or get out of the way of Ike's shot.

Wolfe fired desperately. The bullet clanged off Ike's pistol, knocking the weapon out of Ike's hand, and causing it to go off. The bullet slammed harmlessly into a ponderosa pine several yards to Wolfe's left.

Wolfe fired again, and Ike was smashed back across a boulder behind him, his chest already soaked with blood.

Curly looked very frightened all of a sudden, as Wolfe trained his revolver on him. His fear heightened when Wolfe pulled back the hammer with his thumb. Curly saw death—his own—in Wolfe's eyes, and he almost shook with fright.

111

"I still got one slug left, Curly. I'd be happy to oblige you with it, if you was to insist."

"I . . ."

"Drop the Colt, Curly," Wolfe snapped.

Curly did so immediately. He sighed with relief when Wolfe lowered his own pistol. Still, he had seen what Wolfe could do, and he was not about to move without being told.

Wolfe had stood up and was moving, Colt still ready. He checked on Ike first. The ranch hand was dead, a large hole punched in his chest. Blood was already congealing on the old flannel shirt.

Wolfe moved to Aud, who lay on his back. Aud was not dead, but being shot through the lungs like he was, Wolfe knew he wouldn't last long. The man's face was twisted up with pain, and his chest rose and fell feebly.

Wolfe stopped in front of Curly. He shook his head. "There's been too much killin' here, Curly, but I'm still of a mind to finish off what you and your cronies started."

Curly blanched, as Wolfe continued. "But I ain't the kind of man to kill somebody in cold blood. Not even one who deserves it as much as you." He glared at Curly. "But I hope to hell you've learned some sense here today."

"Reckon I have," Curly croaked through a mouth that was arid due to fear.

"That's good." Wolfe paused, disgusted with all this. He was beginning to wonder a little if perhaps he shouldn't just ride out of Kaibab and never come back. But the thought of the land—and what it meant to him—made that difficult. And the thought of leaving Sally made it impossible. "How are you feelin'?"

"Reckon I'll live. I was only winged." He glanced

112

down at the slight trail of blood across the top of his shoulder, and then back to Wolfe.

"What I want you to do, Curly, is go on back to the ranch house and tell Aaron what happened. You'd be wise, too, to tell the old man. But that's your account. Then you ought to ride on into Kaibab and have Doc Windsor fix you up."

"Yessir," Curly managed.

"I also want you to tell Aaron he'd best not try'n pull such a damnfool stunt again. Good hands are too valuable to lose through such foolishness. And he ain't got a gunman good enough to take me," Wolfe boasted.

"He won't listen."

"I don't really expect him to. But at least he'll be given fair warnin'. Now, go on."

"What about Ike and Aud?"

Wolfe shrugged. "Take 'em with you. What's done with 'em then is up to Aaron—or, more likely, Owen, if he finds out about it. One of 'em'll most likely see they get to Klockschmidt's. Or maybe Owen'll just have 'em buried out here. It don't matter none to me now," Wolfe added with another shrug.

Curly nodded. "Can I have my Colt back?" he asked, almost plaintively. It would not do for a man to go back to the ranch house, or bunkhouse, without his pistol.

Wolfe bent, picked it up and uncocked it. He unloaded it and handed it, butt first, to Curly. "Leave it that way till you get back to the house," Wolfe warned.

Curly nodded again. Without further ado, he tossed Ike and then Aud over their horses. He mounted his own horse and rode out. He wanted to be as far away from Wolfe as he could be.

Wolfe began to relax while he rode back to Kaibab. By the time he had finished his supper and was sitting

113

in the High Country Saloon, drinking his third shot of bourbon, he was feeling quite fine once again.

But the good feelings fled quickly when, a few hours later, Owen Corvallis, his son, and Ev Eyman stormed into the saloon. They spied Wolfe sitting at the table and headed toward him, apparently in fine fettle.

"Damn," Wolfe muttered vehemently. He had had enough trouble for one day. He didn't need this.

"Mind if I sit?" Owen Corvallis asked. Without waiting for an answer, he pulled out a chair and plunked himself down. Aaron and Eyman stood, flanking Owen.

"Suit yourself," Wolfe said dryly.

Orville appeared unbidden with a glass of beer for Corvallis. He set it down on the table and headed back to the bar.

Owen gulped down half the beer. After wiping his mouth on the back of his hand, he burped and then said, "What's the idea of gunnin' down a couple of my boys?"

Wolfe looked up at Aaron and grinned maliciously. Aaron glared back at him. Aaron realized he had made a mistake in coming down here with his father in tow. He had thought it would scare Wolfe off; now he knew he had made a major mistake.

"Your son sent 'em out there to gun me down, Mr. Corvallis," Wolfe said truthfully, eyes locked on Corvallis's.

"That true, Aaron?" Owen asked over his shoulder, not moving his eyes.

"I told you before, Pa, Wolfe's nothin' but a liar."

"Why would he lie?"

"I don't know," Aaron mumbled. He shuffled his feet as he grew fidgety.

"Why would my son send some men to kill you, Mr.

114

Wolfe?" Owen asked.

"Tryin' to run me off, I reckon. You know he ain't happy I've been roamin' around the Lazy O. And you ought to know he ain't happy that I'm courtin' Sally. I figure he thinks that maybe I'll end up marryin' Sally, and you'll give me over the land, and he'll be out his inheritance."

"That's stupid."

"So's your son," Wolfe said bluntly.

"I know," Owen said with a sigh, not caring that Aaron was standing two feet away. "I've tried to do right by him, but . . ." He stopped and finished off his beer. "I still can't believe he'd send three of the boys out to kill you, though."

Wolfe shrugged. "If he had the stones, he would've tried it himself."

"I'd not be all that pleased if such a thing was to happen," Owen said, shaking his head. "Aaron might not be much of a son, but he's the only one I got."

"I understand." Wolfe glanced at Aaron. The young man's face was flushed with rage and shame. The quirt snapped anxiously in his hand, creating an erratic drumming on one denim-covered thigh. "He's thought on it plenty, though. Lucky for you, you got a smart man for a ranch foreman."

"Oh?"

"Ev hadn't of pulled Aaron away from me twice, you'd have no male heir in the family."

"That true, Ev?" Owen asked over his shoulder.

Eyman did not want to answer, but knew he had no other choice. "Reckon so."

"Reckon?"

"It's true, Mr. Corvallis," Eyman said quietly after only a moment's hesitation. "Aaron wanted to take Mr. Wolfe down a couple times, but I think I finally con-

115

vinced him he'd end up dead if he tried. That's why we sent Ike, Curly and Aud out to find Mr. Wolfe and do the job." He stared at Wolfe, not defiant, just a man doing what he had to.

"We?" Owen asked. He was still looking at Wolfe.

"Yessir. About the only way I could talk Aaron out of goin' out after Wolfe himself was to offer him an alternative. I figured," he added, "that you'd rather lose a couple ranch hands than your son."

"You're right, Mr. Wolfe," Owen said straight-faced. "Ev is a pretty smart cookie." He sighed. He had liked none of what he had heard. But he accepted it, since he knew in his heart all of it was true. He just wished there was something he could do to change his son, to make all this better. He had worked far too hard to make the Lazy O Ranch become viable to see it destroyed by a headstrong, foolish son.

"Orville!" he shouted. "Another beer." He waited for it to arrive.

When it did, he took a sip. Setting the mug carefully down, Owen looked into Wolfe's eyes. "Just why do you want this land so much, Mr. Wolfe?" he asked flatly.

Chapter Thirteen

"It's my land, Mr. Corvallis," Wolfe said.

"Booshwa," Corvallis snorted. "You ain't no cowboy, and I reckon you ain't much interested in runnin' a ranch. And I *know* you ain't about to become some sodbuster."

"That's a fact," Wolfe said with a chuckle. "Still, a man's got to have a place to call home. And if it's a sizable chunk of land, well, so much the better." His shoulders rose and fell once, as if to say, "What's a man to do?"

"But why, Luke?" Corvallis questioned. He knew for certain that there was more to all this than Wolfe was saying, and he was frustrated at being kept in the dark. "You ain't about to make your livin' from the land."

"I might just change my mind on that," Wolfe said slowly. He paused a heartbeat, then added, "If I was to get married." He tried hard to keep the smile off his face as he rolled his eyes upward to catch the expression on Aaron's face. It was one of rage—mixed with fear.

"I still don't believe it."

Wolfe shrugged. "All right. Let's just say Gramps went through a hell of lot to get that land. Then my pa went and lost it—or had it stole from him," he added pointedly. He liked Owen Corvallis, but he was still not

117

certain the rancher had not somehow cheated his father. "In either case, I aim to get it back."

"How'd your grandpa come by the land?" Corvallis asked. His interest was real.

"Order us another drink, and I might just tell you," Wolfe said with a grin.

Corvallis, a twinkle in his eye, did so, and when they were served, he said, "Go on."

"Gramps was a mountain man back in the old days of the fur trade. He trapped through most of the Western mountains, includin' much of the parts with some of the big names—Kit Carson, Ewing Young, Bill Williams."

Jeb Wolfe and Bill Williams had trapped this way back in the late thirties. It was then that Jeb Wolfe had first seen the land between the towering San Francisco Peaks and the knob that would later be named after his trapping companion. It was a pleasant land, though cold in the winter they were to find out. Still, there was plenty of wood around, and the place looked like it would make a nice home—if ever any towns grew within a reasonable distance. And, for now, there were plenty of beaver.

They trapped several miles southwest of where Owen Corvallis's house now stood, along the creek that would also bear his partner's name. It was a good area, and one day Williams said, "Maybe we ought to winter here."

"That shines with this chil'," Wolfe said.

In between their trapping and then the curing of hides, Wolfe and Williams roamed throughout the area, looking for just the right spot to build their winter cabin. There were plenty of likely spots, but none that seemed just right.

"I reckon I found it," Wolfe said one day after riding back into camp.

"Whar?"

"Three mile or so north, and to the west just a bit."

The weather was already turning cold, as the weak sun struggled to produce heat, though it was only mid-September. There had even been a few snow flurries already.

Wolfe took Williams to the spot he had found. It was a warm, snug bowl amid sharp, tall cliffs that jutted up thirty or forty feet. The bowl angled sharply off a narrow slash of a canyon, and was mostly hidden, offering plenty of protection. The hole—Wolfe's Hole, they called it—had a creek running through it, and a good spring. Aspens grew all about, their blazing bright colors sharp against the dark green of the pines and piñons dotting the ridges.

"Reckon I'd not be put out to winter in such a place," Williams said in acceptance. "Don't look like none of them red niggurs is about. Thar's plenty of water, wood, even some forage for the horses. It'll do."

They set about building a small, tight cabin up against the cliff to the west, with the front door facing the morning sun. With the narrow, almost invisible "gateway" to the hole, they figured they would be safe from Indians. And they figured the surrounding cliffs would stop some of the bitter wind that was already sweeping regularly down from the north.

Wolfe and Williams managed to keep up with their trap lines, though, despite the work that needed to be done on the cabin. It was prime season for beaver, and the plews they handled were fat, sleek and thick.

"These hyar plews ought to bring in six, maybe seven dollar a pound," Wolfe crowed.

119

Within a month, all the creeks in the vicinity were frozen over, and the beaver getting scarce, sticking in their lodges. Wolfe and Williams contented themselves with fixing equipment, mending clothes, playing cards, yarning, tending their horses, and keeping themselves supplied with meat and firewood. It was a boring existence at times, but both men had been living such a life for so long, they no longer noticed.

Spring seemed to take a long time in coming, though, even to the two patient mountain men. But finally wild flowers began springing up, and the aspens began shooting out buds. Grass poked through the slushy covering of snow, and the days warmed a little. As the creeks and rivers unfroze, Wolfe and Williams went back to their work, pulling out beaver.

"It seem to you thar ain't so many of these critters as there used to be?" Wolfe asked one day, holding up a drowned beaver by the flat tail.

"Waugh!" Williams growled. He had noticed it last fall, but had said nothing, not wanting to worry Wolfe. So he had outwardly crowed over the quality of the beaver they had found then, rather than comment on the lack of quantity. Now, though, he could no longer hide it. "I've made beaver come for a heap of years now; I ain't about to slack off jist 'cause thar ain't as many critters as there once was. I'll make 'em come agin. If thar's beaver to be found in the mountains, this ol' niggur's jist the one to find 'em."

Wolfe knew it to be a fact, too. Old Solitaire was known far and wide throughout the mountains and beyond as a man who most liked solitude. He was also known for making beaver come.

He might show up at rendezvous, of course. Then Old Bill could kick it up with the best of them.

But when the rendezvous was over, Williams most often just disappeared into the vastness of the cold, bitter, harsh Rocky Mountains. He would generally reappear at rendezvous or in some place like Taos in the summer, his mules laden with beaver plews. He never said where he was going; and more than one man had come close to losing his hair when trying to follow the old iconoclast.

Wolfe wondered, as he had numerous times, what he was even doing here with Old Solitaire.

Jeb Wolfe had known Bill Williams, of course. A man couldn't be in the mountains eight years or so like he had been and not know Old Bill. He had kept his distance from Williams, though, not figuring Williams would want a young man hanging around asking questions and such.

So it was with immense surprise that he heard Williams say to him one day at rendezvous two years ago, "Ye seem a quiet coon to me, boy. How's about ye join this old niggur in layin' traps along the Pahsemerol?"

"Well, sure," Wolfe had stammered. He was a free trapper, beholden to no one but himself and the Flathead squaw he had been with for three years.

So they had gone off, Williams, Wolfe, and Winter Swan. Wolfe was never quite sure where he was, other than knowing they usually were within Blackfoot territory. They moved fast and steadily until winter set in. On the way north, Williams had found himself a fat, moon-faced Snake squaw to share his lodge, and the four set up their winter quarters.

Wolfe had more plews than he knew what to do with that rendezvous, and made out well when selling them. He had one hell of a drunken spree, blowing nearly all the money he had earned wading in frigid streams and creeks under the constant threat of the Blackfeet. But he didn't care.

121

When he was ready to leave, he looked around for Williams, but the gaunt, wild-looking mountaineer had gone off already. And had taken Winter Swan with him. When Wolfe next saw Williams, they were at rendezvous again.

Wolfe had been some put out that Williams had left without him the year before. He was almost relieved, though, that the old mountain man had taken the Flathead woman with him. The greedy squaw had become a burden, what with her grasping family always wanting something, and Winter Swan herself always badgering Wolfe for more and more foofaraw. Over the winter he had lost his anger, and was glad to see Williams.

"Jist needed to be off to myself," Williams mumbled when Wolfe had asked about his sudden departure.

"By yourself?" Wolfe laughed. "Then why'd you go'n take Winter Swan?"

"Even a old niggur like me's got to have some comfortin' come the cold of the winter, boy," Williams said, his shallow face solemn, as it always was. Even when he was having a good time, his face never reflected it.

"Where is she?" Wolfe asked, chuckling.

"Gone under," Williams grumbled, stomping off.

Wolfe wasn't too put out, though he did wonder at how it had happened. Williams never said. And there were some stories about Williams, stories of men who had gone trapping with him never to return, while Williams was always hale and hearty. But Wolfe shrugged it all off.

Williams came to Wolfe a week and a half later, as rendezvous was near to breaking up. "I got me an itch to head south. I got me an itch fer a spot of company, too."

And now here he was, a little cranky after a long, cold winter, and looking forward to heading for rendezvous again.

They rode out near the end of March. The ground was slick with mud and new grass, both brought on by the melting of the snow. The days were mild, but the nights still frigid. Wolfe and Williams took their time — Williams leading, pack mules laden with beaver plews and a few supplies tagging along. Wolfe brought up the rear, eyes ever vigilant.

They made it to rendezvous without much further adventure. But instead of the six or seven dollars a pound Wolfe was expecting for their plews, they got two dollars — three for a few of the extra prime plews.

"Such doin's don't shine with this niggur at all," Williams griped. He took his money, had a rip-snorting, weeklong drunk, and rode out. It was the last time Wolfe saw him.

Wolfe was a little more circumspect about all this. It was obvious to him now that the beaver trade was dead. He had little money saved, and not too many prospects — unless he wanted to go out hunting buffalo for the hides. It was not an idea he liked. He managed to hire on with one of the caravans heading back to St. Louis with the year's take of furs.

Once there, he took a job as a clerk in Sublette and Campbell's store.

Soon after that, Wolfe met Miss Rachel McPherson. They were married a few months later. And within a year of their wedding day, their son, Bill — whom Wolfe had named for his old partner — was born.

Over the years, Wolfe had left off for a spell, heading west to trade or just to get away for a few days. The pull of the West was strong within him, and Rachel understood that. And it was something he would continue to do until he no longer could, physically. When he did, he would leave Rachel behind with the children: Bill, the first, born in '39; Jeb Junior, who came along four years later; little Rachel, who made her debut in '45; and finally Amy, two years younger than little Rachel.

Wolfe usually enjoyed these forays, but not all were happy. On one he took in 1847, he stopped at Fort Laramie. There he learned that Old Bill Williams had gone under the year before, dead at the hands of the Utes.

Wolfe had said a silent prayer, and a silent farewell to his old companion. But he had business to tend to, and so he pushed on. But as he rode, he vowed he would be careful of which elk he would shoot for food.

Old Bill Williams—the crazy man of the mountains—had firmly believed for years that when he went under he would come back to the land of the living as an elk. He had even gone so far as to describe exactly what he would look like, lest one of his erstwhile friends kill him for meat one day. The mountain men sitting around the fire whenever Old Solitaire would tell this one, would laugh—though not out loud, at least not in Williams's face.

Still, now that old Bill was dead, Wolfe decided to watch a little more carefully when he was trying to make meat.

Several years later, another old mountain man friend of Wolfe's—Russ Scarborough—showed up. Wolfe had trapped off and on with Scarborough for his first six years or so in the mountains. He liked Scarborough, but could not take him for extended periods. He needed time away from the constantly talking Scarborough.

Scarborough managed to talk a balky Wolfe into heading for California.

They went, but they soon ran out of money since

they spent it freely on whiskey and foofaraw for the señoritas they met.

"You got any plans, Russ, on what we ought to do?" Wolfe asked when they were broke.

Among the options Scarborough mentioned shrewdly to Wolfe was horse stealing. "Such fine animals as they got hereabouts'd bring a fair good price back East."

Wolfe could think of no better idea, and calmed his conscience by telling himself that they were stealing only from the Mexicans. That somehow made it all right. By the spring, they were pushing an unwieldy herd of stolen horses eastward, taking the southern route. It was far more dry and dangerous than the northern route, but they hoped the *caballeros* who were following them—though not too closely after two had been put under by the accurate fire of the former mountain men—would not venture into the awesome desert.

But just after crossing the Colorado River, they found a band of hostile Mojaves chasing after them.

They cached such valuables as they had with them when they bought a little time by releasing the stolen horses. Then they raced like hell to get away from the Indians. Still, it took a long, hot battle, with the two whites fighting for their lives from behind the crumbling walls of an old Indian dwelling.

Chapter Fourteen

"You still ain't told me how your grandpa got the land," Owen Corvallis said. He ordered another round of drinks. Reaching into his jacket pocket, he pulled out two cigars. He handed one across the table to Wolfe and lit one for himself.

"All you've told me was how he spotted the land. The title I got from your pa was all legal and proper. I even made sure of that while we were still in Prescott. How'd he get that title?"

"Gramps give it to him."

Jeb Wolfe thought occasionally about the cache he and Scarborough had left behind. But he was not obsessed by it. The store was doing well, and he was more than well set up for himself. He needed nothing from there. Still, to be cautious, he mentioned it to no one.

He had always meant to go back there and dig up the old cache, but somehow he never got around to it. He had the store to keep running, and after he got back from California, there was another child. All his time was taken up by the mundane activities of life.

The years dragged on, and his mind turned away from the cache mostly, though he remembered the land fondly. Someday, he figured, it would be a good place to begin a store. With all the timber in the area, there would surely be a lumber business one day. That would mean a town. And that would mean a store would be needed. He could wait.

As he grew, Bill Wolfe became more like his father—independent, hard-headed and strong-willed. It led to a little friction between the two, since Jeb had less control over his son than he thought he should have. Of course, Jeb had been that way with his own father, and knew it, so he did not hold it against Bill.

Far more friction came with the arrival of Casey Scarborough. The twelve-year-old boy told the Wolfes how his father had died two years before, and his mother a year ago. Feeling sorry for him, Jeb and Rachel Wolfe took the boy in.

The Wolfes tried hard to make Scarborough one of their own. But Scarborough always remained a little aloof from them, a loner who too often caused more trouble than he should. He was forgiven most often when he apologized, which he did reluctantly, but more than once Wolfe had to take Casey behind the woodshed. Scarborough stoically stood it.

Of Jeb's sons, Bill was closest to Scarborough. But Scarborough even kept his distance from Bill.

Two years after Scarborough arrived, Bill married Betsy Rohmer.

Jeb was bothered that his son had gotten married so young. The old mountain man had hoped his son might show a little more wildness, sow some wild oats before settling down. But he said nothing, figuring Bill had his own life to live.

Bill had been working in the store for a while by the time he got married and was showing signs of having itchy feet. Jeb was proud at that and began to send Bill to take off now and again for a few days to hunt, or on "business," and even trade a little with the tame Indians remaining in the area. Bill seemed to enjoy those times.

Thirteen months after they were married, Bill and Betsy presented Jeb with his first grandson—a boy they named Lucas, after his maternal grandfather. Jeb was a little put out by that. He had hoped all through Betsy's pregnancy that they would name the boy after him. But he put his annoyance aside and accepted his new grandson.

Scarborough seemed to take to Lucas, for some reason, much to the amazement of everyone. But it did not calm him down any nor make a better person of him.

Jeb and Rachel often wondered what to do about Casey, but they came to no solutions. Jeb did not want to just cast the boy out, but he was even more determined to not let the disruptive son of his old friend ruin his marriage and family.

The Civil War changed things.

With the coming of the war, Bill felt he had an opportunity to get out from under his father's rather large shadow. And just after the birth of his second child— Mark—Bill Wolfe headed off for the war, marching away with a company of Union volunteers.

He left behind Betsy, three-year-old Luke, and newborn Mark. Jeb and Rachel, as Bill had known they would, volunteered to care for their daughter-in-law and her children.

Scarborough, several years younger, finally joined the war in 1863—throwing in his lot with the Southern cause.

Jeb was not entirely idle, either. Late in 1863, he learned that Arizona had become a separate territory. Such news got him to thinking about "his" land again.

128

He had always thought of it as his land.

As soon as the weather improved enough for half-way-decent traveling, he hired several men he thought he could trust to run the store. He did not trust Scarborough to do it. Scarborough had been wounded less than a year after joining up and was back at the Wolfe family spread. He was irritated at not having made a name for himself in the war, and took it out on nearly everyone.

Rachel was a pretty independent woman, who could take care of herself, even if she did have a bunch of grandchildren running around. Nothing much could faze her, and Wolfe did not worry about her. He was a little concerned about Betsy, but she would have to make do on her own, or with Rachel's help. His hired hands, two sons and one daughter would also be available.

Since Wolfe could not trust Scarborough with the store, he thought he would take the young man with him to Arizona Territory. Hopefully it would help fix Scarborough—both externally and internally. So he asked Scarborough to come along.

"Why?" Scarborough asked, surly.

Wolfe shrugged. "Might do some good in healin' the wounds of division."

"You just want to try'n talk me into startin' to favor the damn Yankee side in the War of the States," Casey said angrily.

"You fought for what you thought was right, boy. I can't find no fault with that."

So Scarborough finally acquiesced.

The two set out, traveling light—each riding a horse and towing a pack mule with supplies behind him. Wolfe went to "his" land and began laying out its perimeters. He was about half-froze to claim all northern Arizona Territory—from the massive, colorful, grand slash in the Earth to the first town he came to; from the Colorado River to the New Mexico Territory border. But he knew no one would accept that. So he staked out a huge parcel north and mostly east of Bill Williams Mountain.

He found the remains of the cabin he and Williams had wintered in nearly thirty years ago. There wasn't much left, after the Indians, other mountain men, animals and, mostly, Mother Nature, had wreaked their efforts on it. He searched a little, lackadaisically, looking for the cache he and Russ Scarborough had dug to hide their belongings.

But despite his hand-drawn map, kept, folded, in an old, small leather case all these years, he had no luck. Landmarks had changed, the winds and rains and snows had eaten away at the land; and the map had been made days after the fact, when Wolfe had finally had some time.

Besides, he did not want Casey to know what he was up to. He had thought some of finding the cache and giving over half the things to Casey. He expected it was the young man's due, but it did not please him, what with the troublesome way Scarborough had repaid the kindnesses of the Wolfe clan. So he did not look too hard, nor did he give any indication of what he was doing, other than surveying the land for title purposes. Wolfe had decided to pass the land—and hopefully the cache—on to his sons one day. He did not intend Casey to have any part of it, even though Casey was his old partner's son. Young Scarborough had not shown he was worthy, Wolfe figured.

Wolfe gave up the search after a day, shrugging. It did not concern him much any longer. Not when he planned to take title to the land as soon as possible.

130

He spent several days drawing up another map, marking all the creeks, springs, mountains, flats and landmarks he could find. He envisioned a town, and possibly a ranch. He drew marks on his new map of the sites he thought best for a house, a store, roads, water holes and even a train siding—if trains ever got this far west.

Wolfe carefully folded the new map and, with the old, placed it inside the leather carrying case and stuffed it in his pocket. In the morning, he watched the golden sun skim off the jagged San Francisco Peaks. He and Scarborough packed their mules, saddled their horses and rode out, Wolfe leading, an angry Scarborough following.

Four days later they pulled into Prescott, the territorial capital. With little trouble—despite the vastness of the land he had staked out—Wolfe got title to it. The man in the land company did not even bat an eye. When Wolfe questioned him on it, he shrugged and said, "Hell, mister, this territory's so big that'll just about make a decent ranch."

Wolfe cursed himself for not staking out a much larger claim. Then he laughed. Fifty thousand acres, give or take a couple thousand, was plenty for him. He was satisfied. Gratified, he headed for home.

But the trip had seemed to do Scarborough little good. The young man remained as wild and uncommunicative as ever.

Less than a year after they returned to Missouri, Bill Wolfe came home. He had spent four long, bloody years fighting Rebels. He was mustered out as a brevet captain, and something of a hero. But he was, as one would expect, a changed man.

He and Scarborough did not get along at all any more; Wolfe did not mind, but he was enraged when

131

Scarborough started bullying young Luke. Two years later, a disgusted and angry Bill decided to leave.

"I ain't really surprised," Jeb growled when his son told him. He wondered that it hadn't been sooner, what with the troubles between Bill and Casey, and Bill's itchy feet. "You know where you're goin'?"

"Ain't thought much on it yet."

Jeb stood from his fat, soft, comfortable chair. "Wait there," he said. He went into his bedroom and came out with the leather wallet. He handed it to his son.

"What's this?" Bill asked, surprised, taking it.

"Open it."

Bill did so. "It's a land title," he said, amazed.

"Yep." Jeb quickly explained the essentials of where the land was.

"And you're just givin' it over to me?"

"You're all the children I got left," Jeb said gruffly. Jeb Junior had died in the war; his third son had died being born a dozen years back; little Rachel never made it to puberty; and the baby, Amy, succumbed to diphtheria in infancy.

Bill nodded, not knowing what to say exactly.

"When're you plannin' to leave?" Jeb asked.

"Soon's the weather breaks, I guess," Bill said, standing. He had put the paper into the leather wallet, and clutched it tightly. "I'm obliged, Pa," he croaked. He felt awkward, like a young boy trying to please his father again. "I expect I'll have to work a spell somewhere to make enough of a stake to get a ranch—and a store—started," he grinned.

Jeb said nothing. He had some money stashed away, and could probably give his son some without hurting himself and Rachel, but he would not. Bill would have to make his own way through the world, just like he had done himself.

132

* * *

"You know the rest, Mr. Corvallis," Lucas Wolfe said. He leaned back, taking a large swallow of whiskey.

"That's quite a story, Mr. Wolfe," Corvallis said. He was not sure he believed it all, but it was plausible enough. "But it still doesn't explain why you want the land so badly."

Wolfe shrugged: "My grandpa went through a lot of trouble to get this land. He always had plans of buildin' a store here. Even a town." He smiled. "You know, I saw his map once, the one he made when he came here to claim the land. The town he envisioned in that map is almost exactly where Kaibab is now."

Corvallis grinned. "It's the best place around for a town," he chuckled. He finished off his beer and burped again. "Damn, I've had too much beer. Aggie's gonna kill me." He sighed. "Well, Mr. Wolfe, it was a hell of a story. But I still ain't givin' up my land."

"I understand," Wolfe said with a grin. "But I figure if I hang around long enough you'll get tired of me and give me half just to be shed of me. Or," and his grin grew, "I just might up and marry your daughter and move into the house with you."

Corvallis laughed, full and throaty. Behind him, Eyman was bored, and Aaron looked ready to spit nails. "Ain't likely," Corvallis said.

"But we got another problem," Wolfe said when Corvallis had quieted.

"What's that?"

Wolfe looked up at Aaron. Corvallis stared at Wolfe, knowing at whom Wolfe was looking. Corvallis nodded. "Aaron," he said harshly, still looking at Wolfe, "I want you to leave this man be. You understand that?"

133

Aaron's eyes burned hatred as he stared into Wolfe's.

"Do you understand that, boy?" Corvallis asked, his voice taking on an even sharper edge.

"Yessir," Aaron finally mumbled. But Wolfe knew the younger Corvallis was lying.

"Ev?" Corvallis asked.

"Yessir?"

"I want you to make sure Aaron leaves Luke alone. That clear?"

"Yessir."

Corvallis stood. He picked up his hat from the table and clapped it on. "It was an enjoyable evening, Mr. Wolfe. Good night." He turned and strode out. Eyman followed in his relaxed, rolling gait. Aaron glared at Wolfe for a moment before heading after his father. His back was rigid.

Chapter Fifteen

Wolfe headed for the High Country Saloon. It was raining softly, with a chill wind whistling down Corvallis Road. He grinned when he neared the plain doors of the High Country, which were open enticingly. He enjoyed many of the regulars, and he liked Orville.

Needing a change, he ordered a beer instead of his usual whiskey. Orville provided it, and then stayed. The two men chatted quietly, though Orville had to leave occasionally to serve someone before returning to pick up where he and Wolfe had left off.

After an hour, Orville got too busy to be able to talk with Wolfe, who was nursing another beer. Wolfe turned away from the bar and leaned back against it, resting his elbows on it when he was not actually sipping or taking a drag on a cigarette. He watched in comfortable silence as the card games, arguments, chatter and the varied, general activity of a friendly saloon went on all about him.

Two men Wolfe had never seen before entered the saloon, and Wolfe knew right off they were going to be trouble. They marched straight toward him. The bigger of the two said, "Howdy." His voice was soft, boyish. "You know where we might find Lucas Wolfe?"

Wolfe considered lying to the two men. He figured they knew who he was and were just being formally polite. But he decided against it. Better to get this over with. "That'd be me," he said quietly. "Who's askin'?"

"I'm Temple McSorley. My *amigo* here is Farley Garfield." He touched the brim of his hat in an insincere greeting.

McSorley was an inch or two taller than Wolfe, and forty pounds heavier. He was not gigantic, but formidable looking. He had icy blue eyes, almost dead, and Wolfe realized the man was a born killer. He would kill without joy or regret, without emotion or remorse.

Garfield was smaller and slighter than McSorley, and looked older—perhaps forty. He did not seem to be as heartless as McSorley. He could not be ignored, of course, but when the action started—and Wolfe knew that was the only reason these two could be looking for him—McSorley would have to be taken care of first.

Both men were dressed in good wool suits, McSorley's brown with thin white stripes woven in; Garfield's dark blue with the same piping. Each wore a crisp white shirt, string tie and bowler. Their clothes were soiled with the dust of long travel.

Each man also sported an identical set of pearl-handled, .44-caliber Merwin and Hulberts. The pistols were in cross-draw holsters, and both men were well-adept in their use.

"Can't say as I'm pleased to meet you boys." He half-turned to set his mug of beer on the bar. That worried him, since he would have to turn his back to the gunmen, if only momentarily. He turned back without looking like he was hurrying. "What can I do for you?"

"Mr. Corvallis sent us to pay our respects," McSorley said. He had a high, squeaky voice that did not go with his size.

"Owen Corvallis? Or his idiot son, Aaron?"

136

McSorley shrugged. "We just got a wire telling us our services were requested. When we accepted, we were told just who to pay our respects to when we got to Kaibab." He said the last with distaste. Evidently, Wolfe thought, McSorley and Garfield liked big cities like Denver or Cheyenne better than some one-horse town like Kaibab.

Bar patrons, who had followed with their eyes the two gunmen when they entered, suddenly began beating a hasty retreat to the outside. The scrape of chairs mixed with the clank of spurs and the thump of boots on the wood floor. Soon only Wolfe, the two gunmen, and Orville, who felt sort of trapped behind the bar, were left in the saloon.

"Shall we proceed?" McSorley asked. He was far too fastidious for Wolfe's taste; almost effeminate despite his burliness.

"How much did Corvallis pay you?" Wolfe asked, staring at McSorley.

"I don't believe such a thing is any of your concern, Mr. Wolfe," McSorley squeaked.

"It might be."

"How so?"

"I know how much that punk's payin' you, and I just might see to offerin' you more. He grinned. "Maybe a lot more."

"Sorry, Mr. Wolfe. Me and Farley don't work that way." McSorley pulled out a bright red bandanna and wiped his mouth for no reason Wolfe could see. He put it carefully away. "We are honorable men, Mr. Wolfe. Once we take a contract to perform a service, we cannot be swayed from the performance of that service."

"There's one way," Wolfe commented quietly.

"To be sure," McSorley said softly. He paused. "It doesn't matter a whit to either me or Farley if you were

137

to offer us two times what the other has. Or ten times."

Wolfe nodded. "Well, I reckon we can proceed then. Just one more question, though."

"Yes?" McSorley did not look hurried or anxious. Garfield twitched a little as adrenaline began surging through him.

"You want to give me names of some folks where I can send your effects?" Wolfe asked dryly.

McSorley laughed hollowly, acknowledging Wolfe's attempt at humor without actually finding the statement funny. "That won't be necessary. Anything else?"

"Reckon not." Wolfe straightened and moved from the bar. He sidestepped toward the middle of the room. McSorley and Garfield did the same and all three edged backward, putting a bit of distance between them.

"You're the one who's been challenged, Mr. Wolfe," McSorley said in his almost childlike voice. "Therefore, the play is yours."

"It was you boys came callin'," Wolfe said as if bored. Inside he was tense, excited, his muscles and nerves readying themselves for the coming action. He shrugged. "Reckon it's your choice."

"As you wish," McSorley acknowledged. Then he went for a pistol.

McSorley's draw was not the fastest Wolfe had ever seen. In fact, it was downright slow, and Wolfe knew without thinking about it that this professional killer did not need to be a lightning draw. He would be a deadly shot, and utterly cool under fire. That would give him an edge over almost anyone.

Wolfe yanked his Colt out and snapped off a shot. It went wide, and McSorley never flinched. *Take your time, damnit,* Wolfe told himself silently. He thumbed back the hammer and snapped the pistol up to waist level and fired.

Wolfe winced as a slug from McSorley's Merwin and Hulbert seared across the rib just to the left of his heart. But he fired, twice. Without waiting to see the results, Wolfe dived to his left. He landed harder than he had expected, and his breath whooshed out.

Glancing over his shoulder, Wolfe saw that McSorley was down, bleeding heavily. But the big man was trying to struggle up. Wolfe rolled over onto his back and snapped the Colt up again. He fired the last two slugs in it.

Garfield had fired once as Wolfe dived and again as he rolled. Both bullets plowed up a spray of splinters and sawdust. Then Garfield was smacked backward as one of Wolfe's slugs caught him in the midsection. As he went backward, he was forced to double over from the impact. The move placed the top of his head right in the path of Wolfe's second bullet. Garfield went down without ever having uttered a sound here.

Wolfe glanced quickly over at McSorley. The bulky gunman was still trying to rise. He had made it to hands and knees, and was resting, blood dripping from his mouth and nose onto the floor. Wolfe stood, wincing again at the fiery pain in his side. He looked at the wound and realized it was not bad.

Warily keeping an eye on McSorley, Wolfe pulled the empty shells from his Colt and reloaded. Pistol ready, he walked slowly over to McSorley. "I don't know how much time you got left, Mr. McSorley," he said quietly. "But I expect you'd have a better chance at livin' if you was to just rest."

"Must . . . finish . . . business . . ." he gasped, making no effort to look up.

"You're out of business, Mr. McSorley," Wolfe said, hoping his relief was not evident in his voice. He kicked the loose Merwin and Hulbert out of McSorley's reach. "If you'd be so kind as to ease that other pistol out and hand it over, I'd be obliged."

McSorley grunted softly in pain as he shifted his weight from both arms to just his left. With his right hand, he reached down and carefully plucked out his second pistol. He dropped it, and then shoved it out in front of him.

Wolfe kicked that one away, too. "Orville, go get Doc Windsor. Maybe he can do this damn fool some good."

McSorley shook his head, knowing it was useless.

"I don't reckon it'll do you much good either, Mr. McSorley," Wolfe said. "But if there's a chance . . ." Wolfe watched Orville head toward the door. Then he said, "Orville, you best bring Klockschmidt back with you, too."

Wolfe stood and watched McSorley die. The big man remained on hands and knees, his lifeblood splattering the sawdust-covered wood floor, for some minutes. His arms began to wobble before long, and he started to weave. He groaned, and then fell flat on his face as his life expired.

Wolfe was sitting at a table drinking a mug of beer he had gotten for himself behind the bar when Orville, Doc Windsor, and old, beetle-browed Klockschmidt came in. They were followed by what appeared to be half the town—or at least the male half, women not being allowed in the saloon—excepting working girls, of course, a few of whom shoved in.

"You dragged me out of Alma's brothel to look at two dead bodies?' Windsor griped.

"I can use your services, Doc," Wolfe said.

Windsor looked at him in surprise, then came over. He checked Wolfe's wound as Klockschmidt looked over the two bodies. Then the undertaker stepped back to

140

allow the citizenry to inspect the carnage.

Klockschmidt came and sat at the table by Wolfe. "You did goot chob on those two. Ya."

Wolfe shrugged, and winced as Windsor splashed disinfectant on the wound.

Marshal Sam Trumble entered and also sat at the table. He said nothing, but he looked askance at Wolfe. He had intended to lecture the young man again. Until he realized that Wolfe had just shot down two hired gunmen. Trumble decided he was afraid of Wolfe — and with good reason.

"Who vill pay for the funerals, Marshal?" Klockschmidt demanded. "And the burying?"

Trumble shrugged.

"I reckon they got enough cash in their pockets to pay for it all," Wolfe offered helpfully.

Klockschmidt glowered at him. He had intended to pocket the cash the two gunmen carried. And then get the money for the burial from somewhere else, so it would all be profit. Now Wolfe was going to make that difficult. "I doubt they haf much."

"We'll just see," Trumble said, standing. He was relieved to be able to get away from the table — and Wolfe's hard eyes. He shuffled toward McSorley's body, shooing people out of the way. He knelt and went through the man's pockets, pulling out a number of bills. Then he did the same with Garfield.

"Should be more'n enough for the buryin'," Trumble said, gloating. "With plenty left for the city treasury."

"Ach," Klockschmidt cackled. He had been too smart for his own good this time, and now he would have no profit to show. "Gif me mine money. Enough to make two caskets and do all the other tings needed to do it right."

Smirking, Trumble handed him some bills. He stuffed

141

the rest in his shirt.

"You mind if I take one or two of those pistols, Marshal?" Wolfe asked. He had heard that Merwin and Hulberts were good weapons, but he had never tried one. This way he could both try the gun and have a spare. It was beginning to look like he might have a need for an extra gun or two, if things kept up the way they had been.

"Be my guest," Trumble said generously.

"There, all done," Windsor said, straightening. "That thing might pain you some for a few days, but it ain't even as bad as what happened last time."

Wolfe nodded. He stood and walked over toward the bodies. He took both of McSorley's revolvers. He stuffed them in his gunbelt and then went to the bar. "Gimme a bottle, Orville," he said. He took the bottle and headed out, across the street to the hotel, ignoring the eyes that followed his every movement.

He drank half the bottle that night, partly to ease the pain in his side, partly to drown the demons that were beginning to crowd into his consciousness.

Chapter Sixteen

Wolfe felt vastly improved in the morning. With a lighter heart, he saddled his horse and once more made the trip to the Lazy O Ranch. It was a fine, beautiful day, the rain of the night before having drifted off, leaving behind a world that glittered with sunlight reflecting off droplets of water. The rain had cleansed the air, somehow making it more breathable.

Aaron Corvallis and Ev Eyman were standing outside the ranch house, talking and laughing, when Wolfe rode up. Both activities halted when they spied Wolfe.

Wolfe stopped the horse not far from the two men. He leaned forward, resting his forearms on the pommel. "Mornin', boys," he said with mock cheerfulness.

Sally came out of the house, smiling happily at Wolfe's arrival. The brightness in her face faded fast when she saw his wary, stony look.

"Two friends of yours came callin' on me last night, boys," Wolfe said sharply. "While I was at the High Country."

"I got no idea of what you're talking about," Corvallis said, feigning unconcern.

"Booshwa. Those two boys told me they were bringin' me your regards, Aaron." Of course, they hadn't said that exactly, but Wolfe knew it could not have been

143

Owen Corvallis who sent the two gunmen on him.

Aaron gulped, but still tried to brazen it out. "I sent no one calling on you, Mr. Wolfe." He tried to smile in a friendly manner, but it came out as a sour grimace.

"Can the crap, Aaron," Eyman snapped. "Wolfe ain't a fool. I've told you that before." He looked up at Wolfe. "Since you're here, I figure those two wasn't up to the job." It was a question.

"As a matter of fact, Ev, they're both guests of old man Klockschmidt."

Eyman nodded, sort of sadly. It had been his idea. Aaron had wanted to go gunning for Wolfe himself. But Eyman had managed—after considerable argument—to convince Corvallis that Wolfe was far too good for him and that he'd get killed for certain. He then suggested hiring a couple of men who had provided such services for some old friends to do the job for them. Now he was saddened that he had cost two men their lives. Still, he hadn't even known the two gunmen. He was far more concerned that his plan had not worked. Aaron Corvallis was going to be hell to put up with for a while, he knew. And, if Owen got wind of it, he might well be riding the range looking for work.

"What's going on?" Sally asked. She had suspicions, but she was missing something, and that irritated her.

"I'll tell you later," Wolfe said calmly. He was about to say something else when Owen Corvallis came out of the house.

"Mr. Wolfe," Corvallis nodded. He was not surprised to see Wolfe here. But he sensed that something was not right. "Somethin' wrong, Luke?" he asked, half-kindly, half in irritation.

Wolfe looked from Eyman to Aaron to Corvallis. He grinned a little maliciously. "I don't know as if there's somethin' wrong, you understand." He shook his head, the smirk coating his face like cream on a cat's. "In fact, I'd say everything was just fine."

Corvallis raised his eyebrows in question at Wolfe.

"Well," Wolfe began slowly, watching Aaron squirm out of the corner of his eye. "Seems like Aaron here is obeying you for once." Wolfe grinned at Corvallis's surprise—and at Aaron's flash of anger. "He ain't come for me since you talked to him in the High Country the other night."

Wolfe paused, and gloated inwardly at Aaron's look of relief. "But he did the next best thing," Wolfe said unmercifully, his words cutting into Aaron's heart. "He hired a couple of pistoleers to come gunnin' for me."

Corvallis was not surprised. He was a little relieved that Aaron had done that rather than go after Wolfe himself, which is what the father had expected from his hot-headed son.

"I'd suggest you have a talk with Aaron and tell him not to send any more friends to make my acquaintance. It ain't healthy for 'em," he said sarcastically. He smiled humorlessly.

"You can tell me yourself," Aaron snapped, spitting with anger. "You don't need to go through my old man to tell me somethin'. Unless you're scared of me." He sneered to his fullest.

Wolfe laughed. "Scared? Of you? Hell, I'm more afraid of your sister than I am of you." He wasn't sure how well such a statement would go over with Sally, but he could not worry about it now.

Owen Corvallis watched with some interest. He was angry at his son, but thought this might be a good time to really test Aaron's mettle.

"You get down from that horse, and we'll see how tough you are, goddamnit," Aaron blustered.

Wolfe straightened, grinning. He wrapped the reins around the pommel. "It'll be quite interestin' to see if you can do anything for yourself, rather'n send somebody else to do it."

Corvallis stepped in front of his son. "Your pistol, boy," he said sharply. "I'll have no gunplay here."

"What about him?" Aaron demanded, pointing at Wolfe.

"Mr. Wolfe, will you hand your piece over to Mr. Eyman?" Corvallis asked over his shoulder.

Wolfe said nothing. But he unhooked his gunbelt and held it out. Eyman came and took it. Wolfe stared at him hard for a moment. He didn't mind going unarmed when he was going to fight Aaron, but having Eyman holding his pistol made him a little uncomfortable. He shrugged and started to dismount.

Without comment, Aaron peeled off his own gunbelt. He got angry, though, when his father said, "The quirt, too." But he still said nothing, only handed over the leather quirt. His face, however, reflected the deep-seated rage he felt.

"Have at each other, boys," Corvallis said, stepping out of the way.

Aaron spit on his palms, rubbed them together, and then balled his hands into fists. He held them out in front of his nose, rotating them slowly toward Wolfe and back.

Wolfe wiped his hands on his denim pants. He looked a lot more confident than he felt. He was never much of one for fistfighting, though he had handled himself in such a way when the need called for it. He balled his own fists, but left them hanging down at his sides, as he waited for Aaron to make a move.

The younger Corvallis finally did, snapping a fist out. Wolfe was surprised when it caught him on the

146

chin, rocking his head back. His eyes crossed from the impact. Corvallis moved in and pelted him twice more before Wolfe could get his hands up in front of his face and guard against another punch.

Corvallis moved back a few steps, gloating. Wolfe was having a little trouble breathing through the blood in his nose. He swiped his left hand across the leakage, smearing it, then wiped his hands on his pants.

Wolfe was annoyed, but he tried to keep that out of his consciousness. "You tired already?" he asked with a sneer.

Corvallis's eyes widened in anger, and he moved back in toward Wolfe, who was surprised that Corvallis was stalking him rather than charging. He had never seen Aaron Corvallis so disciplined. It worried him, but only a little.

Corvallis flicked a fist at Wolfe, who ducked it. Wolfe bobbed and weaved, avoiding almost all of Corvallis's punches. Once in a while, knuckle would brush his cheek, or skim his forehead. Wolfe began to feel a little better about all this. Once he had Corvallis's rhythm, he decided he could handle himself.

And just about that time—as Wolfe started to get a little cocky—Corvallis changed tactics, and swung a hard, whistling upper cut at Wolfe. Corvallis's fist thumped into Wolfe's solar plexus. Wolfe's breath popped out in one brief burst, and he struggled to inhale.

Corvallis stepped back again and grinned. "What's the matter, Wolfe?" he asked with a smirk. "You got no smart-aleck things to say now, eh?"

Wolfe caught up on his breathing. He straightened. His stomach would be sore come morning, but for now he could ignore it. He grinned, showing none of the frustration and anger he was feeling. "That the best you can do?" he asked.

Fire leapt into Corvallis's eyes, and he looked set to charge wildly, but he caught himself. He, too, grinned, matching Wolfe's maliciousness. "That was just a taste of what I got in store for you, Wolfe," he said, spitting into the dirt.

"Come and do your worst, then," Wolfe snapped. "Unless you're figurin' on standin' there jawin' at me till I fall asleep so you don't have to worry about gettin' your butt thumped."

Corvallis's fists came up and began their slow whirling. He moved forward slowly. Wolfe hunched his shoulders, and brought his own fists up in front of his face. He bent over, hoping that between his shoulders, fists and stance, he might be able to protect himself, if only long enough to think of some way to get out of this trouble.

He found one small opening as Corvallis moved in because Corvallis was getting smug, thinking he had the upper hand. Wolfe's right hand snapped out, and cracked against Corvallis's left cheekbone. Corvallis's eyes widened, more from the surprise of getting hit than from the impact.

"How do you like them apples?" Wolfe crowed. His attitude changed fast when Corvallis came back at him with a flurry that he almost fended off. A few punches broke through, eliciting a soft grunt each time.

But Wolfe managed to cover up, and then spot an opening. He hunched up his shoulders, bent his head and almost doubled over. His fists pounded repeatedly into Corvallis's midsection.

Corvallis was not inactive during the assault. He slammed hard fists down on Wolfe's back, neck and head, battering him. Until he finally managed to smash Wolfe down onto his knees. Wolfe started to topple. As

148

he went over, Corvallis kicked him in the left side.

"Goddamn!" Wolfe roared as pain lanced through him. Corvallis's boot had caught the wound he had suffered the night before from McSorley's bullet.

"What's the matter, Wolfe?" Corvallis asked in false sincerity. "You hurtin'?" He stood, arms akimbo, smirking.

Breathing heavily, Wolfe shoved himself up. He stood, aching all over from the beating. He reached onto his side with his right hand. The hand came away covered with blood. He wiped his hand on his pants. He grimaced, as he explored his lower lip with his tongue. It was already beginning to swell. He snorted a couple times to clear coagulated blood from his nasal passages.

"Well, come on, Wolfe," Corvallis said with an insulting chuckle. "It's about time I finished this." He laughed derisively.

Wolfe balled up his fists again. He moved toward Corvallis, his face hard with pain and anger. Corvallis raised his fists and waited arrogantly. Wolfe edged close, looking tentative.

"This is gonna be fun," Corvallis taunted. "Come on, Wolfe, just a bit closer." He snapped out a jab, then another, his knuckles just brushing Wolfe's hair. Wolfe seemed almost to give up. He stood flatfooted, weaving a little. Corvallis laughed. "Boy, if you ain't some sight, Wolfe." He raised his right fist for the *coup de grace*.

Wolfe moved, feeling a heady relief that he had fooled Corvallis. His left arm snapped up, blocking Corvallis's powerful blow as it descended. "Son of a bitch," Wolfe breathed as his right fist slammed into Corvallis's stomach in a mighty uppercut. The punch doubled Corvallis over, and lifted him off his feet. His breath swooshed out explosively.

Wolfe shoved Corvallis up straighter, and slammed another powerful uppercut into his opponent's abdomen, again lifting him off his feet. Twice more he did the same. Wolfe felt a momentary satisfaction when he felt a rib crack under his fist.

Then he let Corvallis go. Corvallis sank to his knees, desperately trying to suck in a breath. He choked and gasped and made odd noises.

"You ought not to be so trusting," Wolfe gasped. He stood, bent over, his hands resting on his knees. He was breathing heavily. He straightened, chest heaving, and put his hands on his hips a minute. He knew he ought to finish Corvallis off, just pound him into the dry earth. But he was not that vicious, especially not with Owen Corvallis standing right there.

With a last great inhale and exhale, Wolfe turned and walked to Ev Eyman. He held his hand out. Eyman handed over his gunbelt and pistol. "I got enough left for you, if you're of a mind," Wolfe gasped.

"I'll pass," Eyman said seriously. "I ain't no young buck like you two boys. I'll save my energies for more favorable pursuits."

Wolfe nodded. He turned and walked to Sally. "Reckon our picnic's off for today, Sally," he said.

"I can fix you up," she said hopefully. She wanted desperately to comfort Wolfe, but could not be obvious about it.

"Reckon I need Doc Windsor to look at my side."

"Aaron couldn't've kicked you that hard."

"His friends shot me last night. He just happened to kick the same spot."

"Shot?" Sally asked, eyes wide with incredulity.

"Just winged," he said, grimacing as pain from all his hurts telegraphed through him.

"You better have the doc look at it," Sally said

150

"Must be some kind of special fool, Ev," Corvallis said *soto voce,* "that turns down a free drink."

"Best leave off ridin' him, Aaron," Eyman said quietly.

"To hell with you, Ev." Corvallis jolted down the shot in one swift move. He slammed the glass down and, after swallowing, said, "Hit me again, Orville."

As the bartender poured, Corvallis said, "Yessir, must be some kind of extra special fool to turn down a free drink."

Wolfe ignored him, which made Corvallis angry.

"Goddamnit, Wolfe, take the drink. It's free, you goddamn idiot."

"It ain't the price that bothers me, Aaron," Wolfe said flatly. "It's just the one who's payin' is all."

Orville grinned. With his left hand, he moved Wolfe's hand off the glass. The right filled the glass from the bottle. "I'm buyin' this one, Mr. Wolfe," Orville said.

"Well, thank you, Orville," Wolfe said grandly. He raised the small glass carefully to his lips and poured it ever so slowly into him. He smacked his lips as he set the glass back on the bar. "You know, Orville," he said, grinning at the bartender, "there's something extra special about a drink bought for you by a friend." He turned to face Corvallis. "Ain't that right, Aaron?"

Corvallis scowled but said nothing. He drank another shot. "Orville, bring that goddamn bottle back here. And leave it!"

Orville shrugged and set the bottle down in front of Corvallis. He picked up the paper dollar.

Corvallis poured back another short glass of whiskey, the quirt dangling from his wrist while he did. Finished with it, Corvallis twirled the glass in his hand, watching as it caught the light from the lanterns and reflected it in a display much like a kaleidoscope. "You know, Ev," he said, almost as if talking to himself, "there's just no understandin' some folks."

"Oh?"

"Now, you take Mr. Wolfe here." He still twirled the glass, knowing Wolfe was watching him peripherally. "He comes into Kaibab and upsets everything. He comes pokin' around where he don't belong, makin' up all kinds of tall tales and such, just tryin' to get a hold of land that don't belong to him."

"Don't seem right, that's for sure," Eyman commented. He reached for the bottle and poured himself a new drink. "Nope," he added, "seems downright wrong."

"And then," Corvallis said, building up a head of steam of indignation, "when he can't work his will that way—because me and you have foiled his ill-met plans—then . . . *then* he goes after my sister."

"Don't seem right," Eyman mumbled again, seemingly quite embarrassed.

Wolfe got the distinct feeling that Corvallis and Eyman had rehearsed this whole bit, and that Eyman was not happy to be taking part in it.

"No, goddamnit, it don't. Such a man ought to be hung from the nearest ponderosa."

"Ponderosas ain't good for hangin', Aaron, you ought to know that," Eyman said. "No good branches close enough to the ground to make 'em worthwhile."

"Well, aspens, then."

"They're even worse. Too spindly. Never take the weight of a man."

"Hell, we got any trees around here we can use, Ev?"

"A few cottonwoods down by the crick over at the Lazy O," Eyman said helpfully.

"I'll have to consider that," Corvallis said thoughtfully.

"Better consider long and hard," Wolfe noted quietly.

"What?" Corvallis said, feigning surprise, glancing at

154

Wolfe. "Did you say something, Mr. Wolfe?" He turned his head to look at his companion. "Ev, did Mr. Wolfe say something?"

"I believe so."

"Now, what was it you were . . . ?" Corvallis started as he turned his head. But Wolfe was no longer there. Wolfe was down at the far end of the bar, talking with two townsmen.

Fury blazed a rugged trail across Corvallis's face as he glared down the bar at Wolfe, who stood with his back to Corvallis. "Goddamn him," Corvallis breathed.

"Maybe you best let it drop, Aaron," Eyman said. He was not comfortable in his role of Wolfe-baiter.

"No!" Corvallis hissed, without looking at his ranch foreman. "I've come to do a job here, and by Christ, I'll see it done."

"I've been thinkin' about that, Aaron," Eyman said sharply, "and I ain't so sure it's in your best interest to push it too far. I don't know how in hell I let you talk me into this in the first place." He tossed a shot down his throat.

"What's the matter, Ev?" Corvallis asked with a sneer, turning finally. "You scared of Wolfe?"

"You bet your ass I'm scared of him. Anybody with any sense at all would be," he added pointedly, staring at Corvallis.

"If you're that faint-hearted over such business, go on back to the Lazy O, Ev," Corvallis said nastily.

"I do, I'll drag you along."

"Like hell." Corvallis paused a moment. "Look, Ev," he said, in no better mood than he had been, "we tried it your way—twice, if you count the boys from the ranch as bein' your idea, which it was. It didn't work. Now we'll do it my way."

"He'll kill you, Aaron," Eyman said flatly.

"It'll be a cold day in hell before he kills me."

155

Eyman shook his head in stunned amazement. "Christ, how could a smart man like your father have such a goddamn idiot for a son?"

"You callin' me stupid?" Corvallis demanded angrily.

"If the boot fits your foot just right, I reckon you ought to wear it."

"I'll see to you after I finish off Wolfe," Corvallis snapped.

"I can wait," Eyman said dryly.

Corvallis whirled and yelled, "Hey! Wolfe!" Growing more enraged at the lack of attention he was getting, Corvallis roared, "Goddamnit, you chicken-livered son of a bitch, look at me!"

"Maybe you ought to call it a night, eh?" Orville said, wiping up a small puddle on the bar.

"I can have your butt run out of town, too, you know," Corvallis snapped at the bartender. "You just stay behind that bar and mind your own goddamn business. This don't concern you."

Orville shrugged. "You want to get yourself killed, it's no skin off my butt." He grinned lopsidedly at Corvallis before moving away.

Wolfe was still standing several yards away, his back toward Corvallis, talking with the two townsmen. Corvallis hiked up his pants and stepped off, heading for Wolfe. When he got there, he grabbed Wolfe by the shoulder and yanked him around to face him.

Wolfe came around much faster than Corvallis expected, his left fist swinging around in a long, purposeful arc that slammed Corvallis high on the right cheek. The impact knocked Corvallis against the bar, bruising a rib. And before Corvallis could react, Wolfe had slammed him in the mouth with his right fist, staggering Aaron, who lurched backward a few steps before falling heavily on the seat of his pants.

"Your manners could use a heap of improvin',"

156

Wolfe said to Corvallis. Then he turned and went back to talking to the two townsmen.

Corvallis sat, rubbing his sore cheek. He touched the drops of blood leaking from his lower lip. Through the fogginess that had come over him, he heard distant laughter. It took a few moments before he realized the people in the saloon were laughing at him. Anger pierced the fogginess, helping to clear his head.

"Bastard," he muttered. He pushed angrily up, snatching out his Colt as he did so. He was about ready to bring it level at Wolfe's back, when Eyman suddenly loomed between Corvallis and his intended target.

"Put your piece away, Aaron," Eyman said testily. He was tired of all this nonsense. Wolfe had done nothing to the Corvallis family, and he could not understand Aaron's hatred for Wolfe. But Eyman wanted no more part of Aaron's quest to try to best Wolfe. It had gone too far, and he knew Corvallis would get killed if he went up against Wolfe.

"Get the hell out of the way, Ev," Corvallis snarled.

"No," Eyman said simply. "Your father asked me to keep a watch on you. Reckon he knew you'd try'n pull some damnfool stunt like this one sooner or later. But I ain't gonna let you get yourself killed 'cause you're tryin' to prove something to somebody."

"I ain't tryin' to prove nothin'!" Corvallis roared. He was almost shaking with the fury that pulsed through him.

"Like hell."

"You don't think I could take him, do you?" Corvallis said.

"I don't think that," Eyman said with a shrug. "I *know* you can't take him."

"Hell," Corvallis said with a festering sneer, "just 'cause you're afraid of that son of a bitch, don't mean

I am."

"If you had any goddamn sense, you'd be afraid of him," Eyman said bluntly. "He's too good for you, Aaron."

"I can take him, Ev," Corvallis insisted, trying through eagerness to bring Eyman over to his way of thinking. "I *can*."

"No you can't." Eyman rubbed his jaw, thinking. He wished he was better with words, good enough to convince Corvallis of the folly he was contemplating. But Eyman was not a man of many words, nor of varied words. He sighed. "Have you forgotten that he took down Ike, Curly and Aud?"

"No," Corvallis said, unfazed.

"Well, if that wasn't enough to make you think, then, damnit, try'n remember that he also killed McSorley and Garfield."

"So?" Corvallis was irritated. The situation in and of itself bothered him, but making it worse was this litany of fear being expounded by Eyman.

"Christ, Aaron," Eyman said in exasperation. "They were professionals. Goddamn, they made their livin' with their pistols. And Wolfe killed them easy as eating pie. Don't that tell you nothin'?"

"Just tells me they weren't good enough."

"And you figure you are?"

"Yep." Corvallis was brimming over with confidence. That irritated Eyman, who knew better.

"What am I gonna tell your old man after Wolfe puts you in the boneyard, huh?"

Corvallis grinned, but it was a humorless gesture. He was worried, but still his ego would not let him think about failure. "Look, if you're worried about him, back my play, Ev." Corvallis's eyes were fervently aflame. "Then you got nothin' to worry about. He can't take the two of us."

158

"Like hell he can't." But he stood, thinking. There were no more words he could say to Aaron. He shrugged. "Hell with it," he mumbled. "Have it your way." His shoulders sagged and he looked defeated.

Corvallis grinned in victory. "Good thinkin', Ev. Now get the hell out of the way."

"Sure." Eyman moved away from the bar. But as he took a few steps toward the main part of the room, he suddenly reached out. With his left hand, he grabbed Corvallis's pistol and yanked. At the same time, with his other, he punched Corvallis — it was not a hard punch, but it convinced Corvallis to unthinkingly relinquish his pistol.

Corvallis angrily shook off the effects of the blow. "Damnit, Ev," he snapped. "Gimme back my piece."

"Not till you cool off some," Eyman said, stepping back up to the bar.

"You gonna take that from him?" Wolfe called out sarcastically. "I thought you were tougher than that."

Corvallis's ears and face burned with the shame of having had his pistol taken away from him. Suddenly, in a rage, he lashed out, slamming a fist against the side of Eyman's head. As the ranch foreman went down, Corvallis reached out and grabbed his pistol from Eyman's belt. "Fool," he muttered.

Corvallis crouched and began spinning toward Wolfe on the balls of his feet. As he made the move, he thumbed back the Colt's hammer.

Chapter Eighteen

Corvallis fired once—when his index finger contracted involuntarily as two slugs from Wolfe's gun smashed into his chest. The shot went wild.

Wolfe had never even fully turned. While he had been talking to the two townsmen at the bar, he kept a watch on Eyman and Corvallis in the mirror behind the bar. When he saw Eyman go down, he craned his head around. As Corvallis grabbed his pistol from Eyman and spun, Wolfe calmly drew his Colt. Half-turning sideways toward Corvallis, Wolfe had fired.

Silence descended in a rush on the High Country Saloon. It was broken only by several weak moans as Corvallis expired on the dirty floor. Several men tentatively gathered near the body, looking down in horror. Owen Corvallis was sure to make life in Kaibab hell, they figured. At least until the elder Corvallis had Lucas Wolfe lynched. The townsfolk were not happy with what had just transpired, and what it portended for them. And they wanted Wolfe gone: out of the saloon, and out of Kaibab.

Their harsh feelings were, however, mixed with a little relief. Aaron Corvallis had been a thorn in the town's side since its founding, and no one really grieved for the young ranch man. No one would miss him. What did worry them was their own futures, once Owen learned his son had been gunned down.

Wolfe did not know what any of them were thinking, of course, but he could sense the resentment aimed at him. He slid the Colt away, angry at himself, at Aaron Corvallis, at life in Kaibab. None of this was necessary. Even if Owen Corvallis had not given him the land he considered his, Wolfe would not have caused any trouble. He would have hung around a spell, checking things out, courting Sally. He had no intentions of spending the rest of his life in Kaibab — or at the Lazy O Ranch for that matter. He would have, he figured, taken Sally away when the time was right, and they could have lived their lives somewhere else.

But Aaron Corvallis could not leave things alone. He had sent men to beat Wolfe; had sent others to try to kill him. Now Wolfe knew he had the entire town against him. He did not like that feeling of unwelcome. But he would be damned if he turned tail and ran because the people of Kaibab were angry at him for killing Corvallis. He would deal with Owen Corvallis when the time came, and let all else resolve itself.

The two men he had been talking to at the bar had moved off several feet. They were not exactly horrified at what Wolfe had done, but they wanted a little distance between him and them — physically and mentally. Even Orville had drifted down toward the other end of the bar. Wolfe shrugged as he poured himself a shot and tossed it down his throat in one easy motion. He kept his eyes on the mirror as he did. One could never tell in a place like this. Someone would always want to get on the rich man's good side, and might think

161

shooting Wolfe in the back would be a good way to do it.

Wolfe took another drink and then set the glass down. He turned toward the small knot of people gathered at Corvallis's body. Wolfe leaned on his right elbow on the bar. He looked relaxed as he watched the others.

Eyman was kneeling over Aaron's corpse. There were no tears in Eyman's eyes, nor any depth of feeling in his heart. He was worried about having to tell Owen Corvallis that his son was dead, and that did not please him. But, more, he was angry at himself. He had been told to guard Aaron's life, and he had failed in that. He would have to atone for it.

When he stood and faced Wolfe, Eyman's face was hard and crusty with anger and self-hate. His right hand twitched near the butt of his Colt high on his hip.

"Don't," Wolfe said quietly, straightening and becoming more alert.

Eyman said nothing. In dribs and drabs, others who were standing around the body became aware of the tension brewing between Wolfe and Eyman. They watched in frightened excitement before realizing they had better move out of the way. They did so, still watching with interest.

"There's been enough senseless killin', Ev," Wolfe said earnestly, still talking quietly. He no longer cared what people in Kaibab thought of him. He liked—or at least respected—Eyman, and did not want to have to kill him. He knew he would kill Eyman if pushed, and Eyman must know it, too. Wolfe wanted to prevent this bloodshed. He was never one to gloat in the taking of a life. "We don't need to go addin' you to the list of folks waitin' for old man Klockschmidt's services," he added, hoping he could convince Eyman to change his mind.

"I've let Mr. Corvallis down," Eyman finally said, voice rough. "I got to do somethin'."

"No you don't."

"Yeah, I do, Luke," Eyman said sadly.

Wolfe shook his head, but he thought he understood.

Eyman was not afraid, exactly. But he did not want to die either. He knew the futility of his pending action, but at the same time, he felt pushed on to do this, as if it would make amends to Owen Corvallls for his son's death. He stared into Wolfe's eyes. Under different circumstances, he thought they could have become friends.

"Kill him, Ev," someone from the crowd yelled.

"Yeah, gun him down," another roared. Both statements were accompanied by a grumbling roll of agreement.

"You want to get killed for the enjoyment of these varmints, Ev?" Wolfe asked quietly.

"No," Eyman said softly, heaving doubts.

"Don't worry about him, Ev! You can take him," a hoarse, whiskey-soaked voice yelled.

"These bastards just want to see more blood, Ev. I say we disappoint 'em."

"You scared, Wolfe?" Eyman asked. There was no mockery in his voice.

"Can't say as I really am," Wolfe answered confidently. "But if you—if that bunch of stinkin' coyotes over there—want to think so, you go right ahead. I can take it, especially if it'll prevent more killin'."

Eyman thought briefly, chewing on his lower lip. Then he said in little more than a whisper, "Reckon I can't do that, Luke." His hand streaked for the Colt

163

at his side.

Wolfe gave no thought to the distaste he felt for what he was being forced to do. His hand automatically grabbed the Colt and yanked. As the pistol came up, he thumbed back the hammer and pointed it, rather than sighted it, all in a smooth motion, well-oiled from long hours of practice. The index finger squeezed with just the right pressure, and the gun fired. The whole move had taken perhaps half a second.

Wolfe winced as a bullet from Eyman's pistol sliced across his left side, just above his gunbelt. But he paid it no heed as he thumbed back the hammer and fired again through the light haze of powder smoke.

When the smoke cleared, Wolfe saw Eyman flat on his back, Colt in a lifeless hand. His shirt front was coated with thick blood. "Damn," Wolfe muttered. He glanced around the room. Most of the faces were hostile, but no one seemed threatening. He took a few minutes to eject the spent cartridges and reload. He dropped the pistol into the holster.

Alma Fletcher stormed into the saloon, followed by several of her girls. Her entrance shattered the fragile, worried silence that had settled over the High Country. Alma stopped looking down at the two bodies, which lay almost side by side, as if placed there by a gentle hand.

She looked down at the bloody corpses a moment, then looked at Wolfe. She smiled, but it was a meaningless gesture. "There's goin' to be hell to pay over this, Luke," she said.

"I reckon," Wolfe said nonchalantly. He appeared not to care, though he was bothered by all the bloodshed.

"You better get out of Kaibab. Soon."

"When I'm ready, Alma."

"You'll be ready soon, I hope."

"I wouldn't wager much on that."

Alma shrugged. "Have it your way." She sighed and turned to the bartender. "Orville, go and fetch Klockschmidt. And Marshal Trumble, too, I guess. I doubt that bloated windbag will do anything, but I figure we can get him to ride out to the Lazy O and tell Owen what's happened here."

"No," Wolfe said quietly, but firmly.

"Excuse me?" Alma asked, looking at him in surprise, and more than a little annoyance.

"Owen deserves better than that. I'll take the bodies back to the ranch. Owen ought to be the one to make the arrangements with Klockschmidt. Can you get me a wagon?"

"Sure." Alma turned and talked to one of her girls—a hefty woman wearing a cotton chemise covered by a thin silk robe. The woman hurried off. "I'll go with you, Luke," Alma said. Her anger was gone, lost in the knowledge that Wolfe was a smart—and respectful—man. Not many men, especially those as young as Wolfe, would have had the sense—and the courage—to do what he was planning.

"No need for that."

"There might be. Use your head a minute. Owen ain't going to be overjoyed you killed his son—and his foreman."

"So you're gonna go with me to protect me, eh?" Wolfe said with a condescending smile.

"Yes, damnit. And don't look so uppity. I expect Owen's goin' to send some boys after you, but I don't expect he'll kill you if I'm there. It might save your hide—for a time."

Wolfe nodded, chastised. "All right." He was happy

to accept anything that would avoid more bloodshed, even if for only another night. Tomorrow would see something different.

The woman Alma had talked to came back, accompanied by big Charlie Free. "Wagon's ready, Miz Alma," Free rumbled.

"He comin', too?" Wolfe asked, pointing to the big black man.

"Yep." Alma grinned. "A little extra incentive for Owen to mind his manners."

Wolfe nodded. He bent to pick up Eyman's body, but Free stopped him. "You're hurt," Free growled. "I'll see to this."

"Ain't but a scratch," Wolfe grumbled, but he stepped back out of the way.

Within minutes Free had easily—and surprisingly gently—carried the two corpses out and set them in the back of a flat-bed wagon. As he was picking up Eyman's body—he had already taken Aaron's out—Marshal Sam Trumble strolled in, reeking of self-importance. "What's gone on here?" he intoned.

"Go back to your office, Sam," Alma said.

He ignored her. He grabbed one of Free's massive arms. The black man stopped and looked down with contempt as Trumble asked, "Where you goin' with that body, boy?"

"You value that hand, Marshal," Alma said, "you'll get it off Charlie and let him go about his business."

Trumble fairly jumped, as if he realized for the first time exactly what he was doing. His hand moved, and Free walked off. Trumble, gulping, said, "Would one of you folks please tell me what's gone on here."

"Wolfe killed Aaron Corvallis," someone said aloud.

Trumble had already seen Corvallis's body in the wagon outside. And he had known as soon as he

166

walked into the saloon that Wolfe was probably tied up in this somehow. Now he knew for sure. "Mr. Corvallis is gonna be angrier'n hell, boy," Trumble said to Wolfe. He almost chuckled. Everything would be out of his hands now; Owen Corvallis would take care of Lucas Wolfe, and Kaibab could go back to being a peaceful town again. "I'd hate to be in your boots."

"And I'd hate to be in yours, you stupid old fart," Wolfe snapped. He glared at the other people in the saloon, and they suddenly felt embarrassed. Holding out his arm, he waited while Alma slipped her arm through the crook formed by his elbow. With heads high, the two strolled out of the saloon.

Wolfe and Alma crowded onto the front seat of the wagon with Free, who snapped the reins. They made the ride in silence. Wolfe was not sure whether he was grateful or angry that it was still daylight. On one hand, it meant they would not have to make the journey over the rock-rutted road in the dark. On the other, the daylight would do nothing to cover the ghastliness of their cargo when they arrived at their destination.

Heat poured down on them, though it was growing late in the afternoon. Combined with the closeness of three bodies on a single, small wagon seat, they were sweating heavily before they had gotten past the end of the buildings on Corvallis Street.

Wolfe thought it odd, as they pulled onto the dirt lane that led down to the Corvallis house, that when he came out here to meet Sally for their picnics, that the trip seemed interminable. Now, with such serious and painful business at hand, the trip had taken barely minutes. Or so it seemed.

Wolfe could feel his mouth growing dry as they approached the house. He saw Sally come out the front door and wait on the porch, shading her eyes, watching them. She saw Free—and Alma—and opened the door. She called something inside and then went back to waiting. A moment later, Owen came out and stood by her side.

Chapter Nineteen

Charlie Free stopped the wagon. The heat poured down on the three people in the wagon as they sat waiting for the cloud of dust the wagon had spooked up to settle. The dull quiet was pierced by the shriek of a red-tailed hawk high overhead; the soft, persistent clucking of the chickens pecking in the yard; the shuffle and snort of the two horses harnessed to the wagon; the quiet jingle of the harness chains.

Wolfe felt almost sick to his stomach as he watched Owen Corvallis finally move. Corvallis came down the few steps of the porch and walked slowly toward the wagon. Conflicting emotions and thoughts showed on his seamed, proud face.

He was a man torn between grief and relief. Corvallis had known from the time Aaron was ten years old that Aaron would come to a bad end. Corvallis was almost relieved that it was over now, and he would no longer have to wait for it to happen.

Corvallis had been disappointed in his son for years, but he had tried to do his best to make something of Aaron. And, despite his disappointment, Aaron *was* his son, and he felt the loss, though not as much as he thought he should. That made him feel guilty, and he was angry at himself for that.

Corvallis stopped at the back of the wagon and

looked down at his slain son, and at his slain ranch foreman. Guilt rose up in him anew when he realized he probably felt more grief at Eyman's death than he did at his son's. He thought he should do something to avenge the deaths of these two. But he was not sure he wanted to do that. Maybe, he thought, it would be better to just let this all ride. Let it end here. Just go on in and help console Aggie.

Aggie ventured out the door and onto the porch, surprising everyone. Aggie Corvallis had not been known to come out of her house for anything in some years. She was well-dressed and, Wolfe thought, quite an attractive woman, despite her age and the harsh life of the frontier. It was clear to Wolfe where Sally had gotten her fair good looks.

Corvallis headed toward Aggie to try to cut her off, since she was heading down the stairs, a look of horror and worry creasing her otherwise pleasant features. Her hands writhed within each other, showing outwardly the torment the woman felt inside.

"Aggie, don't," Corvallis said softly, acutely embarrassed that these outsiders would see his family troubles.

"It's Aaron, ain't it?" she asked, looking up at her husband. Her face was pained, but her voice had been clear and firm.

"Yes," Corvallis croaked, feeling worse for her than he did for himself. Aggie Runyon had been a vivacious, beautiful young girl when Corvallis had married her and for some years after that. But gradually she had fallen into a seeping melancholy that nothing Corvallis said or did could alter. It had bothered him to see it in her, but he had his own life and dreams.

Aggie had followed him willingly from one place to another, until they wound up in Prescott. But by the

170

time they had finally gotten to what would become the Lazy O Ranch, she was beyond hope of ever regaining her former mental vitality. Other than doting on her children, especially Aaron, she did little but sit in her room or in the parlor. Corvallis had even had to go out and hire a cook and maid. It had strapped them financially early on, but Aggie did not seem to notice. Nor would she have cared if she had known of the burden she had caused.

"I want to see my son," Aggie said firmly.

"I don't think that's wise, Aggie," Corvallis said, sternness creeping into his voice.

"I want to see my son," Aggie said again, insistently.

"He's been shot, and he's covered with blood."

"I don't care."

Corvallis had learned long ago not to argue with his wife. It was pointless, since she never seemed to understand whatever objections he—or anyone else, for that matter—made. She would simply stand her ground, insisting on whatever it was she wanted to do. Until whoever was objecting would grant Aggie her wish.

Corvallis stepped aside, ears burning from the embarrassment. His discomfort was made much more acute by the fact that Alma Fletcher was sitting on the wagon seat watching them. As Aggie had withdrawn more and more into her cocoon of loneliness and depression, Corvallis had looked elsewhere for comfort and feminine companionship. He had found both in the person of Alma Fletcher.

Back when Corvallis had started the Lazy O, Kaibab was not there. That town had only gone up about three years ago. Before that, Corvallis and his cowhands had to go to Flagstaff for much of what they

171

wanted. Anything out of the ordinary had to be brought in from Prescott or Camp Verde. It was in Prescott that Corvallis met Alma. He had visited her as much as possible there, but winters and such it was hard to do so. So when Kaibab sprang into existence — at his insistence and with his cooperation — he had brought Alma and some of her girls to Kaibab. There he visited her frequently.

He had thought for a while that he might be in love with her, but he had enough sense to know it was just loneliness and lust giving him those thoughts. Alma Fletcher was a fine woman, full of life and vivacity; he enjoyed that, both in her bed and out. Many was the time when they would just talk, and he greatly appreciated having someone like her with whom he could unburden himself.

Corvallis's trips to see Alma had diminished in the past year or so, but had not stopped. And, while he was embarrassed as could be that she was seeing such private family matters as this, he did have the fleeting thought that he would have to pick up the frequency of his meetings.

Without looking at Alma, Wolfe or Free, Corvallis went back to where his wife stood. She was weeping silently, great drops of tears falling from her face, her shoulders shaking. Suddenly uncertain of himself, Corvallis stood next to her and put an arm around her shoulders. They stood silent for several minutes before Corvallis finally said softly, "Come on, now, Aggie. It's time you was back inside."

"No," she sniffed. "I want to stay here with my boy."

Gently, but insistently, Corvallis pulled her by the shoulder. "It ain't right that you should be showin' your grief in public," he said. "It's time we brought

172

Aaron inside and saw to him. We'll have old Klock-schmidt come out here soon's possible."

"He should be on his way, Mr. Corvallis," Free said. "I told him before we left Kaibab."

Corvallis nodded and started leading Aggie away from the wagon, toward the house.

"You want I should bring Mr. Aaron inside?" Free asked.

"Thank you, yes."

"What about Mr. Eyman?"

"Take him to the bunkhouse," Corvallis said, stopping just long enough for that one sentence before resuming his journey.

Free easily lifted Aaron and carried him into the house.

Tentatively, Sally finally came off the porch, heading for Wolfe. She had not moved since the wagon had arrived. She stopped, looking up at Wolfe.

"I'm sorry, Sally," Wolfe said quietly.

Sally shrugged.

"Get down there with her," Alma whispered in his ear.

Feeling like a fool for not having thought of it himself, Wolfe hopped down next to Sally. He held out his arms, and she came into his embrace, resting her head on his chest.

Free came back out and was lifting Eyman, when Corvallis also returned. Wolfe let Sally go, and she stepped to his left side, her right hand resting lightly on his arm.

Corvallis looked from his daughter to Wolfe, wondering at the strangeness of life. "Did you kill my son, Mr. Wolfe?" he finally asked.

"Yes, sir," Wolfe said without blinking. "Ev, too."

"Why?" Corvallis was still struggling with his

conflicting emotions.

"I had no choice, Mr. Corvallis." He explained it all as quickly and as painlessly as he could. But he left nothing out, including the fact that Aaron would not back off, no matter what anyone said to him.

Corvallis nodded, understanding. Then he asked, "But why Ev?"

"He felt he had to prove somethin'," Wolfe said simply, not making any fun of the dead man. "He felt he let you down by allowin' Aaron to get himself killed." He shrugged. "He just had to come against me."

Corvallis understood that, too. Sometimes a man had to salvage his honor, even if it meant dying in the process. After all, honor and respect were all a man could really call his own. "He was a good man," Corvallis said softly.

"Yes, he was," Wolfe agreed. "Too damn good to have died for somethin' somebody else started." He paused, and rubbed his nose. He was not comfortable standing here talking to a man whose son he had gunned down less than two hours ago. "I give him every chance to back out of it, Mr. Corvallis," he said quietly. "I really did. I didn't want to shoot either one of 'em. But . . ."

"It's all right," Corvallis said, not at all sure he meant it. But, not at all sure he didn't. He took a deep breath. "I know my son was a hothead, Mr. Wolfe. And, I reckon I knew he'd not come to a good end. I could see what kind of man he'd turned into, and I knew he'd push somebody like you too far one day."

Corvallis wiped sweat off his forehead, and then dried his hand on a pant leg. "I know you would've given Aaron—and Ev, too—a fair chance. Still," he added, looking pained, "I don't reckon it'd be wise for

174

you to come round the Lazy O any more."

"No!" Sally hissed, shocked.

"Hush, daughter.

"I won't hush," she snapped, stamping her foot on the ground. Her fists rested on her full hips, and her face was flushed with anger. "Just 'cause Aaron was foolish enough to get himself killed doesn't mean I should suffer not having my beau come around."

"Don't talk nonsense, girl," Corvallis said harshly. Too much had happened, and he had too much to think about right now to have to deal with a recalcitrant daughter. He watched without interest as Free came back and climbed up onto the wagon.

"It ain't nonsense!"

"Yes it is. You . . ."

"That's enough, Sally," Wolfe said quietly but with strength. When Sally turned her head to look at him, her eyes were wide with surprise. She looked caught between rage and the fear of rejection. "Don't be so disrespectful of your pa," he added.

"But . . ."

"No buts. Not right now. Your pa's got a lot on his mind. He needs time to think all these things through, to see what he has to do."

"You think he'll let you come back after a spell?" Sally asked hopefully.

Sure," Wolfe said soothingly. Wolfe had no intention of not coming around the Lazy O any more. First off, he cared for Sally a great deal. And then there was always the cache for which he had been searching these past weeks.

"Don't wager on it," Corvallis said.

Wolfe glared at him but broke off the arrogant stare. The man must feel some grief, he thought, and it would not be right for him to give Corvallis a hard time right now.

"It'll be all right," Wolfe insisted. He felt sick at the thought of never seeing Sally again, and vowed that it would not happen.

"You'd best be ridin' on now, Mr. Wolfe," Corvallis said in a strained voice.

Wolfe nodded. "Just give me a couple minutes to say goodbye to Sally. Alone." He glared at Sally, lest she retort and possibly spoil things.

Corvallis's head bobbed up, then down, one time. He glanced up at Alma, and Wolfe was surprised to see interest in Corvallis's eyes. *Well, I'll be damned,* he thought. *Old man's Corvallis's got a thing for Alma!* He fought back a grin as Corvallis headed toward the house without another word.

Wolfe, not wanting Alma or Free to hear what he had to say, took Sally's arm and walked off a little way. Dusk was falling, and it would be dark before much longer. "You got to give your pa some time, Sally," Wolfe said. "I know he wasn't all that fond of Aaron, but still, he's just lost a son. And he's got your ma to worry over."

She nodded, chastised, but not much. "But I want to see you," she said.

"You'll see me."

"But Pa said . . ."

"Doesn't matter what he said. We'll give it a few days. He ain't changed his attitude by then, I'll just come on out."

"I'll be waiting."

"I should hope so." He paused, licking his lips, then asked, "You suppose it'd be sinful if you was to give me a farewell kiss out here in the open?"

"Might be," she whispered up at him, eyes cloudy with a desire she was not sure was good for her.

"But," she breathed, "right now I don't give a damn." She hoped she had not shocked Wolfe, but she was not watching. Her eyes were closed, and her lips parted, waiting for him. She was not disappointed.

Chapter Twenty

Wolfe reached for his Colt when he heard the tentative tapping at his door in Fletcher's Hotel. He slid back the hammer and stood just to the side of the door. "Who's there?" he asked, waiting tensely.

"Sally," came back a whisper.

"Come on in," Wolfe said, not relaxing his vigil. For all he knew, she could have every hand from the Lazy O Ranch with her. He didn't really think so, but he could not be certain.

The door opened, and Sally Corvallis slipped into the room, shutting the door behind her. She was pale, and breathing hard, and had a look about her as if she was afraid someone was chasing her. She jumped and turned toward Wolfe when she heard the pistol being uncocked. She stood, gasping in fear and worry, mouth wide, right hand balled and resting on her heaving breasts.

"Sorry," Wolfe said dryly. "But I had to be sure."

"Sure of what?" Sally asked, still shaking a little.

He walked over and stuffed the Colt into the holster. "Sure you didn't bring a bunch of your father's boys over here."

Her eyes widened with shock and anger. "I would never . . ."

"I know you'd not do that," he said soothingly. "But,

hell, Sally, they could have forced you."

"I'd die first," she said stoutly.

Wolfe looked at her seriously a few moments, and then grinned. "I reckon you would." He took up a small towel and wiped the shaving soap residue off his face. Then he grabbed his shirt from the bedpost and put it on. He was conscious that Sally was watching him avidly, and he felt a little embarrassed getting dressed in front of Sally. But he would be damned if he let that embarrassment show.

Sally stepped up to him, and touched a smooth, long fingernail—and then her finger itself—gently on his bare chest, just before he buttoned the shirt up all the way. She shuddered as a spasm of desire gripped her. She was innocent of men, but that did not lessen her yearning.

Wolfe gently lifted her hand away. He, too, was filled with desire, and did not want to tempt himself unnecessarily. Nor did he want to entice Sally into something she would regret. Quickly he finished buttoning his shirt. Turning away from her, he swiftly stuffed his shirttails sloppily into his pants.

He turned back. "What brings you here anyway, Sally?" he asked.

Sally shook her head, as if trying to clear a fog. "Huh?" she mumbled, startled. Then, with worry suddenly splashing across her pretty face, she said, "You've got to get out of Kaibab. Now!"

"Why?" Wolfe asked, somewhat amused. "Oh, and take a seat." He pointed to the plush chair at the table in front of the window.

Sally sat. "They buried Aaron yesterday," she said diffidently. "Out back of the house."

"I'm sorry."

Sally shrugged. "After the burying, Pa got the ranch

179

hands together down in the bunkhouse. I stood outside and listened."

Owen Corvallis was still uncertain of what to do. He had no great desire to get revenge for his son's death, and he did not really want to kill Lucas Wolfe. He liked Wolfe quite a bit, and would have been more than happy to have had him for a son-in-law. That was the way the wind had been blowing before his foolish son had tried gunning Wolfe down.

Despite his own feelings, he knew the ranch hands would expect some sort of retribution against Wolfe. If not for Aaron, then for Eyman. The foreman had been well-liked by the men who worked the Lazy O. He had been competent, hard-working and fair. It was enough to earn the respect of any man.

All the hands had turned out behind the fancy ranch house to attend the burying of Aaron Corvallis in the small family cemetery. And then they all had gone off to the other cemetery—the one where ranch hands and other non-family members were buried. Ike and Aud had been laid to rest there not so long ago; now it was Eyman's time.

"It's gettin' crowded in here," one hand said as dirt was tossed in on Eyman's simple pine casket.

"And all Wolfe's doin', too," another grumbled.

There was more angry rumbling, until finally Corvallis had said, "Let's put Ev to rest in peace, boys. We'll see to the other later."

After the simple ceremony was over, Corvallis led the men back to the bunkhouse. He was still confused and knew he had to do something—or the hands would do something on their own. Corvallis hoped that if he tried to ramrod some retribution, no matter how distasteful, it might prevent a bloodbath of innocents.

"All right, boys," Corvallis said as the hands took seats on chairs or bunks. "First off we got to pick somebody to replace Ev."

"Can't nobody replace Ev," one said to a rumble of agreement.

"That might be. But I need a ramrod for the Lazy O." He paused. "And we'll need somebody to lead when you boys go down to Kaibab." He did not want to say for what.

"To take care of business?" one asked.

"Reckon so," Corvallis said distastefully. How could he tell these men he did not want Wolfe killed? he wondered. But he knew he could not. All he could do was to send them to town and hope that Wolfe had some warning. He thought for a moment that he would warn Wolfe himself—or have Sally do it. But that would give him away. He would have to play this as straight as possible.

Corvallis surveyed the faces arrayed before him. They were hard, weatherbeaten faces, cut through with creases from sun and wind and hard work. And they were tough, unforgiving faces. "Curly," he said. "I reckon you got more time here than anyone else. Think you can handle the job?"

"Reckon so, Mr. Corvallis," Curly mumbled, embarrassed by the chorus of catcalls and whoops that arose around him. He stood and looked around at the men with whom he had worked for almost eight years. Then he looked up at Corvallis. "Yes, sir, I reckon I can," he said more firmly.

"Good." Corvallis did not feel relieved.

"What do you want me to do first, boss?"

"That's your look-out, Curly."

"Boys?" Curly asked, turning in a semicircle, looking

181

at his friends.

"Let's get Wolfe," several shouted in unison. Those who had not joined in, added their voices of approval right after.

"Mr. Corvallis?" Curly asked, turning toward his boss. "That suit you?"

"Reckon it does," Corvallis said. But he found he was beginning to get excited. Maybe, he thought, it was just the grief keeping him from feeling enough rage to want to get revenge. Aaron might've been a poor excuse for a son, and a poor excuse for a ranchman, but still, he was Corvallis's flesh and blood. That counted for something.

"Take a dozen boys with you, Curly," he said, surprising himself that he did. "Ride on in first thing tomorrow." He waited out the rising tide of howling fury spit out by the men. When it died out, he said, "But you boys best listen. There's been a lot of killin' lately. I want you boys to be careful with what you're doin'. You take care of Wolfe and then get the hell back here."

"What else're we gonna do?" Curly asked, grinning. There was always Alma Fletcher's "house" or perhaps one of the saloons.

"What I mean," Corvallis said harshly, "is that I don't want no innocent folks from Kaibab gettin' their butts shot off by a bunch of pistol happy punks, is what."

That served to settle the men some. "Best make yourselves ready, boys," Corvallis said. "Goin' after Wolfe ain't gonna be the same as runnin' down an old coyote." He began feeling uncertain about all this again.

"We'll take care of Wolfe, Mr. Corvallis," one of the men said.

Curly nodded. He felt proud at having been made foreman, but when he remembered his last encounter with Lucas Wolfe, he suddenly got a little weak in the knees. Curly Bodine was not, by nature, a frightened man. But there was something about Wolfe that touched a nerve of fear deep within him.

"Just remember what I said," Corvallis said before stalking out of the bunkhouse into the gathering darkness.

"They ought to be here in less than an hour, Luke," Sally said, urgency creasing her voice.

He nodded.

"You've got to get going," Sally said, even more urgently. "Get out of Kaibab. Head for Flagstaff. No, Prescott. It's bigger."

"What about you?" Wolfe asked, almost amused by this. He recognized the seriousness of it all, but he thought it almost funny that she expected him to turn tail and run. "What're you gonna do?"

"I'll meet . . . you . . ." she said hesitatingly, "in Prescott. If you want . . ." She trailed off, wide eyes staring up at him, pleading for acceptance.

"No," he said firmly.

Sally looked like her life had just been ripped out of her.

"I mean, no, I ain't runnin'," Wolfe said hastily, worried that he had hurt her beyond repair. "Not, no I don't want to meet you somewhere."

A bit of color trickled back into Sally's cheeks. "You want me?" she asked, voice squeaking. "You sure?"

"Yep, I'm sure." He grinned reassuringly.

"Well, you never said."

"I have now."

"I'm glad."

He nodded and reached for his gunbelt. He looked at her and asked bluntly, "Why are you doin' this?"

"I love you," Sally answered simply.

"But I killed your brother," he insisted. He loved Sally Corvallis, and wanted to marry her. But he had to know for sure where she stood on these things.

"My brother was a fool and a bully," she answered, staring up at him. Her eyes were bright. "You know that. And you know there was no love lost between us."

That was all true, and she prayed that he believed her. If he didn't she would have to give him other— equally true—reasons. But how could she tell him that her heart had died for a while when she saw Wolfe sitting alongside Alma Fletcher on the wagon? She was innocent in the ways of love, but she was not so innocent that she could not see that something had gone on between her man and that whore. How could she tell him that? Or how could she tell him how it ate at her insides to know that Wolfe was living in the hotel owned by that woman?

"Will you marry me?" Wolfe asked suddenly.

Her eyes grew big as saucers. "Yes," she whispered. "Yes!" It was said strongly. Then she quickly sobered. "But we've got to get you out of here!"

"I ain't runnin'," he said firmly.

"You'll get killed." Fear gnawed her intestines.

He shrugged. "I run," he said softly, "and they'll only follow me—us. We'll never live in peace. Even if they never find us, the stories'll go around about how I backed down. I couldn't live like that, Sally."

"But . . ."

"No!" He finished hooking on the gunbelt.

Sally stared at him. She was angry and full of fear. But she managed to keep herself under control. With a deep breath, she said, "Then if you're bound and set on goin' out there to get yourself killed . . ." she paused ". . . then I want to be left as your widow." There was no doubt in her eyes.

"You sure?" he asked stupidly.

"Yes!"

Wolfe took the three strides to the door and yanked it open. "Alma!" he bellowed.

A few moments later, Alma Fletcher hurried up, looking frightened. "What's wrong?" she asked, breathing heavily.

"Nothing's wrong," Wolfe grumbled. "Just go fetch Reverend Fordney. Now!"

"What?" Alma asked, surprised.

"Reverend Fordney. Get him."

Alma could not resist asking. "Why?"

" 'Cause he's gonna hitch me'n Sally," Wolfe said in exasperation. There was too little time to be answering so many questions.

"You in a hurry?" Alma asked. She seemed in no hurry to move.

"Yes, goddamnit! Go!"

Alma sensed the urgency and went, shouting orders at Charlie Free, and anyone else within earshot. In Alma's wake, Wolfe calmly checked the loads in his Colt. Then he got the two Merwin and Hulberts he had taken from Temple McSorley. He made sure they were loaded, too. Just after he stuffed them into his gun-belt — one at the small of his back, the other in front — there was a rap at the door.

Tensing, Wolfe motioned Sally into the corner at the same side of the room as the door. Before she could move, though, Alma called, "Open up, Luke. I got the reverend here. Time's a-wastin'."

Wolfe could not quite believe all this was happening.

But he pulled open the door and allowed the Reverend Winthrop Fordney in. He was followed by Alma, Charlie Free, Esther and several other people, who crowded into the room.

"Let's get this *fandango* movin'," Fordney intoned gravely.

Chapter Twenty-one

"I now pronounce you man and wife," the Reverend Fordney said in his basso profundo voice, which seemed strange coming from such a scrawny man. "You may kiss the bride, sir."

Wolfe took full opportunity to do so, pleased that Sally reciprocated with undeterred ardor. The kiss lasted long enough that Fordney coughed in embarrassment. The newlyweds took the cue and broke apart.

"That'll be a dollar, Mr. Wolfe," Fordney said, holding out his hand.

But Wolfe was not paying him any heed. He was, instead, staring warmly at his new wife. She had never looked more beautiful to him, though her face was streaked with sweat, dust and tears. Her hair was straggling out from the knot in which she had put it this morning. She had lost her bonnet somewhere on the trail, she had told him earlier. She wore a simple, though eye-pleasing calico dress of blue flowers against an off-white background. Her bright blue eyes were wide with wonder.

"Here, Reverend," Alma Fletcher said with a grin, holding out a paper dollar bill. "And thank you."

"Anytime," he said in quite somber tones. He looked at the couple. "I don't suppose this union will be blessed with longevity, will it?"

"There's a small chance it will," Alma said quietly.

"But I wouldn't wager more than a little on it."

Fordney nodded. "Well," he said seriously, "I'd better be on my way." He was still uncomfortable here. He had not wanted to perform the marriage. He was certain that Owen Corvallis would not be pleased that Fordney had joined Corvallis's daughter and this drifting gunman in holy wedlock. But Charlie Free's massive fist held under his nose had convinced the good minister, and he did his duty as fast as he could. Now he wanted to be away from here.

Wolfe and Sally were still not paying anyone else any mind. They clutched each other, knowing Wolfe must leave in a few minutes.

"Sorry," he whispered into her ear.

"About what?" she asked in the same tones.

"This wasn't exactly a fittin' weddin' for you, Sally. No flowers. No ring. Wasn't even done in a church. You deserve better. A lot better." He was abashed.

She pulled back from him a little so she could look into his eyes. "You forgot to mention I ain't wearin' a wedding dress neither," she said, not caring any longer if the others heard. "But none of that matters, Luke. What matters to me is that I'm your wife." Tears sprang unbidden into her eyes. "And now you're going to go out and get yourself killed."

Wolfe glanced around the room. He was uncomfortable under the eyes of the others. But he was trapped. He looked back at Sally. "I ain't *aimin'* to get killed, Sally," he said softly.

"Then run, Luke," she insisted. She did nothing to wipe away her tears.

"We've been through that," he said gruffly. He felt bad for her, but he guessed a woman would never understand what it meant for a man like him to run away. If he did that, he would not be able to face himself again. And if he ran, then he would no longer be the man she had fallen in love with and married.

She nodded, trying with limited success to stop the tears. She was horrified that her face, puffed and reddened from crying, would be the last thing he saw. No, she wanted him to remember her better. She wiped at her wet cheeks. Gratefully she took the small, perfumed handkerchief one of Alma's girls handed her and dried her eyes and face with it.

"Reckon it was time I was gone, Sally," Wolfe said, realizing his mouth was dry. He wasn't afraid to go out there and face whatever was coming. But leaving Sally here was the hardest thing he had ever had to do.

Sally nodded again. She stepped up close to him, gripped his shirt in her small fists and bent her head back. He accepted her inviting cue and bent his head so he could kiss her. She took the lead this time, her sweet mouth trying to devour his. When he finally pulled away, she whispered, "You just remember what you got waitin' here for you."

"I will," he muttered. He grabbed his hat, and stuck it on. With his mind cluttered by thoughts of Sally and brain fogged by desire for her, he left. By the time he hit the front door of the hotel, he had managed—reluctantly and with great difficulty—to put Sally, and the promises she offered, mostly from his mind.

He strode into the dusty street and stopped about halfway across Corvallis Road. With slow, deliberate movements, he rolled and lit a cigarette.

Wolfe ignored the people of Kaibab who stopped to stare at him, wondering what this crazy young gunman was up to. People riding horses or wheeling their wagons along the street avoided him.

A mangy old dog came up and started sniffing at him. When it looked ready to raise its leg toward

189

Wolfe, he growled, "Git away from me, you ragged-ass bag of bones." He scowled. The animal did not appear to be at all deterred by the name-calling, so Wolfe dropped the smoldering remains of the cigarette on its head. The dog yelped once and loped off, long ears flapping.

"Goddamn dawg," Wolfe muttered. He rolled and lit another cigarette and stood waiting patiently, staring down the road stretching out before him. More and more people began lining Corvallis Road, watching him in wonder. He ignored them still.

Then he saw a drifting cloud of dust floating rapidly toward Kaibab, and he knew his wait was almost over. He dropped the cigarette into the dirt at his feet and pulled two pistols, but did not cock them.

A dozen men thundered into town, with Curly Bodine in the lead. He spotted Wolfe and held up his hand. The men stopped hard, ten yards in front of Wolfe. A billowing puff of dust rose from under horses' hooves and lingered around the men for a few minutes before the wind blew it off.

Wolfe stood waiting, his hands down at his side. In his right was his Colt Peacemaker; in his left, one of the Merwin and Hulberts. "Sure you brought enough boys with you, Curly?" he asked when things had settled down a little.

"I reckon," Bodine said. He seemed almost arrogant.

"That's good." Wolfe scratched his right temple with the muzzle of his Colt. "Any of these boys you don't favor much?"

"Why?" Bodine asked, suspicious.

Wolfe shrugged, and grinned ingratiatingly. "Well, unless y'all are gonna say howdy to me and then ride on back to the Lazy O, a couple of these boys are gonna be ready for the boneyard before all this is over.

190

Thought maybe if you didn't favor some of these boys, I'd take them out first."

Bodine chuckled. He leaned forward, his forearms on the saddlehorn. "You're pretty funny, Wolfe," he said. "But I reckon we've all had about enough of your humor. You've caused a hell of a lot of trouble for Mr. Corvallis, and you've killed several good men. Now it's time for your comeuppance."

"What've you got planned?"

"There's a fine, fat cottonwood over yonder on the corner," Bodine said. He leaned back and pointed to the southeast corner of Corvallis Road and Williams Street. "Folks have said it'd make a good hangin' tree. Reckon we'll be findin' out quick enough." He grinned confidently.

"You're mighty damn cocky," Wolfe said. He hesitated a heartbeat, then added, "For a dead man."

"Starr, bring the rope up," Bodine ordered. He glared at Wolfe, his face hard. "It ain't me that's the dead man here, Wolfe," he commented.

A young, small man rode forward, dangling a noose in his hands. His clothes were too big for him, and he looked like he was barely old enough to grow fuzz on his cheeks.

"Best stop there, boy, and take a minute to listen," Wolfe said coldly. Starr did, doubt clouding his eyes under the huge hat he wore. "You best know, boy, that if you move any closer, I'm gonna shoot you dead." He sneered and turned his gaze toward Bodine. "But you, Curly, are gonna get the first slug."

"You talk mighty big for a man's facin' death," Bodine said arrogantly.

"I ain't afraid of dyin', Curly." It was true, too. More times than he could count he had faced death, and never once did he worry about it or fear it. He did

191

not wish for it, and he would do whatever he could to stave it off. But it did not faze him to know he was close to death.

Of course, he had some things in his favor, despite facing odds of twelve to one. For one thing, he wasn't afraid of dying. Most of the others would be. For another, they were cowpunchers, not pistoleers. Wolfe had made his way through his young life as best he could. And often in the past five years, that had included using his pistol to get by. Bodine's men were used to using their pistols to scare cattle into line, or to kill rattlesnakes and such. They were not used to gunning down other men—especially men who were firing back with deadly accuracy.

Then there was the fact that the mass of men was packed together. At least half would not be able to fire without hitting one of their companions. That, in itself, lessened the odds considerably.

"Cole," Bodine said, "You and Harv bring your ropes up. Lasso the son of a bitch, and we'll see how much trouble he causes us then."

Wolfe waited just long enough to make sure the two men were actually heading for him slowly, shaking out their lassos, one coming past each side of Bodine. He could not—would not—let them get their ropes on him. And these boys would be good with those ropes. He had little time to act.

"Bye, boys," he said quietly. He snapped the Colt up and calmly put a bullet through Harv's forehead. The cowboy never knew what hit him. He just tumbled silently back over his horse's rump and lay in a bleeding pile on the ground.

Time seemed to stop for a moment. Then all hell broke loss.

"You bastard!" Cole roared. He viciously spurred his

horse forward, swinging the rope loop over his head.

Wolfe dropped to one knee and snapped off two quick shots. He didn't know which shot—or if both—hit Cole, but the cowpuncher suddenly was no longer on his horse. Wolfe waited to see no more. He fired the last three slugs from the Colt, hitting a horse and winging another cowpuncher.

"Damn," he muttered as he jammed the Colt into his holster. He had hoped for better success. But the swirling clot of horses and men were hard to get a fix on. Especially when they were partially obscured by the cloying veil of dust. Horses whinnied, and Wolfe was aware that people were screaming and running for cover. Several shots whizzed by him, but he was not hit.

Wolfe shifted the Merwin and Hulbert to his right hand. He could shoot with his left when he had to, but he was a far better shot from the right side.

A gust of wind cleared the cloud away, like the parting of a curtain, for a moment. He spotted Bodine shouting orders and pointing. *"Adios,"* he mumbled. He aimed and fired once. The bullet punctured Bodine's head an inch above the right ear. Bodine fell and was trampled by his horse.

A bullet ripped through the cloth of Wolfe's shirt between the biceps and ribs on the right side. He decided it was time to seek cover. He spun to his right and ran, hoping he could make Fletcher's Hotel in safety. As he ran, he heard the heavier crack of a rifle. Glancing over his shoulder, he saw one of the cowboys go down.

He cranked his head back and concentrated on the door of the hotel. It seemed a thousand miles away, and getting farther away with each step. He heard the rifle crack several more times, but he was not sure if whoever was firing had hit anything.

193

Suddenly a horseman was in front of him. Wolfe jerked to a stop. The cowboy, the lower half of his face covered by a bandanna, fired his pistol at Wolfe. But the horse had reared, and it threw the shot wide.

"Damn," Wolfe roared. He whipped the Merwin and Hulbert up and fired. He swore again as he saw a burst of blood from the cowboy's leg, just above the knee. The cowpuncher howled. The cowboy fired again as he spurred the horse forward. That shot, too, went wide.

And then the horseman was gone. Wolfe took a deep breath, choking on the dust that hung in the air like mist after a rain. He spit out a mouthful of dust in annoyance.

Wolfe started running again. He began to think he would make it to the hotel—and the sanctuary it offered.

Fire suddenly seared across his leg, and it buckled on him. He went down in a heap. Cursing, he shoved himself back up, glancing down. He saw the wound was not bad, though it stung like hell. Still, it wasn't bleeding much, nor was the bone broken. He ran on again.

Another trail of flame seared its way across him, this time on the back of his shoulders. But he was still going. He was within five yards of the hotel door now, and his breath was coming hard. Dust clogged his throat, and his chest ached from the exertion and the dust pouring into it.

He hoped Alma had not locked the door of the hotel behind him after he had left. But suddenly it didn't matter. A great, blinding burst of light exploded in front of his eyes, and he felt himself falling. He was conscious of throwing out his arms to break the fall. Then blackness overcame him, and the world was gone, blotted out.

Chapter Twenty-two

Wolfe woke up slowly, fighting to stay in the world of darkness, while at the same time battling to be free of it. There was something compelling, comforting about the warm, soft blackness in which he was now dwelling. He was reluctant to give that up and re-enter the world. Especially when that world included bright lights, loud voices, and intense pain.

But he could not stay in the safe haven of the dark cocoon forever, he knew. There might be more danger. And he would have to be ready for it. Battling off the sense of dread that threatened him, he grudgingly cracked his eyelids. He waited out the flood of pain, and let his eyes adjust to the light before he opened the eyelids fully.

Roaring pain pounded in his skull, ricocheting inside from one ear to the other, crashing and pounding. The agony made his stomach far more queasy than he wanted to admit even to himself. He shut his eyes again, hoping it would serve to quell the violent lurching in his abdomen.

When the roiling had settled down to mere tidal waves, he opened his eyes again. Sally was hovering over him, her usually open face dark with worry. "Are you all right?" Sally asked, concern making her voice quiver.

"Just dandy," Wolfe mumbled. "Ready to take you to our weddin' dance." He remembered the wedding. It was odd almost beyond belief to realize that he was now a husband. Good lord, he thought. He had never thought such a thing would happen.

The wedding had been quick, and then what? he wondered. Then he remembered meeting Owen Corvallis's ranch hands outside. There was the fight—and then the cover of darkness.

"He'll be fine, Sally," Alma Fletcher said, stepping into Wolfe's field of view. "If he can wisecrack like that, he ain't in no danger." She grinned.

Wolfe looked from one woman to the other. He wondered what was going on here between these two. And what had gone on. He would have to find out, but that could wait. First he needed to know how he had gotten back to his room at the hotel.

"What happened?" he asked, dry mouth making the words splinter as they came out.

"Don't you know?" Sally asked. She was afraid his skull was cracked and might never be right again.

"I know what went on up till the time I went down—and out," he said with some irritation. He did not like this feeling of not knowing what had happened; of having been helpless, even if only for a short time.

"Just about the time you fell, the ranch hands turned tail and skedaddled," Alma said. She figured—correctly—that Sally was too upset and worried about her new husband to be able to explain things to him.

"Why?" he asked. "They had me down, and outnumbered. I would've been easy pickin's."

"You had help."

Wolfe closed his eyes, once again grateful for the darkness it brought. There had been other gunshots, he remembered now. Someone with a rifle had come to his

196

aid, shooting from . . . Where? And who? "Somebody was firin' a rifle," he whispered. "Got at least one of the bastards."

"Big Charlie," Sally said brightly, as if determined to break the gloom that had settled over the hotel since the gunfight. "From down in the lobby."

Wolfe opened his eyes and strained his neck to look up. Charlie Free stood in a corner, grinning. Cradled in his arms was a .45-caliber Marlin lever action rifle.

"Thanks, Charlie," Wolfe croaked, letting his head sink back onto the pillow.

"My pleasure," Free commented. He seemed bored, as if such things happened every day.

"Then what?" Wolfe asked. The pain in his head was immense, and was making him sick again.

"Soon's those boys kicked up their heels, Sally was out of here like a lightnin' bolt," Alma said with a growly laugh. "By the time me and Charlie got there, she was tryin' to drag you in here all by herself."

"You did let Charlie help, didn't you?" Wolfe asked, looking at his new wife. Not only was he now a husband, he had a wife. It was a strange thought to him yet. Wife. He rolled the word around in his mind a bit. It wasn't so bad, he guessed. Wife. Mrs. Sally Wolfe. No, he thought, definitely not so bad.

"Yes," Sally said very quietly, casting down her eyes in embarrassment.

"Good," he said sincerely. He shut his eyes just a moment, hoping the agony would go away. But it wouldn't. "How long have I been out?" he asked.

"Not long," Alma answered calmly. "Little more than a half-hour maybe."

"How bad?" he asked, not sure he wanted to know. At the moment, he thought he would prefer being dead. It would sure as hell be a lot less painful, he

197

reasoned. Of course, then he wouldn't have Sally for a wife any longer if he was dead, and that was not a pleasant thought at all.

"Hell, I've seen lots worse after a brawl over at the High Country," Alma said with a chuckle. When Sally looked over at her in horror, Alma said with emphasis, "A little humor's good for a body, girl. Even one's been hurt some. *Especially* one's been hurt some. Shoot, he was a lot worse off after he got whupped outside the hotel here that time."

Wolfe knew the former to be true. Alma Fletcher was an astute enough woman that if she had thought Wolfe was close to dying, she would try to make him comfortable, ease his pains as best she could, even sympathize with him. But if she figured he wasn't hurt all that bad—just had some paining from the wounds—she could afford a little humor. Laughter might hurt his head considerably right at the moment, but it still let him know that he would be fine. She would not coddle him, though, if he wasn't bad off; so he figured he must be doing as well as could be expected.

"You two gettin' along all right?" he asked. He just had to know what had transpired between the two women while he had been outside. He watched Sally.

"Sure as hell we are," Alma said with her deep, lusty, throaty laugh accompanying the words. Sally's face grew pink with the embarrassment.

"Care to tell me about it, Sally?" Wolfe asked, interested not only in knowing, but also in Sally's reaction.

Sally shook her head. Her long, strawberry hair, now loose, swung back and forth, partly obscuring her face—and its deepening color of discomfort.

"It ain't nothin' you'd be interested in, Luke Wolfe," Alma said with another chuckle. "Once you'd gone off to make a hero—or a bag of bones—of yourself, me

198

and Sally set out to comfort each other. We both know you and all . . ." she grinned at him, and he thought it was done lecherously. He stole a glance at Sally, but she still seemed to be in shock a little.

"So we talked of many things—women's talk and such," Alma said. She grinned. "We learned some things about each other, didn't we, honey?" Alma smiled at Sally. Her fondness for Sally was evident in it.

"Yes," Sally said, still abashed, but wanting her new-found affection for Alma to be known.

Wolfe knew far more had transpired between them than either woman was letting on, but he knew he would never be a part of it. They would tell him only what they wanted to—if anything. He would have to accept that or live in frustration. He had far greater things to worry about. His only concern was that Sally would find out about the time he had spent with Alma. It worried him that Sally might be hurt by that.

"You never did say how bad off I was," he commented.

"Flesh wound on your left leg," Alma said. "Another across your upper back. The worst—and it ain't all that bad—is the one that took you down. A slug from somebody's gun winged you across the side of the head."

So that's where the pain in my head is coming from, he thought. "My skull's not cracked?" he asked, a note of concern in his voice. He reached up and touched the bandages wound around his head.

"No," Alma said reassuringly. "Doc Windsor's been here and gone. He checked you over pretty well. Cleaned up the wounds and bandaged you. Said your head was fine."

Wolfe nodded, and realized right off that such a

199

move had been a mistake. But despite the pain, he felt better. It was a relief to know his head was not cracked open. The pain he could live with—he hoped. "Did the doc happen to leave somethin' to ease the painin' in my head?" he asked hopefully.

"As a matter of fact, he did," Alma said. But she made no move to get it.

Wolfe looked at her questioningly for a moment, but Alma was looking at Sally, a half-smile on her lips.

Sally suddenly looked like she had been poked with a red-hot branding iron. She jumped up, realizing that Alma expected her to get the powder Doc Windsor had left. After all, she was now Wolfe's wife. It was her place to do this for her husband. She almost ran to the small table a few steps away and grabbed the vial of powder. Carefully she poured some of the powder into a glass and then filled the glass with water. She carried it to Wolfe. "Here, Mr. Wolfe," she said tentatively.

"Thank you, Mrs. Wolfe," he said pointedly, grinning.

She looked shocked—shocked at the fact of it; and shocked that she had forgotten. But he did not seem upset. She smiled. It was nice being Mrs. Wolfe, she decided.

"That's better," Wolfe said quietly. He shoved himself up so he was sitting, leaning back against the headboard of the bed. Pain sent colored dots swirling before his eyes, and a powerful throbbing lancing through his head. He shut his eyes and breathed deeply, trying to keep down his breakfast. Finally he opened his eyes. With a grateful, wan smile, he took the glass.

"Sure hope this damn stuff helps," he muttered. He drank it down all at once, wincing at its taste. With a sigh that he had managed it, he handed the glass back to Sally. "Again, thank you, Mrs. Wolfe," he said.

Sally beamed and dipped in a curtsy. "You're welcome, Mr. Wolfe."

Wolfe felt the darkness coming over him again, and he almost panicked. Then he realized that it was only sleep drawing near. The pain seemed to be farther away now, and drowsiness settled heavily on his shoulder.

He was aware—barely—that Free had come over, set the rifle down, and then eased Wolfe flat on the bed. "Thanks," Wolfe mumbled.

"You rest," a worried Sally said, placing a hand gently on the bandages that swathed his head. "We'll watch over you."

Wolfe thought he said thank you, but he could not be sure. Then he was asleep.

He awoke, he didn't know how much later, to a knocking on the door. The pain in his head was gone, except for a dull throbbing. "Who's there?" he heard Free call.

"Owen Corvallis," came the reply.

"Damn," Wolfe muttered. He tumbled out of bed and realized belatedly that he was naked. Somebody—and he hoped it was Free—had stripped him down to both get at his wounds, and because his clothes were a mass of blood and dirt. He knew there was no going back now, so he grabbed the pair of red longjohns Alma held out to him.

Alma was grinning widely. With a glance, Wolfe could see that Free was grinning, too. Wolfe gulped. As he struggled into the garment, he peeked at Sally. She was standing, head down, hair covering what portion of her face that might otherwise be visible. He burned with shame as he realized she must be giggling, since her hair was bobbing up and down.

The knocking came again. "Luke!" Corvallis shouted from outside. "Luke! Open up."

"Hold your horses," Wolfe said. He felt somewhat relieved to have some clothes on. He went to the bureau and pulled out a pair of denim pants. In seconds, he had them on and felt more comfortable. As he buckled on his gunbelt, he yelled at the door, "You alone, Corvallis?"

"Yes." Wolfe checked his revolver, making sure it was loaded. Then he motioned to Sally and Alma to get into the northwest corner of the room. The door was in the west wall, and he figured that corner was the safest. The women moved silently, Alma looking unconcerned, Sally frightened. Free stood, Marlin rifle ready just to the right of the door as it would open.

With the Colt held loosely in hand, Wolfe stepped up to the door. Corvallis was pounding on it again. Without warning, Wolfe yanked the door open, leaving Owen Corvallis standing with his fist still raised in the air.

Corvallis blanched as he saw Wolfe's pistol only inches from his nose. He stood stock still, afraid.

Chapter Twenty-three

"Come on in," Wolfe said, moving the Colt enough to allow Corvallis to enter.

Corvallis stepped inside, looking around in some distaste—a barefoot Wolfe, his head bandaged, with only the torso of his longjohns covering his top: Charlie Free casually aiming a .45-caliber rifle at him; Alma Fletcher, with whom he shared too many memories; and his daughter, looking distraught.

Wolfe stuck his head carefully out the door and then looked around.

"I told you I came alone," Corvallis said gruffly, a touch of anger in his voice, watching Wolfe.

"I know," Wolfe said disinterestedly as he came back in and closed the door firmly behind him. "Have a seat, Mr. Corvallis," he said, sliding the Colt into his holster. "I reckon you know everyone here."

"Sally," Corvallis said roughly, indicating that he wanted no argument, "go on downstairs. A few of the boys are waiting outside. I have business to discuss with Mr. Wolfe."

"No," Sally said flatly, shocking her father. "Luke and I . . ." she started, but she stopped when Wolfe shook his head at her and mouthed the word, "Wait."

She did not finish.

"What do you mean, no?" Corvallis demanded. "Do what I told you, girl." He was quite angry now.

"No."

Corvallis didn't know what to do. He was not used to such defiance. He certainly could not hit his daughter; he was far too fond of her for that, and he did not think such behavior was proper. Besides, it might set Wolfe off, and there was no telling what that crazy gunman would do. After all, Wolfe had just stood off a dozen men, killing five of them, and wounding several others. He would not have changed his opinion much, even had he known that Free was responsible for killing two of the ranch hands and wounding at least one other.

"Best just take a seat, Owen," Alma said. The look she gave Corvallis shocked Sally, though she already knew that Alma had been involved with her father. It was one of the many things they had talked about in that short time Wolfe had been gone, and in that eternity when he had lain in his bed, unconscious. Still, hearing it stunned her a little. She would, she told herself firmly, have to get over it.

Corvallis looked from his defiant daughter, who was sitting in the plush chair by the table at the window; to the bold, brassy Alma Fletcher, whom he realized he had not seen enough of lately; and on to Wolfe, who watched him alertly. He shrugged and took the other chair at the small table, across from his daughter.

"We'll just leave you folks be," Alma said. "Let's go, Charlie." At the door she stopped and turned. "Just watch your manners, Owen," she said softly, but the warning was there. "I don't want no trouble from you — or your men downstairs."

Corvallis nodded.

There was only one other chair in the room. Alma had had Free bring it in for her to sit on when Wolfe had gotten hurt. Wolfe shoved the chair over toward the table and sat in it. "Well?" he asked, looking at Corvallis.

"Well, Mr. Wolfe?" Corvallis countered.

"It's got to end, Owen," Wolfe said sadly. All this killing was wearing on him.

"I didn't start it, Luke," Corvallis said quietly.

"Neither did I," Wolfe said bluntly.

Corvallis sighed heavily. The weight of all these troubles sat heavily on him, and at the moment he felt every one of his fifty-two years. "I know my son was a gun-happy fool, Luke. But he was my son, and I've lost him," Corvallis said. He did not sound very convincing.

"You're going to lose your daughter, too," Wolfe said without any sympathy. "We were married this morning, and I figure to take Sally away from here—if necessary—as soon as all this is settled."

Corvallis sat, mouth gaping. Shock buzzed through his system, and he found himself short of breath.

"Pa?" Sally asked, suddenly alarmed. She stood and reached across the table, fearfully placing a hand on her father's arm. "Pa? You all right?"

Corvallis patted Sally's hand absent-mindedly. "Yes, yes," he mumbled, trying to absorb what he had just heard. He sat, trying to sort out the jumble of impressions, fears, worries, thoughts, emotions and information. But he could make no sense of it all. "Married?" he asked, his voice cracking.

"Yes, Pa," Sally said quietly, almost ashamed. She began to feel as if she had betrayed her father. She did not regret marrying Wolfe, but she began to wonder if it had not been done too fast. "This morning. Here.

205

Reverend Fordney . . ." She drifted off, knowing her father would not want to hear the details of her marriage right now. He was having enough trouble just accepting the fact of its reality.

"Why?" Corvallis asked, stunned yet.

"I asked her," Wolfe said. He, too, felt a little bad now about having done it the way they had. But it could not be changed now. "And," he added pointedly, "it looked like she was gonna be a widow within an hour of us gettin' wed."

"Curly and the boys," Corvallis said dully.

"Yes, sir."

Corvallis sat in thought for some time. Wolfe got up and found a bottle of bourbon he had stashed away. He brought it and two dirty glasses to the table. He filled the glasses and handed one to Corvallis, who took it with a nod. Wolfe sat and raised his glass toward Corvallis. The rancher returned the gesture and then downed the drink in one swallow.

Corvallis set the glass down. "You're right, Mr. Wolfe," he said. "This has to end. Here. And now."

"I'd like that. But it's got to come from you."

"I know," Corvallis said, pained at all the death and anguish that had come about.

"You sure you want to do that, Owen?"

"Yes." The single word was filled with pain.

"After all that's gone on?"

Corvallis nodded, not trusting his voice for the moment.

"You gonna be able to control your boys?" Wolfe asked sharply. "I reckon there's gonna be some of 'em not too fond of me after this afternoon. I take no pride in it, Owen . . ." He shrugged.

"They'll listen," Corvallis said with determination. Some animation returned to his face. "Or they'll ride

206

for someone else, somewhere else." He shook his head, his anger building steadily. Mostly anger at himself. He had been weak for too long. He had become so used to Aggie's odd ways, and backing off from confrontation with the fragile woman, that he seemed to have forgotten what had brought him so far along in life. Strength. And determination. They were the keys. And, by God, he vowed, silently, he would get them back and use them.

"You know, Luke," Corvallis said quietly. "I never wanted to send Curly and the others down here." He paused, ashamed at not having had enough courage to have stopped all this a long time ago. He explained his reservations—and the reasons he finally came up with to allow the men to come to town after Wolfe.

"I thought that if you heard they were coming and ran, it'd all be over. Or, at worse, if they lynched you it would end." He was close to tears—both from rage and frustration. "Damn, how could I have been so stupid?"

Wolfe believed Corvallis. There was just something about the man's demeanor—and the pain he wore so evidently on his craggy face—that could not be faked. Wolfe poured them each another glass of whiskey, and they touched glasses before drinking. "To the end of it," Wolfe said quietly.

Corvallis nodded and sipped. He looked at Sally and said, "I'm glad you took off and warned him, daughter." He wanted to tell her that he had wanted to warn Wolfe, but he could not say it.

"Me, too," she said with a grin that brightened her tear-stained face. She had been crying soundlessly at the exchange between the two men she loved.

"Can't say the same, though," Corvallis added ruefully, "at the method or timing of your marriage."

"We can have it done up proper later," Sally said,

dabbing at her eyes and blowing her nose. "If Luke's willing."

"If that's what you want, Sally," Wolfe said with a crooked smile.

"I'd like that."

They fell silent again, and Wolfe filled the two glasses again. They drank quietly.

"Well," Corvallis said dryly after the glass was empty, "I reckon you're gonna get your land sooner or later. I got no son now, and you're my son-in-law . . ." He shrugged.

Maybe that wasn't all that bad, Corvallis thought. Wolfe was a strong, daring man, and anyone would be proud to have him as a son-in-law—or as a son. And maybe he would become a grandfather at long last.

"But," Corvallis said with a grin, "you're going to have to wait a spell. It'll be time enough when I'm dead and gone."

"I can wait," Wolfe said. He was in no hurry now. Since he was married to Sally, he would have free run of the Lazy O Ranch. Perhaps Corvallis would even have them live there. He would have plenty of time to explore.

That thought was pleasing to Wolfe. But it was also disturbing, he found. Corvallis had been kind to him, even if the rancher had been unable to control his son. And he was trying now to make amends such as he could. There was no reason not to let Corvallis in on the deal. He noticed that Corvallis was watching him warily, and he raised his eyebrows in a question at the rancher.

"There's more to this land than you've let on, isn't there?" Corvallis asked after several moments' hesitation.

"What makes you say that?"

Corvallis shrugged. He ran an index finger around the rim of the glass, round and round. "Things just don't add up is all. I've said before you ain't the kind of man who'll take easy to farmin' or ranchin'. But there's other things. All your pokin' around over at the Lazy O. Why? You can't be lookin' for some cache of beaver pelts or personal items your grandpa left there forty years ago. And you can't be lookin' for some old camp he had. You ain't that sentimental."

"Reckon I ain't," Wolfe laughed. He was starting to relax for the first time in months. Even his head, which had started aching again, couldn't disturb the relief he was beginning to feel.

"There're other reasons," Corvallis continued. He, too, was beginning to feel better. The troubles of the past several weeks seemed far away, the deaths and bloodshed somehow not real.

"Like what?" Wolfe reached for the bottle again, but then did not grasp it. He figured it was not far past noon, though he wasn't sure. He had already had three stiff drinks, and had not eaten since breakfast. He had reached his limit for the time being. He sat back.

"Well," Corvallis said slowly, "you've spent a heap of time out at the Lazy O. Much of it," he added with a comforting smile at Sally, "with my daughter, I reckon. But there were plenty of times, I heard, when you were nosin' around on your own. A man don't spend that much time with something like that for no good reason. And a man especially doesn't do such things after he's been warned to stay away by the owner of the ranch." Corvallis grinned reassuringly, letting Wolfe know he was not angry at Wolfe's transgression.

"What?" Wolfe asked sharply, sitting straight upright, alert.

"I got reports you were out there twice since you . . .

since Aaron .." He decided there was no point in continuing. Wolfe would know the day he was talking about.

"I ain't been out there since that day," Wolfe said, cocking his head suspiciously.

"You haven't?" Corvallis asked in wonder. "But, if you . . ." The ranch hands had told him they had seen someone hanging around the Lazy O. The man had a palomino. Wolfe was the only man they knew of with a palomino and an interest in checking out the Lazy O Ranch. Maybe Wolfe was lying to him.

"No," Wolfe said flatly. He, too, wondered. Perhaps those uneasy feelings he had gotten occasionally had some validity.

"Then who . . . ?"

I don't know," Wolfe snapped. He considered telling Corvallis everything. But he was not sure. The land would be his now one day, and he could wait. Or could he? But he could tell by the look on Corvallis's face that the ranch owner did not really believe him when he said he had not been out to the ranch lately. Maybe he should tell Corvallis the whole story. That would convince him he was telling the truth, and probably solve several other problems at the same time. Wolfe decided he would find out who had been on the ranch and resolve that problem on his own. "I reckon," he added, "It was just some saddle tramp passin' through and found a comfortable spot to rest his bones a couple days." He shrugged. "Your boys were on the lookout for me, saw some dude with a palomino and just thought it was me."

"Reckon that's it," Corvallis said, though he was not convinced. Wolfe suddenly made up his mind. Corvallis—and especially Sally—deserved to know. "You're right, though, Owen," he said softly. "I got more of an

210

interest in the Lazy O than just the land."

"Oh?" Corvallis asked, interested.

Sally's eyes glittered with expectation.

Chapter Twenty-four

"Gold," Wolfe said, letting the single word hang enticingly in the air for a few moments, watching Corvallis's face with glee. "Gold, Mr. Corvallis."

"Gold?" Corvallis asked, eyes bright. Thoughts tumbled around in his brain, all of them unabashedly greedy.

"Gold," Wolfe reiterated.

"Maybe you better tell me about it, Luke."

Wolfe nodded. He stood and walked across the room to the bedside nightstand and picked up his fixings. Back at the big table by the window, he sat and leaned back in his chair. He talked as he rolled and then lighted his cigarette. "I wasn't exactly full truthful with you last time I told you why Gramps got the land," he said with a grin.

"That's obvious," Corvallis said dryly. "Now."

Wolfe dragged on the smoke and then blew it out. "Well. Gramps did take off with Russ Scarborough, his old friend from his mountain man days. And they did lead a wagon train of immigrants. And they did go to California."

It was 1850 when Scarborough stopped by Jeb Wolfe's store. "I'm leadin' wagon train out to Californy," he said in his jarbled language. "I could do with some old mountaineer knows his ways around trails and Injins and such-ever like. Will you ride?"

"I ain't sure," Wolfe shrugged. "I got me a wife, and some young 'uns now. I can't go traipsin' off just at the drop of a hat."

"Hell, it'll be shinin' times — jist like the ol' days," Scarborough said, eyes eager. "Ain't you got no hankerin' to see them peaceable Injins and them bean-eaters out there?"

"Reckon I do," Wolfe said skeptically, catching some of Scarborough's infectious enthusiasm. He grinned at his friend, who was more than half-froze to get on the trail. Scarborough was tall and skinny, and his thinning, mostly white hair once was thick, full and an orangish red. He was some years older than Wolfe, but they had always got on well.

Wolfe really wasn't much interested in tagging along, until Scarborough said, "Hell, Jeb, I ain't goin' to Californy just to lead a bunch of westerin' folk. Shoot, no. Why'd I do that? Damn foolishness. Ain't you heard?"

"Heard what?" Wolfe asked, not really understanding half of Scarborough's blabbering, as usual.

"There's gold out there, Jeb," Scarborough said, eyes glittering with greed. "Just lyin' 'round on the ground waitin' to be picked up and toted off."

"How come Jed Smith never mentioned it?" Wolfe asked suspiciously. "He was out there more'n once in the old days. He would've told us others."

"Hell, that Bible-thumpin' ol' fart just didn't know whar to look is all. Idjit couldn't even find beaver."

"I don't know," Wolfe said skeptically, shaking his head. It would, he thought, be nice to find a pot of gold and be able to live the good, easy life. Be more like Bob Campbell or the Chouteaus, with their fancy houses and such. Let somebody else run the store.

He glanced over at his wife, Rachel, who was listening, he knew, without seeming to. He would miss her terribly while he was gone. And he'd have to be gone at least a year. Maybe two. He hated to admit it — and would not admit it to anyone but himself, and, perhaps, Rachel — but for a freedom-loving man like him, he quite enjoyed being tied down here — as long as it was with Rachel.

Besides, he wondered, who would run the store for him while he was gone? Rachel could do some of it, but she would need help. He looked at Rachel again, and, like usual, she seemed to be reading his thoughts. She almost imperceptibly darted her chin toward the window. Wolfe looked out and saw his oldest son, Bill, working out in the yard. Bill was only eleven, though he would be twelve in a few months. Wolfe shook his head at Rachel, indicating he thought Bill was too young.

Scarborough, lost in his dream of finding gold, was paying them little mind. Rachel looked at Wolfe and nodded. "Yes he is," she seemed to say.

"Why'n't you go out to the corncrib and fetch us up a bottle, Russ," Wolfe said to his friend.

Scarborough was startled at having been brought back to reality. But he nodded, and hurried off. A bottle in the hand, he thought, was even better than gold in his dreams.

"You don't think he's too young, Rachel?" Wolfe asked when Scarborough had gone.

"You was workin' for your pa when you were his age."

"That wasn't the same. This here's a lot more responsibility than I had back then."

"We'll make do."

214

Wolfe thought a few moments, then asked, "You want I should go?" he asked.

"No, I don't *want* you should go," Rachel said, coming up and resting her hands on his broad shoulders. "I'll miss you somethin' awful. But I can tell you want to go, and I'll not stand in your way."

Unlike most men these days, Jeb Wolfe knew exactly how lucky he was to have such a woman as his wife. He looked down at her lovingly. She was no longer young. Then, again, neither was he. In fact, he had more than six years on her. Her face was lined with work, wear and time, though she was only in her early thirties. But he did not mind the lines. They gave Rachel character. She had never been what could be called a beautiful woman, but she was always handsome in a tall, plain sort of way. It was a look he liked. She was still handsome, grown more so to him with her fuller breasts and thicker hips brought on by childbearing.

Wolfe was torn. He did not want to leave Rachel; he enjoyed being with her, having her warm in his bed, always there when he needed her. And he liked doing for her, too.

Still, the pull of the West was strong. It was something in his blood. It had been a long time since he had been out to the mountains. He had made his forays out onto the plains to hunt and to the trading posts up the Missouri. But none had taken him back to those Shining Mountains. In his mind's eye he could see those glimmering purple mountains, peaks glittering with pristine snow; camps with buffalo tongue baking in the coals of a fire; smell manure and castoreum, and fresh killed buffalo; see the brightness of blood on a green glade and the sparkle of the dew in a mountain meadow; feel the hard, cold wind on his face.

"You won't mind?" he asked, voice as far away as

the mountains.

"No," she said. She would miss him, it was true, but she knew how deep his desire ran. She was also confident enough in herself to know he would come back to her.

Wolfe and Scarborough rode out the next morning before dawn filtered down. Wolfe and Rachel had said their unembarrassed goodbyes while a grinning Scarborough sat atop his ugly black mule watching. Rachel kissed Wolfe the way she had done when they were first married, holding out infinitely lustful promise. When Wolfe headed for his horse, he had a little trouble walking because of the excitement Rachel had created in him.

"I can wait a little, Jeb," Scarborough said with a disgustingly lecherous grin.

"Bah," he growled at Scarborough. But as they rode out of the chicken-crowded yard, Wolfe looked back and smiled warmly at his wife, wishing he had taken the time to go back into the house with her for a few minutes.

Their journey was mostly uneventful, and they left off the wild-eyed immigrants, all of whom had gold fever far worse than Scarborough. They stood in the middle of the main street of Sacramento looking around. The place was utterly mad with gold fever.

"You still want to head up into them hills lookin' for gold, Russ?" Wolfe asked.

"Reckon not," Scarborough said in disgust. All this madness was too much for him. People were leaving the city as fast as they arrived. Hundreds, thousands, streaming in and then out, all heading into the Sierra Nevada in a wild search for the yellow metal. Scarborough was, despite his greed, rather a simple man. He knew that if this many people were roaming the mountains looking for gold, it would be slim pickings for him and Wolfe.

"Me neither."

"What're we gonna do?"

"We'll think of somethin'," Wolfe said with a shrug.

They lived pretty high for a while, but with the prices being charged in Sacramento, their money ran out just after winter arrived. Wolfe thought of opening a store to supply the miners, but he had no money to get started. So he took a job at someone else's store. That lasted a week before he quit. Besides being too independent and having been his own boss for so long, he just couldn't charge these poor, benighted people the prices being asked.

Scarborough had taken work in a blacksmith shop. That lasted even less time than Wolfe's job at the store. He came in drunk from a lunch break once and listened quietly for a few minutes as the blacksmith who owned the shop berated him unmercifully in front of the other men. Scarborough took it for perhaps five minutes, then he calmly picked up a short-handled sledgehammer and cracked the blacksmith's head with it.

One of the other workers charged Scarborough, who calmly drew his new .36-caliber Colt revolver and shot the man down. The others stayed where they were. Scarborough sauntered out, but then ran next door to the livery stable. He hurriedly saddled his mule and skedaddled.

Wolfe had wondered where Scarborough had gotten off to when his friend did not return to the room that night or the next. But he figured Scarborough had just gone off on a bender for a while.

Scarborough returned nearly a week later, under the cover of night. He explained what had happened.

217

"Well, you did a heap of runnin' for nothin'," Wolfe said. "The 'smith's got a stove-up head, but he'll live. The other'n's still alive, too. Damn, you always were a piss-poor shot, Russ."

"Bah," Scarborough grumbled. He told Wolfe he had been living in a small camp several miles outside of town. He even displayed some gold.

"You took to minin' after all, Russ?" Wolfe asked, surprised.

"Hell, no," Scarborough said indignantly. "I've decided scrabblin' around in the dirt lookin' for gold don't shine with this old niggur at all."

"Well where'd that gold come from?" Wolfe thought he knew.

Scarborough grinned. "I 'found' it," he said with a shrug.

"Stole it is more like it," Wolfe said. He was not sure if he was angry or not.

"Well," Scarborough said, drawing the word out. He knew Wolfe would have reservations about such things. "I ain't hurt nobody. It's easy. All you do is find yourself somebody carryin' a little color ridin' down from one of the minin' camps. Flash your pistol at 'em, maybe knock 'em over the head, and relieve 'em of their gold. Hell, I don't even take all of it. I figure it's only right to leave 'em a little. I ain't greedy."

"They hang people 'round here for such doin's, Russ," Wolfe said. He had faced death many times before, and wasn't afraid of it. But he never went out tempting the fates with foolishness, either.

"Hell, Jeb, they just hang people that steal whole wagon loads of gold, or take everything a man's got." He grinned. "That's another reason I leave them somethin'. They ride into town here and tell the law they been robbed — but tell 'em the robber left 'em some

218

gold, and nobody'll believe 'em." He laughed at his ingenuity.

It was true. Anyone who gave such a tale to the law would be considered *loco*. Scarborough had come up with a good plan, and Wolfe began to think it was workable. He was intrigued. Besides, the thought of working in another store—or doing any job working for someone else—was repugnant. Not that he was a thief by nature, but such doings sounded better to him all the time. He thought about it for several days, though, and then hunger made the decision for him.

With the advent of the heart of winter, their pickings were slim. Most of the mining camps shut down for the most part, and travel was almost impossible. But they had made enough early on—and on their journey south to Fresno. They had wanted to get out of Sacramento so they did not have to worry about Scarborough being arrested because of what he had done at the blacksmith's shop. They wintered in Fresno, living off the gold they had acquired.

They were running low on the precious metal by the time spring came, and Wolfe had lost his inhibitions about acquiring the gold through theft. He and Scarborough went back to that profession with enthusiasm. On one of their forays, they wound up taking several horses so their victims—a bit more angry and bloodthirsty than others Wolfe and Scarborough had encountered—could not follow them. That got them to thinking. There was a considerable market for horses in California. But there was a bigger one for the animals back in Independence and environs, the jumping off point for most of the gold-rushers.

Wolfe missed Rachel, and wanted to get home to her. So he said to Scarborough, "How about we pull a few more jobs, take what gold we got, grab some horses

219

and head back for the states?"

"Reckon that'd be all right."

They increased the frequency of their holdups, and added horse-stealin' forays to their repertoire. Within two weeks, they had a sufficient amount of gold, they thought, and more horses than they could comfortably handle. In addition, a vigilance committee — formed by men of the small mining camps in the area that housed victims of their raids — took off after them.

Wolfe and Scarborough headed southeast, choosing to chance the desert rather than the mountains. The mountains contained too many mining camps, where word would get around of their activities. And they hoped that by taking the desert, they might discourage the posse.

They made it across the Colorado River, leaving the posse behind. But shortly afterward, a party of Mojaves attacked them. While Wolfe pushed the stolen horses eastward, Scarborough fought off that attack. Bolstered by reinforcements, the Mojaves chased after the two former mountain men, and the two forces began a series of running battles.

With hard running, and some luck, Wolfe and Scarborough put a little distance between themselves and the Indians. As they moved into more familiar land, Wolfe said, "We best take time to cache what valuables we got before them niggurs catch up to us."

"We stop to cache our plunder now," Scarborough shouted over their pounding horses, "and our hair's gonna be hangin' in some Mojave's lodge."

It took some talking, but Scarborough was finally convinced. "You got any ideas where?" he asked, still unhappy. He looked around at the barrenness of the flat land covered by sage and scrub pine.

Wolfe pointed east and a little north. "Me and Bill

Williams wintered up that way a long time back. Somewhere near there would be a good place."

"Then let's go."

Wolfe hesitated, then said, "We ain't gonna outrun them niggurs with all these horses and the pack mules slowin' us down."

Scarborough growled, but knew Wolfe was right. "What're you suggestin'?" he asked roughly.

"We let 'em go," Wolfe said bluntly.

"We went through a heap to get them beasts."

"I know, but we ain't gonna live long enough to sell 'em if we keep 'em with us."

"Shoot," Scarborough snapped. But he fired off his pistol and yelled, chasing the horses off.

Chapter Twenty-five

"Gramps got back to St. Charles all right," Luke Wolfe said. "And, as far as he knew then, Scarborough made it out safely, too. A few years later, Scarborough's boy Casey told Gramps that his old man had gotten killed in a card game down in Texas." He finished another cigarette and crushed it out on the top of the table.

"Didn't they ever hook up together again and go back to get the gold?" Sally asked. She was still bright-eyed with wonder and excitement.

"Reckon not," Wolfe shrugged. "Gramps never said for sure why. But from what I've heard, Scarborough died only two years later. When Gramps got back, he had nothin' to show for his year away. Fortunately, Grammer had kept the store goin' well, so Gramps just stepped back in and took up where he left off. He figured, or so he said, that Scarborough, who also came back with nothin', went to work to build up a stake to get back out there. But he wasn't no good with money, and probably gambled or drank away whatever he had made, and never got back around to it."

He shrugged. "Then, when Casey came along, Gramps didn't figure there was any hurry, I guess. I reckon he kept meanin' to go back on his own, once he held title to the land. But he never did."

Corvallis sat nodding. It was all clear to him now. "So that's why all the nosin' around," he muttered, not really angry, just musing.

"Yep," Wolfe said. He grinned. "Now that you know, I expect some help findin' it."

Corvallis laughed. "I got no troubles with that. But I expect a fair share."

"Me, too," Sally piped up brightly.

"You're my wife now, Sally," Wolfe said with a smile. "My share is your share." He paused. "I wouldn't have told you about it, Owen, if I wasn't plannin' on givin' you a share."

"I know."

"Damn, I'm gettin' hungry," Wolfe said. The hunger was making his head hurt a little again. All in all, for what he had been through today, he felt marvelous. It was even hard for him to remember that only six hours or so ago, he had been facing death out on Corvallis Road. It would have seemed like a bad dream to him if not for the light throbbing in his head and the bandages.

"Me, too," Sally said, realizing it. She had bolted down her breakfast this morning, hardly chewing it, since she wanted to get to Kaibab and warn Wolfe. With mention of food, though, her stomach sent up some unladylike rumblings. She flushed.

"Let's go next door," Wolfe suggested.

"What about the gold?" Corvallis asked.

"We'll talk about it after we eat," Wolfe said. He stood and walked to the bureau. He pulled out a new cotton shirt—the only decent one he had now—and put it on. He stuffed it into his pants. Then he found a pair of dirty socks on the floor and put them on before adding his boots. "Well, I'm ready," he said, standing.

Corvallis, still sitting at the table, looked at his

daughter. Red-faced, he asked, "Would you mind if I was to invite Miz Fletcher to join us?" He was clearly embarrassed.

Sally was shocked that he would even ask such a thing. How could he treat his wife—her mother—that way? Sally wondered. Even more, why bother to ask her? "I . . ." She stopped, not really knowing what to say.

Corvallis was aware that Wolfe was watching him and his daughter with interest, but he felt the need to try to explain. "I know you don't think such a thing is proper, Sally," he said quietly. He sighed. "But there's times things go on between a man and woman . . ." His embarrassment was acute. "Well, Sally, your ma ain't been exactly wifely toward me for some years now. She . . ." He had to stop; his discomfit had tangled his tongue.

Sally thought back, and realized with a shudder that her father probably was telling the truth. It was not a common thing for husbands and wives to display much affection in public, but even such rigid moral codes that existed here could not account for the fact that she had never, ever seen her mother and father exchange a warm glance or a loving word. Her mother had been caring toward her and her brother, but never toward Owen. With her husband, Aggie Corvallis had been aloof and withdrawn.

"It's all right, Pa," she said, her sudden understanding making her quite sympathetic toward her father. And she vowed silently that she would never allow herself to become like her mother.

Corvallis beamed as he stood. He led the way out of the room, with Wolfe and Sally following, walking arm in arm. In the lobby, Corvallis hurried ahead of his daughter and son-in-law. He spoke quietly, earnestly with Alma Fletcher for a few moments. Alma grinned and nodded. She came out from behind her desk.

Corvallis once again led the way. He was followed by Alma, then Wolfe and Sally, still with arms linked. As he passed through the doorway, Wolfe was alert, and his right hand rested on his Colt. But Corvallis was already shouting to his men, who had been waiting outside all this time. "Go on home, boys," he said jovially. "Things're settled."

One of the hands spotted Wolfe and pointed at him. "What'n hell's he doin' here alive?" the man asked in a loud voice.

"He's my guest," Corvallis said sternly.

"He killed Curly," the hand said. "And Harv and . . ."

"You boys started it," Corvallis roared.

"Like hell," another hand shouted back at his boss. "It was your doin'."

"If that was my doin', then so's this," Corvallis bellowed, overriding the angry clamor from the four cowpokes. "It's over."

"Not till that bastard's hangin' dead from a tree," the first cowpuncher snapped. The others growled assent.

Corvallis pulled his new .38-caliber pocket Remington from the shoulder holster worn under his striped wool suit coat. "First one moves'll be a guest of old Klockschmidt right off," he barked. "Now you boys listen to me. I lost more'n all of you. I lost a son. And I lost two foremen. I don't mind losin' a third, Jace. You push me too far, and they'll plant you alongside the others."

Corvallis paused. Then, "Mr. Wolfe here's married my daughter. That makes him family. Any of you boys—or anybody left back at the ranch—don't like that, you can ride on. I'll pay you right now, if you want."

"But, boss," Jace protested. "He killed all those men. He . . ."

Corvallis sighed. "That was all my fault, Jace," he admitted, feeling relief when he did. "I should've never let it go that far. My son and Ev pushed Mr. Wolfe too far, and Luke killed them for their troubles. I should've let it end there. But I didn't. And as a result, a bunch of my ranch hands got killed, too. I ain't real proud of that, but it's water under the bridge. We'll let it drop. Either accept that, or leave." He hefted his shiny, nickel-plated Remington. "Or make a play."

Jace looked like he was considering the latter. He changed his mind as Wolfe suddenly was standing next to Corvallis. Wolfe's Colt was still in the holster, but his hand rested on it.

"Ah, hell," Jace said, spitting. He grabbed his saddle-horn and swung up into his saddle. "The boys ain't gonna like this," he snapped.

"You're the new foreman, Jace," Corvallis said coolly. "Make 'em like it. Or run 'em off."

"Shoot," Jace snarled. He jerked the reins hard, snapping the horse's head around. He jammed his spurs into the horse, and the animal bolted forward. The three other cowpokes leaped into their saddles and raced after Jace, almost knocking down an old woman in their charge.

"Fools," Corvallis said. He stuffed his gun away and turned toward the restaurant, Alma at his side. Wolfe allowed Sally to take his arm again and followed them. Things should be real interesting out at the Lazy O, he thought. He would have to talk to Sally about staying in town—at least for a while, to lessen the possibility of trouble.

The four ate well—at Corvallis's expense. During the meal, they allowed their tensions to dwindle, until they

226

were laughing and having a fine old time, relieved. Sally had the hardest time of it. She was confused and emotions soared through her, one banging into another, each fighting for its rightful place of dominance.

She was happy—almost deliriously so—to be married to Wolfe. But at the same time, she was sharing lunch with a woman who had been made love to by her husband—and her father. Still, she liked Alma a lot. She understood why her father spent time with Alma, but she felt sorry for her mother, too. She was afraid that if she did not measure up to his standards, that Wolfe would, like her father had, turn to Alma, or someone like her.

It was almost too much for her, and she thought her mind would spin into craziness. Then she looked at Wolfe, and he smiled at her. He leaned over and whispered, "You needn't worry about any of it."

She grinned as relief washed over her. She hadn't realized she had been so transparent, but it no longer mattered. She knew Wolfe loved her, so Alma was not a threat to her. And her father's life was his own. She had too many things to occupy her time now: she had to learn to become a wife—and a woman—plus there was the gold to be found. She would be plenty busy without having to worry about all these other things.

After their meal, the four went back to the hotel. Alma, despite knowing that something was up with her friends, stayed in the lobby. She was curious, but not bitter. She figured it was family business. She sort of wished, though, that something would happen to Aggie Corvallis. If that occurred, she felt sure Owen would ask her to marry him. It was a pleasurable thought. But she shrugged. She was not about to do anything to Aggie, and so she would have to be content with life as it was. And it was far from bad.

In Wolfe's room, Wolfe, Corvallis and Sally sat at the table again. Wolfe poured himself and Corvallis another drink. When it was finished, Corvallis asked, "Well, where do we look?"

Wolfe reached into his pocket and pulled out a small leather wallet. From it he took the map Jeb Wolfe had made so many years ago. He stood and spread the fading map out on the table. Corvallis and Sally also stood, crowding up on each side of Wolfe.

Wolfe stabbed a finger at the map. "There it is," he said. "Or so Gramps told me."

Corvallis shoved Wolfe out of the way so he was centered at the map. He bent over, peering carefully at the paper. "Can't make out too much on here," he said.

"You just need your glasses, Pa," Sally said. "Let me look."

Corvallis stepped aside and gave his position to Sally. She bent and peered at the map. The writing, what little there was of it, was faded and hard to read. But she thought she could begin to place some of the symbols. "Look, Pa," he said, pointing out a spot with a slim, delicate index finger, "it's that little spring west of the house, nestled down among them aspens in that canyon."

"Damned canyon," Corvallis muttered at Wolfe. "Goddamn cattle're always gettin' down in there. Takes us days to get 'em out with all those trees, brush and such in there." He bent and looked. "Sure enough, Sally," he said.

"You know the spot?" Wolfe asked. For the first time since he had arrived in Kaibab, he felt excitement at the prospect of finding the gold. He had never really believed it would be possible, though he was determined to make every effort to find it.

"Quite well," Corvallis said.

228

"You think they could've buried the gold there?" Wolfe asked.

Corvallis shrugged. "It's an out of the way place. Accessible, but not easily seen. Could be a good place, I guess." He thought. "Depends, I guess, on how much time they had, and how close they were. But, knowing your grandpa was a mountain man and had made the map, I would reckon he knew what he was doin'."

"Then let's go," Wolfe said.

"No," Sally said firmly, spinning away from the map to face him.

"No?" he questioned.

"No," she emphasized. "You've been hurt and you need some rest. Tomorrow's soon enough."

In his excitement at being so close to the gold, he had virtually forgotten his wounds—and this morning's battle that had caused them. Now that Sally had mentioned them, though, they started hurting again, and he secretly felt relieved that she had vetoed his idea. "Yes, ma'am," he said, trying to sound meek, but not managing it.

"Don't worry about it," Corvallis said with a laugh. "It ain't the last time you'll be told what to do by a woman. I can guarantee you that." He chuckled some more, then added, "Besides, that gold's been there thirty-some years. Another day ain't gonna make a difference."

Wolfe looked at Corvallis slyly. "And I suppose you'll be goin' back to the Lazy O, eh?" He grinned. "So you can get an early start on the search?"

"That's an idea," Corvallis said, rubbing his chin, as if in thought. Then he grinned. "Actually, I thought I'd stay right here at Alma's hotel." He winked at Wolfe, where Sally could not see. "We can all ride out together tomorrow morning."

229

"Sounds fair." Wolfe took a deep breath and let it out slowly. "Well, Owen," he said, feeling awkward, "it's been a long day, with more than its share of excitement. I expect I could do with some rest."

"And," Sally said bluntly, though she blushed furiously, "it's our weddin' night, Pa."

Corvallis fought back the smile that threatened to overtake him and left.

"I thought he'd never go," Sally said, walking up to Wolfe.

Chapter Twenty-six

Wolfe was sweating like a stuck hog, perspiration pouring down his skin. He had taken off his shirt and tossed it aside, and the top of his longjohns was soaked. He tossed another shovelful of dirt onto the growing mound, and then jabbed the spade into the soil at his feet.

"Goddamn," he breathed. He pulled a bandanna from his back pocket and wiped his sopping face. "Christ, Owen, I thought it wasn't supposed to get this hot up here in the high country."

"You just ain't used to workin' is all," Corvallis laughed. He was sitting in the shade of an aspen, sipping from a canteen. Sally sat nearby, waving a paper fan in front of her face. She giggled.

They had come back to the ranch early. In fact, Corvallis had come pounding on Wolfe's door before dawn. Since it had been his wedding night, Wolfe had been awake until the wee hours, experimenting with his new bride. Grumbling, he had gotten up and stumbled to the door. Without a great deal of humor, he opened it.

"Time's a-wastin', Luke," Owen said cheerily. He, too, had been up rather late, entertaining—and being entertained by—Alma Fletcher. It had made him feel like a new man. Wolfe looked a lot worse off than the much older Corvallis, but, of course, Corvallis had not been shot less than twenty-four hours ago.

"It's the middle of the night, for pity's sake," Wolfe grumbled. He was acutely conscious that Sally was lying, naked and desirous, in the bed behind him.

"Like hell. It'll be daylight before long."

"Go away, Pa," Sally called out from the bed.

"Bah," Corvallis growled good-naturedly.

"Give us an hour or so," Wolfe said somewhat contritely. "We'll have breakfast and then head out."

Corvallis grumbled but agreed. He left. Wolfe shut the door, waited a few seconds and then opened it again. He peeked out and grinned. Alma Fletcher was just pulling Corvallis back into her room. Wolfe shut the door and went back to bed—and Sally's waiting arms.

Alma must have kept Corvallis well-occupied, Wolfe thought, for it was almost an hour and a half before the rancher rapped on the door again. Wolfe and Sally, dressed and ready to go, went through the door together. They smiled in their new knowledge of each other, and at the satisfied look on Corvallis's face.

After breakfast, they saddled their horses and rode to the ranch. They stopped at the barn for two shovels, several canteens of water, and some food. Then Corvallis led the way toward the canyon.

Wolfe had the bothersome feeling that someone was watching—or following—them. He dropped back a bit. He looked behind him frequently, trying to spot anything that would indicate they were not the only people here. But he neither saw nor heard anything out of the ordinary. He finally shrugged, putting it down to nervousness at the thought of actually finding the gold soon.

He did not really believe that someone had been following him all along, or that someone with a palomino had misled the ranch hands into thinking he had been at the ranch recently. Still, the possibility existed, and he had had this odd sensation before.

Wolfe finally growled at himself in annoyance. The last time he had had the sensation, he *had* found someone following him—Sally. He was just nervy, he guessed.

The one real entrance to the canyon was a gentle slope, and Wolfe hardly noticed they were moving into it. But the canyon sloped down quickly until the walls on either side rose forty feet high. At the far end, the canyon seemed to end.

Wolfe looked at Corvallis in confusion. "You sure this is it, Owen?" he asked.

"Yep," Corvallis said with a grin.

"But . . ." He stopped, thinking. "You told me it was hell's own work to get cattle out of here. This don't look so bad."

Corvallis grinned again. "Follow me," he said.

The canyon hooked hard left, and passed through a narrow opening, almost invisible since it was obscured by brush. Wolfe nodded.

Just through the "gate," as Wolfe thought of it, they skirted a jumbled heap of boulders that had fallen from the cliff. Corvallis stopped, and Sally and Wolfe pulled up alongside and stopped also.

The back wall rose up as high as the other walls. From above, Wolfe thought, the canyon must look like a giant knife wound in the earth, with this bowl the point of the initial stabbing.

A short way in front of the back wall, nestled in amongst the trees, were a spring and the remains of a cabin. A creek ran up to the spring. Aspens, tall and wiry, rose up nearly as tall as the lip of the cliff sides. Some ponderosa pines were scattered through the aspens, and dotted the rim above. In front of the ruins of the cabin was a small open glade, roughly circular, perhaps twenty feet across at any point. To the left in front of the glade was a huge cottonwood.

The three dismounted and drank water from their canteens. It was hot, and would get worse. Wolfe pulled out his map, and the trio gathered around to look at it.

"Best I can tell from this," Corvallis said, "is that it'd be over there by that big cottonwood." He pointed.

"The map says to look for a small cottonwood near the spring."

"When did they make the cache, Luke?" Corvallis asked, making a face at Wolfe.

"Fifty, fifty-one. Why?"

"That was more than thirty years ago, Luke," Corvallis said, as if teaching a foolish child. "That damn cottonwood wouldn't have been half the size it is now."

Wolfe felt incredibly stupid. But it was never something he had thought of. "Christ, what a fool I am," he mumbled. In more normal tones he said, "That must be it." He took a last look at his map, folded it up and stuffed it into his pocket.

They mounted and rode forward. The towering cottonwood was ten feet from the spring, just at the edge of the glade. It would seem, Wolfe thought, as they neared the tree, a likely spot for a cache.

They stopped again and tied their horses to trees. Corvallis tossed a shovel to Wolfe and said, "Have at it, Luke." He grinned as he sat himself on a rock in the shade.

"Ain't you gonna help?" Wolfe griped.

"I've done my part," Corvallis said, settling in.

"Like hell," Wolfe said, but he was not really angry. He grabbed the shovel and walked to the tree. He went to the northeast side and rested his back against the trunk. His heart pounded with excitement. He measured off six paces. With a deep breath, he jabbed the spade into the earth and levered out the first blade of dirt.

He began to sweat as he worked. He dug in a three-foot circle in the shade of the tree's wide foliage. He persevered, though he grumbled often at the less-than-helpful comments offered by his wife and father-in-law. His enthusiasm and excitement wore off, wilting under the heat and exertion like an icicle in the August sun.

After an hour of digging, his head was throbbing mildly again. His leg ached, and the back of his shoulders stung from where sweat dripped into the wound there. In addition, his arm, back and leg muscles began to quiver from all the exertion. He could not understand how his grandfather and Scarborough had dug the cache, buried the gold and then covered it up well enough to not be found again in so quick a time when they knew a bunch of Indians was looking for them.

He was two feet down, and had enlarged the circle to about six feet when he finally tossed the shovel down. "I need a rest," he said, stepping out of the hole. He pulled his shirt off and hung it over a bush nearby.

As Wolfe mopped his face with his bandanna, Sally came to him with a canteen of water. He took it gratefully and swallowed deeply. Then he poured some over his head and face, enjoying its coolness. He took a few minutes to smoke a cigarette—and share a few quick snorts from Corvallis's flask while Sally filled her canteen at the spring. Then he went back to work, somewhat refreshed.

After another hour and a half of digging, Wolfe was getting quite discouraged. He began cursing more, arguing with and yelling at every rock or tree root he hit. The deeper he got, the harder the digging. He was down about three feet now, and began to wonder if he had the right spot. Jeb Wolfe and Scarborough could not have had time to dig much deeper than this, he figured.

"Come and eat," Sally finally said, smiling at him.

Wolfe grudgingly agreed. While he had lost his zest for the search, and he was beginning to doubt the gold's existence, he was the type of man to never give something up once he started it. But he knew a break and some food would be helpful right now.

He walked down to the spring, tearing the bandage off his head while he walked. When he got there, he lay down on his stomach and plunged his face into the shallow pool of cold, fresh water. He brought his head up, shaking it vigorously from side to side. Still prone, he drank deeply, slurping up the spring water. Then he strolled back to where Corvallis and Sally waited.

He sat on the blanket opposite Sally and next to Corvallis. Sally began passing out pieces of salted beef and some biscuits. They ate silently.

When they were finished, Wolfe rolled and lit a cigarette. He puffed a few moments, thinking. Then he said quietly, "You know, Owen, I don't think this's the right spot."

"Why?"

"Hell, Gramps and Scarborough were diggin' knowin' they had a band of Injins nearby half-froze to raise their hair," Wolfe said, shaking his head, disgusted that he had led them on a wild-goose chase.

"Half-froze?" Corvallis asked with a smile.

"An expression Gramps used a lot. Means hellbent or something similar."

"Oh," Corvallis said, nodding.

"Anyway, with that, they couldn't've dug too deep."

"Even in a place like this," Corvallis said thought-

236

fully, "a lot of soil can blow around. Hell, in thirty years, you could get a couple feet of dirt blow in from above." He pointed, and everyone looked at the sharp edge of the canyon against the solid blue of the sky.

"You think I ought to go down farther?" Wolfe asked, uncertain whether he should—or wanted to—make the effort.

"You want the gold?" Corvallis countered.

Wolfe grinned, his mind made up. He flicked the cigarette away and blew out a stream of smoke. Suddenly a flask was thrust before his face.

"Maybe a belt of this'll help ease your labors," Corvallis said with a chuckle.

"Reckon it would," Wolfe said, taking it and swallowing a healthy dose. He handed it back and wiped his mouth off on the back of his hand. "Well, that hole ain't gettin' dug with me settin' here on my butt like this." He stood, and with renewed vigor grabbed his shovel.

He dug furiously at first, but quickly slowed down as his muscles complained. He got into a steady, smooth rhythm: sink the blade, jam it down with a boot, flex and then jerk the dirt up over the rim of the hole. He almost lost himself, letting his mind float free, doing the work almost automatically.

He had no idea how much time had passed since he had eaten, but suddenly the shovel thunked into something solid. His hands, blistering a little from all the spade work, stung when the blade hit whatever it was. "Goddamn rocks," he mumbled. He pulled the shovel out and moved it a few inches, hoping to get around the rock and get it loose. He hit something again.

Wolfe came out of his fog. What the hell? he wondered. He scraped dirt away from the solid surface he had encountered. This was no rock, he realized.

Quickly he cleared away more dirt from the top of the object. Within minutes, it was evident that what he had found was a metal box of some kind. He felt his heart pounding. This must be it! he thought, excitement coursing through him.

He dug wildly around the perimeter of the box, sending shovelfuls of dirt flying wildly. Sally and Corvallis, sitting nearby, saw the dirt shower, and chuckled at each other. Wolfe must've gotten angry again at all the work and was taking it out on the dirt.

Suddenly Wolfe knelt. He grabbed the handles of the box and tugged, helping it to break through the last of the dirt that held it. "Eureka!" he roared.

Sally and Corvallis leaped up from their seats and ran to the hole. They gazed down, seeing Wolfe pulling on a metal box. Sally bounced in exhilaration, while Corvallis radiated excitement.

Suddenly a voice said, "Come on out of the hole, Lucas."

Wolfe stood slowly, a chill gripping his heart. He looked past Corvallis and Sally, who seemed frozen in fear, and saw a man, pistol out and cocked, walking toward them. He was leading a palomino.

"Uncle Casey," Wolfe said tightly.

Chapter Twenty-seven

"I take it you know this man, Luke," Corvallis said, voice betraying his fear. The man holding the gun on them was not the type to inspire confidence.

"Yep," Wolfe said in distaste, stepping up out of the hole. He stood at Sally's right; her father was to her left. "Much as I hate to admit it."

"He the one you've mentioned before? Your grandfather's friend's son?" Corvallis asked, never taking his eyes off the gunman.

"Yep, goddamnit." He sighed. "Owen, meet Casey Scarborough, the son of Gramps's old partner, Russ. Casey, this is Owen Corvallis. And," he added after a moment's pause, "my wife, Sally."

Wolfe looked at his "uncle." Scarborough was roughly Wolfe's height, and weight, but somewhat paunchy with age—which was about forty. He wore a filthy, red wool shirt and a pair of equally soiled twill pants. His boots were scuffed, and his hat was stained with sweat and faded to an indistinguishable color. He wore a long canvas duster, open and flapping a little in the slight breeze. He had not shaved for at least a week.

"I heard you were dead, Casey," Wolfe said slowly. He wiped his sweating hands on his pants, inching his right hand up toward the Colt.

"I don't look very goddamn dead, do I?" Casey snarled. He had a voice that sounded something like a broken saw with several missing teeth cutting through a hardwood log.

"You smell it, though," Wolfe said humorlessly.

"Still the smart-ass little punk, ain't you?" Scarborough laughed gruffly, showing some missing and broken teeth. He was an altogether unsavory character. "And I'd keep your hand away from that Colt." There was no need for him to complete the threat.

Wolfe froze, eyes glittering. His hands twitched, but stayed where they were. "What do you want here, Casey?" he asked harshly.

Scarborough laughed gruffly again, the sound offensive to Wolfe and the others. "Same goddamn thing you do, boy." The last word dripped hatred and derision.

"What're you talkin' about?" Wolfe asked, trying to project innocence.

"Gold, boy. I want the gold. I want *my* gold."

"We got no gold here, Casey," Wolfe said, still trying to appear guileless.

Again the hideous laugh. "I suppose, boy, that you're jist out here diggin' fer your health."

"Lion trap," Wolfe said dryly. "We've had a few pumas ravagin' the stock of late. We want to catch 'em."

"Can the crap, boy. I been watchin' you a spell. I know goddamn well there ain't no lions been botherin' the stock." He spit a thick stream of tobacco juice into the dust, the trail of it splattering across his chin. He paid it no mind.

"How'd you find out about it?" Wolfe asked, angry, but trying to keep the feeling in check. He was dead sure he would have to kill Casey to get out of this mess, and he did not want to be too tense to make his play when the time came.

"It was years ago, I first got the hint." He got a faraway look in his eyes, but Wolfe was not foolish enough to think Scarborough was paying so little atten-

240

tion that Wolfe could try something.

Casey Scarborough was almost ten years old when he overheard his father, drunk as he so often was, bragging about his buried treasure of gold. He told his equally drunken cohort how he and Jeb Wolfe had outwitted the stupid Mojaves and buried their hoard. And how he was going to get his stake together and go back out to that wild land and get that gold.

The boy was not sure he believed the old man. But soon after that, old Russ Scarborough disappeared for a while. When Casey asked his mother where his father had gone, she had answered cryptically, "Back to the mountains, boy." The words had been slurred since she was drunk, as she usually was, and in between entertaining her men friends.

When Scarborough returned home to Jackass Flats, Texas, he seemed defeated, crushed. He would not talk about where he had gone or what had happened. But he became even more obstreperous than usual, and often got into drunken brawls over the slightest things. He drank more than before, too, and his relationship with Round-Heels Ethel, Casey's mother, deteriorated until the marriage seemed to consist solely of arguments, fights and screaming matches.

One night, though, Casey's father did not come home. Late that night Sheriff Tull arrived and spoke quietly to Round-Heels Ethel for a bit. Casey's mother screamed, and Casey snuck up close to the door that separated him from his mother and the sheriff, in time to hear: "He was cheatin' again, Ethel. And drunk as usual. The other dude called him out. Russ pulled his gun, but he was too goddamn drunk to shoot straight. He got off two shots before the other boy put him in the boneyard."

The sheriff left Scarborough's pistol, which Casey stole the next morning, knowing that if it was left around, his mother would sell it for another drink.

A year later, Ethel herself died, drowning in her own vomit after a particularly heavy night of drinking. Casey, almost a man already, though he was just ten years old, packed up what few things he had, kicked over a burning coal-oil lamp, stole a horse and rode out as the rickety shack he had called home burned behind him. He had no idea really where to go, so he just wandered.

But all the time, he had held the thought of the gold his father had talked about. If he had the gold—and it must be real, for his father had said so—well, the possibilities were endless, even for a boy-man.

He had heard Jeb Wolfe's name from his father frequently, but only the once in connection with the gold. But his father had mentioned more than once that Wolfe lived up in Missouri, so Casey turned his horse in that direction.

Jeb Wolfe took the poor waif in, after hearing the sad story of how the boy's father and mother had died. Casey mentioned nothing about the gold. He was already cunning enough to know how—and when—to keep his mouth shut.

He persevered in the harsh household, as he saw it. He felt an outsider, even after many years in the house. Many was the time he planned to run away, but the thought of his father's gold always kept him put. He would endure anything to get that gold.

Casey could not see that Jeb and Rachel Wolfe—and their children—would be glad to make him part of the family. But old Jeb Wolfe had certain rules and standards he expected to be kept. Casey was unwilling—or unable—to keep them, so he was frequently in trouble. More than once he stoically accepted the unfairness of

242

the strap Wolfe laid across his backside.

He took to "brother" Bill's child, Luke, right off, knowing he surprised the entire Wolfe clan with it. But even he did not know why. It just happened. That was all he knew, and so he accepted it.

He saw the Civil War as his means of salvation. He had watched with hate and annoyance as Bill Wolfe rode off with his fancy blue uniform. Scarborough, born in Texas, was a Southerner through and through. But he joined up on the Rebels' side more to annoy the Wolfe family than anything else.

He had heard of William Quantrill and Bill Anderson and their forays. Such things excited him immensely. And it was to them that he went. He used to laugh, thinking how the foolish Jeb Wolfe had never learned that Scarborough was never a regular in the Confederate Army.

He got wounded and so went to the only home he knew—the Wolfe place—to recover. Several months later, Wolfe asked Scarborough to go to Arizona Territory with him. His father had never mentioned Arizona Territory, but just the way Wolfe was talking led Scarborough to believe that Wolfe was going for the gold.

Scarborough was scared, afraid he might betray himself. If Wolfe was really going to pick up the gold after all these years, Scarborough certainly wanted to be along. All he would have to do was let Wolfe lead him to the gold, dig it up, and then shoot Wolfe dead. He could ride off happily with the gold.

But while he was excited, Scarborough did not want to seem too anxious, lest Wolfe suspect Scarborough knew about the gold.

Scarborough had finally let himself be persuaded, and they left. He was heavily disappointed when no gold was found, though he did try to implant into his mind the lay of the land. He suspected several spots that might have the cache, since Wolfe had spent no more time looking in one place over another.

All he needed now was the map, he figured. With that, and having seen the land, he would be able to find the gold. He tried several times in the next couple of years to steal the map, but he always failed.

After they returned to Missouri, Bill came home. But the two men did not get along at all. Scarborough, frustrated at his lack of luck, began taking it out on young Luke. And Scarborough was happy when Bill decided to leave. He even watched surreptitiously from outside the door as Wolfe gave his son some papers. Scarborough assumed it was the map to the gold.

Still, Scarborough managed to bide his time some more, waiting, long after Bill and his family—except Luke—had left.

But he could not control his temper, and Scarborough became an increasingly wild man. Wolfe began to suspect Scarborough was involved in illegal activities, but he could never be sure—until one afternoon, three years after Bill had left, when Wolfe caught Scarborough in the midst of raping a town girl in the back room of the store.

Wolfe was still immensely strong, despite his age, and he was made more so by the blinding rage he felt. He grabbed Scarborough and pulled him off the girl, who screamed once Scarborough's hand was gone from her face. Wolfe flung Scarborough roughly on the floor, as the girl ran out. Scarborough went for his pistol, but Wolfe had his out first.

"I won't abide such doin's from any niggur, anywhere," Wolfe snarled. "Especially in my home or my store. You're too goddamn big and old to whup, boy. And I'm about half-froze to give ye a lead pill in your meat bag. But since you're the son of an old friend, I'll not kill ye now. But if I find ye around my property in

244

fifteen minutes by the clock, you'll be dead in sixteen."

He relieved Scarborough of his pistol and stalked out, burning with a desire to kill his son's friend. Twenty years ago he would have done so without a qualm, no matter whose son he was. But now, he wasn't sure why he didn't, only that he didn't.

Twelve minutes later, Scarborough was riding away, whipping his horse. He had an extra shirt, some coffee, sugar, flour and jerky in a sack hanging from his saddle, and an empty pistol—his father's—in his belt.

In some one-horse town in Arkansas, Scarborough met up with three men he had ridden with in the Civil War. They, like he, had lived on the far side of the law in the six years since the end of the war. They joined up, and continued their outlaw ways, robbing banks, stages and trains, then escaping into the Indian nations.

Finally with something of a stake, Scarborough told his companions about the gold that he figured was his. They rode on into Arizona Territory. Scarborough knew where Jeb had claimed the land, so he went there first, but the land was barren.

From letters Bill had sent home before Scarborough had been tossed out by Jeb Wolfe, he knew Bill had been working in Prescott. Scarborough led his three cohorts to that city, only to learn that Bill Wolfe was no longer there. It took almost two years of searching—taking time out for a new spate of robberies, rapes and other assorted felonies—before Scarborough found the Bill Wolfe family.

"Howdy, Bill," Scarborough said, riding up to the farm house in the eastern section of the territory. He grinned, hopefully disarmingly.

"What're you doin' here, Casey?" Wolfe asked, suspicious, and wary. He had never liked Scarborough much, and he did not take to the three unsavory companions he had with him now.

245

"Let's let bygones be bygones, Bill," Scarborough said, trying to be friendly.

"It's too late for that." Wolfe shrugged. "But we ain't ever turned anybody away without a meal." He felt afraid and was not sure why. He knew he should not let these men stay, even for a little while, but it was true the Wolfes had never turned people away hungry.

All his fears were given purpose that night when Scarborough shot Elsie, Wolfe's youngest child, to death in her bed. The gunshot woke the rest of the family, and they were herded into the kitchen of the log house.

"Where's the gold, Bill?" Scarborough demanded.

"What gold?" Wolfe asked, confused, and speaking truthfully.

Scarborough did not believe Wolfe each time he said he knew nothing about the gold. The outlaw grew more and more angry about it, and finally ordered one of his henchmen to kill Galen, the younger son.

Wolfe's eyes grew very wide with fear and rage. "I don't know nothin' about no gold!" he roared, shuffling over a little, getting between the outlaws and Betsy and Mark and Betty, trying to protect his family.

But Scarborough was crazed now, and soon the Wolfe clan had been slaughtered. Wolfe had fought as well as he could, but he had little chance to do anything when confronted by the maniacal fury of four armed men.

Just before he went down, his lifeblood flowing out and blackness creeping over him, Wolfe saw one of the outlaws wrestling Betsy to the floor. Another was tearing off her nightclothes, giggling with degenerate glee.

As Wolfe felt death wash over him, he heard Betsy scream. It was the last thing he ever heard.

Chapter Twenty-eight

"Apaches killed Bill and his family," Luke Wolfe said obstinately, staggered by the story he had just heard, and not wanting to believe it. Rage coursed through his veins as if it was part of his blood.

"Hell," Scarborough said with his disgusting laugh, "that's just what I told that old fart Jeb."

After slaughtering Bill Wolfe and his family, Scarborough and his three cronies ransacked the house looking for maps or anything that might help them find the gold. But it was to no avail. They hacked at the bodies, and then set the place on fire, hoping to make it look like Apaches had done the devilish deeds.

Then the four outlaws rode off. Somewhere in New Mexico, one of the men got on Scarborough's nerves, and Casey cold-bloodedly murdered him. Laughing, the other three continued on. But several weeks later, Scarborough decided to head for Missouri, and left his two friends in some wretched saloon deep in the Indian Nations.

He rode on to St. Charles and walked straight into Jeb Wolfe's store. He stood quietly, an arrogant grin on his face, waiting for Wolfe to spot him.

It didn't take long. Wolfe's face darkened with anger

when he spotted Scarborough. "Git the hell out of my store," Wolfe roared, snatching up a scattergun from under the counter. "And git the hell out of St. Charles."

"Hold on now, old man," Scarborough said smugly. "I got news you might want to hear."

"Say and then git out."

"Bill and his family was killed by Apaches," he said, almost grinning.

Wolfe's face blanched, but he otherwise kept his composure. "You've said it, now drag your butt out of here."

Scarborough's eyes bugged out as rage throbbed in his blood. He wanted desperately to gun Wolfe down. But that scattergun never wavered.

He spun and stomped out, spurs jangling. He leaped on his horse and roared out of town, nearly killing several people along the way. He had come up here thinking that maybe now that Wolfe knew his son and the whole family was dead, he might relent and consider Scarborough as an heir, perhaps even get the map he needed. He realized now that he had been foolish to think that, and that made him all the more angry. He knew his mental faculties were limited, but he hated to have it pointed out to him.

So angry was he, that he was unable to think clearly. Several months later, after he had hooked back up with his two outlaw companions again, he began to think about the situation. Wolfe had no one left, except his wife. And Luke! It came to Scarborough in a flash, and he almost shook with excitement. How could he not have thought of it before?

Scarborough was not very smart, but he had a certain natural cunning. He knew he could not go back to St. Charles to find Luke, who might not even be there.

That was the first thing—finding out where Luke was. So he concocted a plan to have one of his two partners—Asa Capert—go to St. Charles. Scarborough and the third partner—Clu Morgan—would wait outside the town.

Capert spent three days in St. Charles drinking and whoring. When Capert got back to his friends, Scarborough was beside himself with anger. "What did you find out?" he asked, snarling as he paced around their small camp.

"Luke ain't here," Capert said with a semi-grin. He was hungover and in no mood for taking any crap from Scarborough. "He left out a year ago. Maybe more."

"Where?" Scarborough demanded, trying to keep his never cool temper somewhat in check. He was not having any more success with it now than he usually did.

"Hide huntin'. Could be anywhere from Canada to Mexico."

"It took you three days to find that out?" Scarborough screamed in rage. He was practically spitting in his anger.

"Hell," Capert said, grinning crudely, "a body's got to have some nourishment and such."

"Dumb bastard," Scarborough muttered. He drew his Colt and shot Capert in the forehead. He squatted at the fire and grabbed a piece of roasting venison. Morgan, across the fire, had not even glanced up from his eating.

Scarborough spent perhaps a year searching for Luke Wolfe without success. But by that time, Morgan was itching to pull some more holdups. What money they had gotten from their early raids was long since gone, and they were getting by on small, penny ante robberies and such.

"Go on, then, Clu," Scarborough said nonchalantly.

"I'll keep lookin' a bit longer."

Morgan nodded. He saddled his horse, put on his bedroll and small sack of food, mounted up and rode out. He hadn't gotten ten feet before Scarborough shot him in the back.

Scarborough sat and drank some coffee. He had no remorse whatsoever. Indeed, he even felt a little relief in knowing that there no longer existed anyone who could connect him to the murders of the Wolfe family down in Arizona Territory; or to any of the robberies the gang had pulled all over the west.

Scarborough kept up a desultory search for Luke over the next several years, but without luck. Along the way, he raped and pillaged and robbed his way from eastern Missouri to the mining camps of Arizona and Nevada Territories; from lower Texas to Iowa. He was in a Kansas cow town, wetting his dry, when he overheard some grizzled old man say, "Now that old Jeb Wolfe's on his last legs, thar ain't a many of us ol' mountaineers left." The old man shook his head, seeing the good days of the beaver trade in the high, shining mountains fading faster than his eyesight.

Scarborough moved up next to the old man and bought him a drink. "I used to know an old man named Jeb Wolfe," Scarborough said. "I heard you sayin' a Jeb Wolfe was ailin'? I was wonderin' if maybe it weren't the same feller."

"I don't know but one. Been keepin' a store up to St. Charles for some years."

"My friend did, too. Must be the same. I'm much obliged, old-timer. I'll have to call on ol' Jeb."

Scarborough bought the man another drink and then hurried outside. He jumped on his horse, and made the best time he could back to St. Charles. He entered the town under cover of darkness. He poked around at the

250

store and the house, and finally went to a nearby saloon. He did not think anyone would recognize him, since he had been gone so long. He was right.

He stood at the bar, keeping his ears open. And it soon became apparent that old Jeb Wolfe had passed away about two weeks ago. Scarborough stewed, angry, trying to use all his feeble wits to come up with a plan. When he did, he grinned, and finished his drink.

He strolled casually over to the Wolfe home. It was a big place, and fairly fancy, though not ostentatious. His only worry was that Luke would be there. But if he was, Scarborough was prepared to deal with that. He unconsciously patted his Colt.

He rapped on the door, and a few minutes later Rachel opened the door. She was no longer handsome, though if anyone had cared to check close enough, he might have seen vestiges of Rachel's former attractiveness. But at sixty-six years old and after a life lived on or near the frontier, her handsomeness had been robbed.

But she was still a formidable woman, having lost little of her vigor or feistiness. And she was not at all pleased to see Casey Scarborough at her door. "What do you want here, Casey?" she asked, bracing herself to try to keep Scarborough from bursting through the door.

"Lookin' for Luke," Scarborough said relatively calmly, trying to keep himself in control.

"He ain't here."

That was all Scarborough needed to hear. He slammed a shoulder against the door, forcing his way in, and almost knocking Rachel down in the process. He stormed into the room, and Rachel backed up warily, but there was no fear on her face. She finally stopped and glared at him.

Scarborough pulled out his knife, and ran a thumb along the flat side of the blade. "I'm gonna ask you some questions, Rachel," he said with a sneer. "If I don't get the right answers, or I don't get any answers, well . . ." He grinned wickedly. "I've used this on folks before."

Rachel sneered back. "You don't scare me, boy," she said in a clear, firm voice.

"You don't think I'll kill you?"

"Don't matter none." Rachel looked infinitely sad. "I'm too old to fear death. And with my Jeb gone . . ." She shrugged her broad, bony shoulders.

Scarborough was not about to be deterred. "Jeb had a stash of gold somewhere," he said. "I need the map."

"I ain't got no map."

"I swear to Christ I'll carve you up, old woman," Scarborough snarled.

"Go ahead," Rachel said, unafraid. She stared at him and shook her head. "Lord, you always was a dumb one."

That sent Scarborough's anger soaring, and he nearly plunged the knife in Rachel's breast. But he caught himself. "What do you mean?" he squawked.

"Why in hell would Jeb give me a map to some buried gold?" she asked, as if Scarborough was an idiot. "An old lady like me's gonna go lookin' for gold somewhere in God knows where?"

"Reckon not," Scarborough mumbled. "But," he added, as a light went on in his feeble brain, "he might've give it over to you to give to Luke."

"Might have," Rachel said without blinking. "But he didn't."

"Where's Luke?" Scarborough demanded, his frustration making his anger boil up.

"Gone."

"Gone where?"

"Arizona Territory. Bill lost some land of ours in a card game a few years back. Jeb asked Luke to try'n get it back for himself." She thought Scarborough might know that Luke was heading down there for the gold. But she had utmost confidence in her grandson. He had been a buffalo hunter, lawman, gunfighter. He could take care of himself against some scum like Casey Scarborough. Indeed, she felt almost as if she was boasting, trying to goad Scarborough into finding Luke.

Scarborough knew where Luke was heading now. All he had to do was get down to that land he had once seen with Jeb and follow Luke around. "Thanks," Scarborough sneered. He plunged the knife into Rachel's chest a dozen times.

Lucas Wolfe did not even think. He just acted. With his left arm, he shoved Sally as hard as he could. She yelped as she slammed into her father, and both tumbled toward the hole.

As Wolfe had hoped, the movement momentarily distracted Casey Scarborough. Still, Scarborough had enough presence left to fire right away. Wolfe heard Corvallis shout with pain, and he hoped his father-in-law was all right.

But Wolfe had not stopped or even slowed to analyze things. He was still moving, shifting a step to his right, crouching, drawing the Colt and firing three times. As he fired, he shouted, "Die, you yellow-hearted son of a bitch! Die!"

Scarborough jerked and twitched as three slugs slammed into him, punching holes in his shoulder, chest, and guts. He managed to get off another shot, but hit nothing.

253

Wolfe rose and cocked the Colt. He walked slowly over to Scarborough. His "uncle" lay there, still alive, but in obvious pain. "You're just lucky I had a decent upbringin', Casey," Wolfe said quietly, looking down at Scarborough. The wounded man's chest rose and fell weakly. "Or I'd cut your stones off and shove 'em down your throat."

Scarborough spit at Wolfe, the bloody sputum splattering the knee of Wolfe's pants.

"Somebody should've done this years ago, Casey," Wolfe said quietly. He drew a bead and fired, feeling a certain sense of satisfaction as the neat little hole suddenly appeared dead center in Scarborough's forehead.

As Wolfe turned, Corvallis was standing, with Sally's help. One pant leg was bloody and he favored it as he tried to stand. "You all right, Owen?" Wolfe asked.

"Yes," Corvallis said in annoyance. "Damn thing."

Wolfe smiled and walked up to them. "Sorry, but I reckon I lost my head there."

"It's all right," Corvallis said. His ashen face still revealed the fear he had felt. "He was quite the desperado, wasn't he?"

"He thought so." Wolfe sighed. "Damn, and all this for nothin'."

"What?" Corvallis asked, surprised.

"There ain't no gold in that box, Owen." Wolfe smiled ruefully.

"How do you know?" Corvallis asked, panicking a little. "Did you look inside?"

"Just a glance. There ain't no gold. Just a note from Casey's old man."

"What's it say?" Corvallis asked. He felt his life crashing down around him.

"It's hard to read," Wolfe said, stepping into the hole. He flipped the lid open and pulled out a yellowed

254

piece of paper. "It's dated 1853, looks like March. Russ says he took out the gold in bags. Easier to carry. Says he left the note in case Jeb came on his own. Says he's takin' the gold back to Texas and leave it there, then go and find Gramps. That's all."

"What in hell could've happened to it?" Corvallis asked, growing angry now. Someone had stolen his gold!

"Could've lost it along the way. Could've had it took from him by bandits. Could've been any number of things." He grinned. "What in hell are you lookin' so down in the mouth about?"

"That bastard stole my—our—gold." He was growing more and more furious.

"Hell, we can't have lost what we never had, Owen." He tried to laugh, but it came out strangled. He grew serious. "Damn stuff's been nothin' but trouble and grief anyway. It got Casey here killed. It probably got old Russ killed. And it got my whole family killed." He looked terribly sad.

Sally worked herself out from under her father's arm, leaving him to fend for himself. He looked about ready to say something, but then clamped his mouth shut. Sally walked up to Wolfe and lightly grabbed the front of his shirt.

"Not your *whole* family," Sally said softly, kissing him.